BREAKING WICKED

Crooked Brook Book Two

E.J. Nickson

www.BOROUGHSPUBLISHINGGROUP.com

PUBLISHER'S NOTE: This is a work of fiction. Names, characters, places and incidents either are the product of the author's imagination or are used fictitiously. Any resemblance to actual events, locales, business establishments or persons, living or dead, is coincidental. Boroughs Publishing Group does not have any control over and does not assume responsibility for author or third-party websites, blogs or critiques or their content.

BREAKING WICKED
Copyright © 2021 E.J. Nickson

ISBN: 978-1-953810-47-2

For Nicholas – do what you love even if it doesn't always love you back

ACKNOWLEDGMENTS

Thank you to my husband who keeps the place from burning down while I'm on a wine induced writing tear. Knowing you and building a life with you has made me a better human, and that's something for which I'll never be able to express enough gratitude. Thank you to my son for creating the need to go on wine induced writing tears, but also for showing me that genuine awe for the little things is possible and necessary.

I'd also like to thank my mother for showing me how strong a woman really can be, and for enthusiastically reading anything I've written in a way that encouraged me to write more, even when the first draft was crap. Big thank you to M for welcoming me back into the horse business after my ill-advised dalliance with cubicles and human resource departments. You generously brought me back home.

My heart is full of sincere appreciation for all of my dear friends who had excitement for this process even when I wouldn't allow myself to feel the same. You know who you are: H, Double A and L. A1, thank you for all the wino nights that gave me the liquid courage to move forward, and for your wizard skills once I was started on this path.

I am so thankful to Boroughs Publishing Group for taking a chance on an untested, not so young, author, and to my editor. I owe this journey to you and the leap of faith you were willing to take.

BREAKING WICKED

CHAPTER 1

A three-thousand-acre cattle ranch in the middle of Montana is quiet at night, so the sound of a woman yelling, "Bastard" carried well on the warm midsummer air. Trix was rounding the corner of the barn on his way back from the main house as the barn door flew open and she came crashing through it right into him. He caught the top of her arms to steady her, and she practically hissed when he did. Katherine Grant, a pit viper among women. Her green eyes were fierce with rage, no doubt due to the cold reception she'd received this evening. The Crooked Brook Ranch crew had gathered around a bonfire to celebrate a visit from out-of-town guests, and their lighthearted plans did not leave room for the calculating harpy who had torn the heart out of one of their own. If Trix had to guess, the bastard in question was her ex-boyfriend, and Trix's best friend, Winn. Trix hoped Winn had flat out told her to get lost after she'd spent the beginning part of the evening trying to catch his eye with flirty hair tosses and soft eyes which made naughty promises.

"Get out of my way, Trix," Katherine demanded. "I'm leaving."

"Evening not working out as you planned?"

"Not your business."

Trix noticed Katherine's long dark hair was curled into the kind of wave that looked easy and natural, but probably took hours to create. She was wearing dramatic makeup, which made her jade eyes glow.

"You look mighty...what's the phrase I'm looking for? Gussied up? Seems you took a little too much time getting ready for a country bonfire," Trix teased.

"I'm not in the mood for what passes for wit around here," she said, pinning a hard stare on him.

"Do you need a ride?"

"No."

They turned toward the large open area behind the barn where his friends had gathered around the firepit about a hundred feet from where they stood. Katherine's cousin, Maddie, was sitting on her boyfriend's lap and laughing as she wrapped her arms around his neck. Katherine's face pinched. Maddie was her ride, and was likely to pitch a fit if Katherine tried to make her leave now.

"You sure? 'Cause Maddie looks pretty cozy," Trix said, following her gaze. "Seems it's me or hitchhiking."

"You hate me," Katherine countered.

"You cheated on my best friend. Doesn't mean I want you snatched up and murdered in a windowless van."

Katherine rolled her eyes, but then gestured away from the group toward the main house and the driveway.

Trix chuckled. "All right. Let's go."

He started walking toward the front of the property not looking back to see if she would follow. He hopped into the driver's side of the ranch's old beat-up orange farm truck and pulled the keys from the visor as he waited for her to get in.

***

Katherine clicked her seatbelt and stared straight ahead, refusing to acknowledge Trix as he started the truck. The night had been an unmitigated disaster. Her desperate attempt to regain her high school sweetheart's affections had blown up in her face. She'd tried everything in her arsenal from soft and willing to trying to bait him into a fight so they could temporarily crash against one another. Nothing had worked. Winn had brushed her off, his anger over their past overriding any response to her advances. Chewing the inside of her lip, she tried to formulate her next move. *Always working an angle*, she chastised herself, but refused to stop her mind from plotting.

As the truck's headlights lit up the front of the main house, her gaze traveled along the house's cedar siding and huge wrap-around front porch. So much of her life was spent in and around that home. Mae's home. The one where Katherine had felt more loved than she did under her own family's roof. She took a deep breath, beating back memories of lazy days rocking in chairs on the porch, evenings shucking corn in the warm kitchen, and playful nights shooting pool in the basement.

Mae Becker owned Crooked Brook Ranch, and not only had she kept the business afloat after the death of her husband, she'd used it to create a family out of thin air. Collecting lost men from around the country to work the ranch and grow into themselves. Mae didn't bring people together: she brought the *right* people together.

The twelve men who lived under that roof were closer than most blood relatives. They would do anything for one another, and they guarded their manufactured family with a fierceness Katherine hadn't understood until she'd been a part of it. If she were honest with herself, maybe it wasn't until she was ousted and looking in, that she truly understood the value in it.

She would never be a part of them again. She'd made sure of that when she blew up her relationship with Winn. Now all that remained was a smoking pile of emotional rubble. She looked at Trix as he threw the truck in reverse. Make that rubble, resentment, and inescapable country courtesy.

Trix was an interesting case. For as long as she'd known him, he had been her boyfriend's best friend, yet they were a study in contrast. Winn's disheveled dark blond hair and amber eyes added to his rugged good looks, while Trix had a refined attractiveness to him, with short dark hair and several days of stubble framing full lips. There was something stark about his sharp cheekbones and ridiculously long black lashes framing his light blue eyes. She wondered if he might represent an opportunity. Not like it would be a hardship to spend more time with him. Maybe there was an angle to work there.

***

Trix felt Katherine's calculating eyes on him as he turned the truck down the drive. There was never a moment when she wasn't crafting some wicked move. Many folks had correctly predicted Katherine's relationship with the man she'd left Winn for wouldn't last. They'd also assumed it was only a matter of time before she tried to insinuate herself back into Winn's life. Trix wondered what her scheme would be now her efforts had been rejected. As was his nature, Trix figured he may as well poke the bear. "So, it's been a while since you sauntered round our parts." He smiled when her eyes narrowed.

"Are you asking a question, Jacob?"

"Ah, good parry using my real name, KG," he countered.

"Now who's deflecting with names? If you've got something to say, say it. No need to throw in one of your silly pet names." It was true. Trix did have a habit of assigning everyone he met a nickname or two.

"Ah, seems like only yesterday we used to be able to enjoy this without the knowledge you were a super villain spoiling the banter."

"Simpler times." Her tone seemed annoyed, but she didn't dispute it.

"Seriously though," Trix insisted, "you did shit the bed on this one."

"Still don't hear a question," she said, sounding bored.

"Fine, how about this one. How's Blake?" Trix knew bringing up Blake—the arms she'd run into at the end of her relationship with Winn—was a low blow. Trix couldn't help his smile as Katherine turned in her seat to pin a hard glare at him. He liked getting under her skin.

"Amazing in bed." Katherine was trying to get a rise out of him by belittling Winn.

"Unlikely," he responded, not taking the bait.

"Didn't know you ranked your male friends' sexual prowess."

"Blake's not my friend," he stated.

"Still more energy than I thought you'd spend on another man's sex life."

He shrugged. "Everyone needs a hobby."

"Thought your undying mission was to get women into bed."

He chuckled. "If you say so, KG"

Katherine crossed her arms over her chest and turned to stare out her window at the dark wheat fields as they whipped by. Trix wondered what was bouncing around in her head while he waited to see if she would fill the silence between them.

"How is he?" Katherine asked softly.

Trix let out a long breath. When he'd offered her a ride, he knew the thirty-minute drive would be longer than their appetites for childish mocking.

"If you'd asked a few months ago I would have said he was a mess," Trix admitted.

She winced at that, but he couldn't gauge if it was because of the pain she'd caused or the implication he was moving beyond that pain.

"And now?"

"Now, the mess is more... manageable."

"Alexandra makes it manageable?" she asked, referring to the spitfire redhead from Chicago who had been vacationing at the ranch. Now Trix began to fill in the blanks on her blow up with Winn. Maybe Katherine tried to glean from with Winn how he was feeling about Alex. Which begged the question: had Winn been truthful, or had he played it cool and not let on how important Alex was to him?

"Maybe she does. He wasn't going to stay destroyed forever, no matter how badly you broke him."

Katherine nodded, but her gaze remained focused out the window.

Trix went on, "At first it seemed like Alex being there was complicating things. Now I wonder if she's not the ginger jolt he needed to get out of his slump."

"Good," Katherine mumbled.

Trix furrowed his brow. Was it good because she genuinely wanted Winn to move on, or good because Alex was moving back to Chicago at the end of the summer and Winn would be repaired but unattached?

They slipped back into an uneasy silence as they turned onto County Road HH, and eventually into the trailerpark where she lived. She didn't seem surprised Trix knew where she was staying. Her shoulders sagged slightly, and he could feel the steam leaking from her bravado. She'd chosen a hard line to walk: pretending she was better than everyone else while en route to a dilapidated, six-hundred-square-foot aluminum cube she called home. Trix wasn't one to judge, but was sure she didn't know that about him.

When they were inside the entrance of *Rolling Acres Mobile Home Park,* she reached down to unclick her seatbelt.

"Here's good." She was reaching for the door handle before he'd stopped.

Trix had no idea which trailer was hers, and had been on the verge of asking when she started to leave the truck.

"It's one of these?" he asked gesturing toward the first few trailers. Trix looked down the rows and rows of identical mobile homes. The park went on for at least a half mile in both directions.

"Don't worry. I've got it from here."

"You sure?"

"Yep. Thanks for the ride, Jacob." She smiled a little sadly as she climbed out of the cab, adding, "and for the honesty." Then she shut the door in his face.

CHAPTER 2

Katherine closed the truck door and watched the dome light fade over Trix's puzzled expression. She waited until he drove away before she took off down the long row of trailers. Her family's home was about a quarter of a mile down, but the walk saved her from letting Trix put eyes on the tilted and decrepit place where she lived. Winn was the only one who knew, and despite what he thought of her now, she was confident his honor sealed the vault on her living conditions.

As she passed the Markey's trailer, Katherine heard the sound of shouting and a bottle crashing against a wall. Then their dogs started barking, and Charlene screamed at them to shut up. Katherine walked on unphased, thinking the cops would probably be called to the park again tonight. *What else was new?*

Jimmy Markey slammed open the screen door while yelling over his shoulder, "Pay for it yourself, bitch." He clunked his way down the half-rotted steps wearing only a tattered pair of cargo shorts and flip flops, a long neck bottle dangling from his hand. His hairy belly bounced with the movement and Katherine tried to suppress a sneer at the all-too common sight. Seeing her, Jimmy grinned, revealing a meth-assisted gap in his teeth.

"Hey there, Kitty Kat," he said, sarcastically.

"Screw you, Jimmy," she answered without slowing.

"Screw you, you trashy bitch."

"The hypocrisy of that statement is truly astonishing." She forced a chuckle, her glare glued straight ahead.

"You think you're fancy. Like we ain't living the same life, sweetheart," he said.

Katherine slowed, and turned to say, "You should put on a shirt before the COP's camera crew shows up this time."

"One of these days that nasty mouth is gonna earn you an ass whoopin'."

"Not today." Katherine continued walking, making sure she kept her stride unhurried as she cleared his lot.

Every one of these trailerpark pseudo-alphas were cut from the same cloth. All bark until you backed down, then they would bite. None of them had the gonads to actually come at you if you weren't already down.

Katherine craved a life where she wasn't constantly surrounded by the lowest form of society. Her conscience reminded her she'd had a chance, but she'd walked away. Or more accurately, she'd pulled the pin from a grenade, tossed it over her shoulder, then walked away.

What a stupid girl.

She shook her head trying to clear it of blameful thoughts. Guilt never solved anything, and what she needed right now was a solution.

Her mind wandered back to Crooked Brook and the ride home with Trix. She tried to picture his face on one of these tank-top wearing, beer bellied, perma-grimy bodies. The look so common it was essentially the redneck uniform. Her brain rebelled, not wanting a face like his to settle on shoulders like that.

Nevertheless, she smiled imagining Trix's vanity taking the hit when his dark hair receded to bald, and his firm athletic frame was replaced with rounded folds. The game would be less fun if Trix didn't know he was so good looking, but his ego beamed every time he flashed his perfect dimpled smile, or when those blue eyes twinkled at everything they landed on.

Maybe Trix being knocked down a peg or two would become one of her favorite mental fantasies. But the real question was: could he be part of a solution? Tonight had made it clear, Winn was not a viable option. Katherine didn't actually want to be back with Winn, but she was in trouble. Winn and his family were the strongest most reliable people she knew. Until she convinced at least one of them to forgive her, she had no one. No one to lean on. No one to help.

Reaching her family's trailer, she let out a long breath. There was no chance anyone under that rusted roof would help her. As always, she would help herself, regardless of what it cost someone else.

A thin line of smoke slowly drifted up from the back of the trailer, which meant Daddy was outside burning trash. In other words: he was avoiding her mother who must have already run through a sixer.

Another day stuck on stupid, a cycle which had become the ordinary since her brother Kyle had gotten locked up on drug charges over a year ago. They were the dysfunctional poor, playing their roles perfectly, waiting for the end of their miserable existence in the form of a premature death due to booze, violence, morbid obesity or a combination of the three.

Welcome home.

***

On the drive back to the ranch, Trix wrestled over his talk with Katherine. He was thrown by what felt like her genuine interest in Winn's current headspace. When she'd shown up uninvited at the bonfire, he was pissed, as was the rest of the crew, but he'd known there must be something brewing in her life. Katherine was well aware of her pariah status, so why would she risk the ridicule and show up anyway? She worked at appearing carefree and erratic, but usually there was a well thought out, albeit self-serving plan driving her actions. What was it this time?

Likely, she regretted her decision to leave Winn for that smarmy bastard, Blake Martin. Rightly so. The guy was an asshole who graduated from being Winn's high school sports rival to the man who stole his girlfriend and was successfully putting his horse training business in the gutter. Basically, Blake's father owned the county and was using that influence to strong arm Winn's clients into taking their business to his son.

Despite the long list of Blake's irredeemable qualities, Katherine had chosen him. It'd been a year since her unimaginative gold digger move. It was no secret the Martin family money wasn't going to run out any time soon, and to a girl living in a trailerpark, trading up to the luxury cowboy model was probably an attractive move.

The current gossip was Blake Martin's true nature—aggressive, cheating and downright mean—may've been more than even the formidable Katherine Grant could manage. If the theory was correct, Katherine and Blake had been on the outs for months, but if she wanted to come crawling back to Winn, this was the wrong time to do it. Winn and Alex had the appearance of oil and water at the moment, but Trix had a feeling eventually those repelling magnets would flip, and the attraction would be impossible to ignore.

What could Trix do to mitigate the Katherine factor?

He had a lot of faith in Winn and hoped the man's pride wouldn't allow Katherine back into his life. However, men have done stranger things for a face like Katherine Grant's.

Trix turned the truck to pass under the worn wood and steel sign overhead proudly announcing arrival at *Crooked Brook Ranch*. He looked over the impressive property with the same awe he felt when he first saw it.

A traditional working cattle ranch was something to behold. The hundred-year-old main house was so large every full-time member of the crew, plus Mae, lived there. There were acres of flowing hay fields in the front of the property, and dozens of outbuildings housing animals and farm equipment in the back. Everything was plunked down in the middle of an endless sea of pastureland so vast it was almost incomprehensible.

A familiar warmth filled him. A chest-deep feeling that came with knowing he was exactly where he was supposed to be. Crooked Brook hadn't been his home for long, but in the three years since he stepped foot on the property, this place had become his sanctuary and the place where his family lived. Not his real family, but the right family.

The one who loved him in a way he'd never known growing up in a cold, clinical penthouse. He would've never predicted sharing an old country house with loud raucous ranchers would be more peaceful than anything he'd known. He owed Mae for that. His favorite grizzled sage who cracked the whip over them wore many hats, including ranch owner and surrogate mother to more than a few of them. He smiled to himself imagining the tough loving way her hard glare scolded, and the masterful way she pulled it off.

His gaze traveled the long fence line of the dark fields and he pulled in a deep breath from the open truck window. This was his peace. A strange unexpected peace he'd accidentally stumbled across in the middle of nowhere Montana. In that moment it felt indestructible, and his pride at building this life for himself was dizzying. Such a thing would've been incomprehensible only a few years ago.

Welcome home.

Trix walked around the house toward the back of the property to see if the bonfire festivities were still going on. It was only eleven at night, but ranchers tended to party and end early so the six a.m. chores hurt less. The large working area of Crooked Brook Ranch came into view. The immense cattle barn to his right was dark, but the machine shop and equipment garage's large flood lights lit up the middle of the yard where a few fruit trees and Mae's greenhouse were nestled. The horse barn was to his left, and still had all of its interior lights on. It seemed strange Winn would be in there over an hour after Katherine had stormed out.

The barn door opened, and Winn came through with Alex, and another one of their ranchers, Bishop. Trix noticed his friend Bishop looked like he was trying to calmly walk away from a bank robbery.

"Hey guys," Trix called to them.

"Hey, where'd you run off to?" Alex asked.

"Ran an errand," he half-truthed easily. "What's up? Bishop looks guilty as sin."

Alex looked to Bishop like she was seeking approval. After a long moment, he nodded, a broad smile spreading across his face.

"Bishop is going to propose to Belle," Alex said quietly enough to not let her voice carry.

"Oh hey, man. That's awesome. Congratulations," Trix said, extending his hand to shake Bishop's. Trix adored Bishop's girlfriend Belle, everyone did.

"Why does everyone keep saying that?" Bishop asked. "She hasn't said yes yet."

"She will," Alex and Winn said at the same time.

Trix nodded his agreement. "When?"

"As soon as Alex gets a plan together," Bishop confessed. "We're going to do a fancy thing here to set the mood for her to say yes."

"She'd say yes if you asked in the middle of a burger at Hank's Diner," Trix joked, nudging Bishop in the ribs. Then turning his attention to Alex, he asked, "Can I help?"

"I'm going to get a shopping list together, but we're going to need help setting up too."

"Consider me your servant." Trix smiled.

"Always." Alex laughed as Trix swung a friendly arm around her shoulder.

Trix snuck a peak at Winn to see if he'd react, but as usual, Winn was too guarded to show if the move rubbed him the wrong way.

I'll help flip these magnets, Trix thought before bringing his attention back to Alex.

"Back to fire and beer, Red?" he asked, using the obvious nickname she'd been given as soon as she arrived earlier that summer in all her feisty redheaded glory.

Alex nodded, her eyes quickly darting to Winn before turning to smile up at Trix.

"How about you?" Trix asked Winn.

He shook his head. "I'm done for the night."

Trix knew Katherine's visit had to've been emotionally draining, and Winn was a solitary, stew-on-it kind of guy. Trix didn't push. "Night," he said.

Winn nodded, and walked away.

CHAPTER 3

A few weeks later it was time for the proposal dinner. Trix and another member of the ranch crew had been tasked with going into town to pick up a few last-minute items, including a nice bottle of wine, candles, and fresh flowers. The romance gods were being generous. Not only had they found a bottle of wine that cost more than nine dollars, they'd also talked Mrs. Jenkins into letting them have a fist full of roses from her garden at the village hall, which doubled as post office/police station. As they walked into the street, his fellow errand boy, Junior, nodded at the diner. "Let's swing by Hank's and grab a burger. I want to see Maddie before we head home."

Trix checked his watch to make sure the pitstop wouldn't get them gutted for throwing off Alex's timetable. He should've anticipated this. Junior could never get this close to where his girlfriend worked without sneaking in a visit.

The bell chimed as the pair walked through the door and the smell of grease and disinfectant met them in the entryway.

"Hank," Junior called to the bald-headed man at the grill.

"Boys," was the generic reply Hank used, despite having served them each more than an entire cow's worth of hamburger over the last few years.

Trix scanned the room and saw Katherine taking an order from a gentleman seated in a booth near the counter. She wore the classic small-town diner uniform: a light-yellow, button-up dress with an oversized white scalloped collar and navy apron. Her hair was pulled up into a messy mass at the top of her head which appeared to be secured by a pencil stuck through the middle. She brushed a few stray strands out of her eyes as she nodded then wrote down whatever the man had ordered.

"Fine choice there. I'm sure your arteries will forgive you when you're dead," she teased.

The heavy-set gentleman laughed, and she gave him a little wink. "You're a mean woman," he chuckled, then took a swipe like maybe he was going to give her rump a swat.

Katherine dodged the move easily. "Chuck, if you do that again, I'm going tell Joanie and you won't get laid for a year." She shook her pen in his face with an easy grin on her own.

Trix couldn't help but smile at the scene. Katherine had every regular here eating out of the palm of her hand.

Like a succubus, he reminded himself.

Maddie appeared from the backroom and let out a little yip when she saw Junior. She bounced over and planted a lingering kiss on him, but was interrupted by a sharp slap on the counter bell and Hank yelling, "Order up."

"Sitting at the counter?" Katherine asked, breezing past them, already knowing the answer was yes. Trix and Junior nodded and took up two stools. Out of habit, Trix picked up the menu. It was unnecessary since the fifteen items on offer hadn't changed since he moved into town. Maddie made her way around the counter and leaned over, putting her elbows down in front of Junior.

"Burgers?" she asked.

They nodded. Trix added, "I'll have a coffee too, please."

Junior said, "Coke," and reached up to lightly poke Maddie's nose. Trix found the move weird, but dumb men in love were, well, dumb.

Maddie clipped their order to the wheel above the serving window and Katherine sauntered up with a pot of coffee in her hand, flipping over a mug. "What are you guys doing in town?" she asked, filling Trix's cup.

"Pretty important stealth mission," Trix said as he watched Junior and Maddie resume mumbling and making eyes at each other over the counter.

"For the proposal tonight?" Katherine asked, catching him off guard. "Maddie told me."

Trix knew Maddie couldn't keep a secret, and seeing as how she was Katherine's cousin, he supposed it shouldn't be a shock she'd blabbed all about it.

"Yeah. It's going to be pretty epic, far as I can tell," he said. "If anyone deserves a happily ever after it's Belle and Bishop."

"Trix, it sounds like maybe you're a romantic at heart," Katherine accused.

"Aren't we all?" he asked. Hank slapped the bell.

"Not really," she said flatly and turned to retrieve their order. She put down the plates in front of them and Trix doctored his burger with ketchup. He looked up and found her watching him. "What?"

"I was thinking, you're a pretty good friend," Katherine said.

Trix watched her for signs of artifice. It didn't sit well she was being sincere.

"Guess that's what it's like when you look out for someone other than yourself," he said.

He took a big bite of burger and tried to swallow it along with the guilt for taking a jab that felt a little too on the nose.

Katherine's brows lifted. "Ah, well done. Now you can say you've fulfilled your role as Winn's protective best friend by being nasty to me."

He narrowed his eyes, annoyed she'd put so fine a point on it. He did feel compelled to be mean to her out of a sense of duty to Winn.

"You say that like you don't deserve of it," Trix pointed out.

"I suppose." She shrugged. "But every crime has a statute of limitations."

"It's hard to gain forgiveness when you don't ask for it," he stated and took another bite. The burger sat in his mouth like sawdust.

"Deep thoughts from a mailorder cowboy," she said, sounding disinterested, her gaze scanning the roomful of customers.

He choked down the food and had to laugh despite himself. "Mailorder cowboy. That's pretty good, KG."

"It's a pretty common phrase, but I suspect you wouldn't know." They both seemed to relax as they fell into the familiar territory of trading less painful barbs.

Trix chuckled and realized Junior was watching them while Maddie was helping a customer. Trix cleared his throat. He knew Junior also struggled with how to act around Katherine. Junior was stuck between the *we hate Katherine* camp and the *she's related to my girlfriend* camp. Trix wondered what Junior was thinking, then shifted his focus to his food.

***

Trix had completed his rehearsal dinner assignments, and had helped Winn and Bishop get into their tuxes. His part in this little scheme was done and he was unsure of what to do next. Alex had convinced Belle to come over under the pretense she needed help picking out a formal dress for a fictitious event in Chicago and was going to use Maddie to help push a dressed-up, unwitting Belle out of Alex's room, down the stairs, through the kitchen and into the backyard. Trix wanted to watch the goings-on but was unclear about the best way to do it without inserting himself where he didn't belong.

He walked into the front room next to the base of the stairs and saw Mae in one of the overstuffed chairs by the fireplace. She'd wrapped herself in a blanket, and as usual, had a book on her lap. Glancing up at him she nodded her head at the other chair. If Mae thought this was the best place to wait, it was probably the best place to wait.

"Ready for mission ball and chain?" Trix asked.

Mae considered him for a beat. "Ready to pretend you're not panicked about the first one of you taking the plunge?"

Trix crimped his brow. Mae had an uncanny feel for what was going on in the minds of the men she employed and pseudo-adopted. It felt odd she believed Trix would be upset about Bishop getting engaged. He opened his mouth to explain her gut was off, but he was interrupted by the sound of Alex, Belle, and Maddie coming down the stairs. When the women finally appeared, Alex was so wrapped up in herding Belle to the kitchen and back porch she didn't see him and Mae.

Mae held his gaze for a beat before she gave him a knowing grin, and then stood. He joined her, and they followed behind the women as they went through the dining room and into the kitchen.

With flourish, Alex called out, "Hey what's that? What's going on outside?" Trix snickered at Alex's abysmal acting.

Before Belle could protest, Alex and Maddie whisked her through the back door into the romantic set up, while Trix and Mae leaned over the kitchen counter to watch through the window.

Mae's accusation was scratching at the back of Trix's mind. She was wrong, wasn't she? He knew Bishop and Belle were a perfect match, the kind of high school sweethearts who marry and live together seventy years before dying in the same bed on the same day surrounded by a pack of children and grandchildren.

He was happy for his friend. Genuinely.

His thoughts were quickly overshadowed when he saw Winn and Alex lay eyes on each other. Earlier Trix had earned himself a punch in the arm when he told Winn the tux looked good on him. Watching Alex holding her breath, he knew she agreed. Alex also knocked it out the park. Her dress was simple and elegant, showing off her petite frame. Her make-up and hair accentuated her delicate beauty.

Trix smiled to himself when it appeared Winn forgot how to breathe. His gaze was glued to Alex. The air between the two seemed thick and tense.

I officially consider those magnets flipped.

Eventually they came to their senses enough to proceed with the evening's plan. Winn played a song on the guitar and they sang together as Belle and Bishop slow danced. Then Winn and Alex walked away, giving Bishop privacy as he got down on one knee.

"They're going to have cute babies," Mae mused next to him.

"Hope they'll look more like Belle," Trix joked.

"I wasn't talking about them." Mae slid him a sideways grin and Trix had to laugh.

"Think Alex and Winn are ready to get over themselves?" he asked.

"If not, I'm going to have to ramp up my meddling," Mae threatened.

"Let's hope it doesn't come to that," Trix chuckled, and then turned his attention back Bishop and Belle.

He couldn't make out the words, but whatever Bishop was saying had Belle tearing up, which seemed like a good sign. When he produced the ring, Belle nodded through her tears as he put it on her finger.

Trix smiled, feeling proud and happy for them. Mae was wrong, Trix had no qualms about one of the guys getting engaged, but he had to admit he felt strangely detached from the whole process. A missus and a happily-ever-after were things he never dreamed of having. He wasn't opposed to it, but he didn't' think about it. He couldn't even picture it. Settling down with the woman he loved was a great concept, but it was the same as abstract art and interpretive dance when it came to relevance in his own life.

He hadn't had great role models. His parents' relationship was more a corporate merger than a happy marriage. Maybe that's why it felt peculiar to watch friends his age, or younger, find someone they'd be willing to attach themselves to for the rest of their lives.

Mae pulled him from his own thoughts when she asked, "Well now what?"

"It does feel a little like if you're not falling in love at this moment, there's nothing to do." He laughed.

She nodded and lifted her brows. "You wanna play Scrabble?"

Trix shrugged. "Guess that's a good a plan as any."

After taking an unsurprising thrashing, Trix went to bed feeling a twinge of something he couldn't put his finger on. Damn Mae's intuition and the bug it had planted in his brain. Maybe he was feeling a little unsettled, but it wasn't because he was unhappy with his life. Actually, he didn't want a single thing to change. Just because good things were happening for the people around him, didn't mean his life was going to be different. Right?

***

The next morning Trix joined the crew in the dining room for breakfast. He loved when everyone in the house ate meals together. It was particularly fun on days like this when the air was filled with a contagious joyousness as people congratulated Bishop. Alex hadn't come down yet, and Trix kept trying to catch Winn's eye to glean what'd happened between them after they'd disappeared into the darkness last night. It seemed Winn was making an effort to not look at anyone. He sat with his back to the table, knee bouncing at a breakneck pace, his eyes laser focused on the bottom of the stairs.

When Alex appeared, Winn walked over and pulled her into a seriously deep, and not breakfast-appropriate, kiss. Trix looked to Mae, who let a brief smile pull at her lips before winking at him. When Alex and Winn broke away from one another the entire assemblage sat in stunned silence.

Trix decided someone needed to break up the weirdness and show some support for this new development. "Well, it's about goddamn time," he called, and the group returned to a loud and happy gathering.

CHAPTER 4

Everyone was settling into a routine made easier since Winn and Alex had given into the force drawing them together. Instead of having to make room for them to avoid one another, they worked together, which made everyone's life easier. It'd been only two days since these recent developments, and Trix was relieved Alex and Winn's relationship, and Bishop's new status as a fiancé, weren't upsetting life as he knew it. Perhaps his strange sense of foreboding about change had been an overreaction to the emotional day and a knee-jerk reaction to Mae's flippant comment.

That morning they'd all risen earlier than usual to herd the sales cattle into semi trucks to take to auction. A few hours later they were driving onto the fairgrounds and Trix was transported back in time to almost three years to the day when he'd been on a self-imposed hiatus from his real life and driving without a destination through Montana. He'd left the highway following signs promising an auction and rodeo. There he figured he'd find some good food, a few drinks, and perhaps he'd be lucky enough to find some temporary company.

That was the day Trix was pulled into Mae's world and the day he started his new life with the folks he now considered to be the most important people in it. He hadn't left Montana since.

As Trix stood in the stock auction office with Mae, he laughed at himself remembering how absurd it'd been to stop mid road-trip to take a job he knew nothing about in one of the flyover states. He'd had no intention of staying put anywhere ever again, but when Mae had ordained he belonged at Crooked Brook, he'd followed her directions without questioning a damn thing. Back then he didn't know Mae had a way of moving people through her world as if they were marionettes. Maybe someday she'd be wrong, and people would start to bristle under her meddling, but from what he knew,

Mae had been a human puppeteer for damn near fifty years and hadn't been wrong yet.

Mae seemed to hear his thoughts as they walked out of the office and into the crowds. "Happy anniversary," she said, as if she'd been along for the ride in his head since they arrived.

"Witch," he laughed.

"Go get us some coffee," she chuckled and then pointed at the bleachers where they would sit for the auction, an unspoken order to meet her there.

***

The sale of Crooked Brook's cattle encountered a hiccup, which seemed to be orchestrated by Blake Martin's father. Ted Martin was a wealthy rancher who was trying to push Mae out of the cattle business by leaning on the buyers to leave her stock on the table. Despite Ted's plotting, they managed to sell what they'd brought, but at disappointing prices. Frustration with the events was short lived when everyone's attention was diverted at Alex'd confession she'd engineered what amounted to a cowboy pissing contest between Winn and Blake.

"You did what?" Trix had to work to keep himself from yelling.

"Okay," she said, hands up in surrender, looking between Trix and Mae. "Okay, hear me out." Alex tried to explain, "I get it. This River Rock mare is a monster, but Winn is good. He can do this."

"What exactly happened?" Mae asked calmly.

"In front of Blake's dad, I suggested to the guy who bought the mare it was a shame this stunning horse's babies wouldn't be worth as much money. You know, because she has this reputation as an un-ridable nightmare. I left the challenge out in the open and Ted Martin ran with it, claiming if the mare could be broken it should be his son who did it. I told him Winn was the best man for the job and he could prove it here and now."

"You're asking Winn to break a famously un-breakable horse. Here. In front of a crowd to prove he's a better horseman than Blake?" Trix did nothing to hide his displeasure.

"Ah-huh. Blake can't break the mare. Winn can. You know Winn's business has been hemorrhaging clients all because Ted Martin is spreading rumors and leaning on people to take their business to Blake. This kind of display will take away any doubts that Winn is the best horse trainer in the state." Suddenly she looked less sure. "Right?"

"That's a big risk to take with someone else's reputation and safety, Alexandra," Mae reprimanded.

"Blake's going first," Alex said.

"Good. Maybe the mare will kill him, and we won't have to go through with the rest of this," Trix said gruffly.

Alex's face blanched.

"Wish I was kidding, Red."

"He can do this," Alex whispered, almost to herself.

Mae reached out and grabbed Alex's hand. "Winn will do the right thing," she said. Alex nodded and walked away, he guessed to find Winn for some kind of please-don't-die pep talk.

Trix leaned over to Mae. "Now we know Winn has it bad for Red. He would have throttled anyone else who tried a stunt like this."

Mae looked up, a spark of mischief behind the worry in her eyes. "Agreed."

***

Of course, and as always, Mae told it true. Winn did the right thing. First, Blake had entered the round pen with the notorious mare to try to break her spirit with his brutal and inhumane training tactics. Which he did in front of a growing audience and a seething Winn. But after getting his ass handed to him by the horse, Blake had to relinquish his turn. During his time in the pen, Winn had succeeded in constructing a tentative truce with the previously overly aggressive mare, but he did not try to saddle or ride her as Alex had promised he would.

Doing the right thing had earned Winn a significant amount of trash-talk from Blake, who should have been off nursing his ego and potential head injury, but instead was next to the round pen to heckle Winn for not having the guts to ride the mare. That harassment had led to the second gauntlet of the day being thrown. Winn told him they could hash out their macho pecking order in the rodeo ring atop the bareback broncs instead.

An already exciting evening had a little more spice thrown into the mix.

***

Katherine and Maddie found a place in the stands near the judges, and Katherine felt a familiar tinge of anxiety forming in her gut. She'd been with Winn when he did some amateur rodeo events in high school and she wasn't sure her heart could take watching him do it again. On the other hand, the potential to watch Blake get trampled wasn't something she was going to pass up. Katherine had watched the horse breaking showdown from afar, unsurprised by Blake's cruelty toward the animal, and Winn's compassion for it. During the spectacle she found her attention frequently returning to the redhead who was obviously Winn's new romantic interest. When Katherine had confronted Winn during the bonfire, he'd downplayed his feelings for Alex, but here it was clear they were together.

She had to acknowledge the begrudging respect she felt. Not only had the petite city girl stepped up, toe to toe, with Ted Martin, it appeared she'd weathered whatever temper tantrum Winn would've thrown when he learned of her interference. Neither task was for the faint of heart. Deep down Katherine knew Winn deserved to have a fierce defender in his corner and she was amazed her reaction wasn't to somehow intrude in their budding relationship. Now as she sat waiting for the rodeo to start, she felt a little sorry for Alex, knowing the city girl had no idea how traumatic it would be to watch someone you love put their life on the line for bragging rights.

Katherine's gaze drifted through the crowd until it landed on Mae, and was unnerved to find the older woman watching her. One of the byproducts of leaving Winn was the loss of the nurturing influence Mae had in Katherine's life. While she missed a lot from being with Winn, the hole Mae used to occupy was one of the most painful. She held eye contact for a several long moments and tried to glean something from Mae's expression, but she had a spectacular poker face, and Katherine couldn't tell what, if anything, was being conveyed by the look.

You've got bigger problems than disapproval from a mother figure, she reminded herself and she looked away first.

Next to her, Maddie bounced with excitement. "Oh, looks like Winn is going first," she chirped. "Think he's still got it?"

"Of course he does," Katherine said with a confidence she didn't feel.

Winn rode his first bronc for the required eight seconds and Katherine sighed with relief before she realized he had gotten his hand hung up in the rope and wasn't getting off like he should. Her stomach pumped extra acid through the excruciating seconds it took him to free himself. Alex was also watching Winn in the ring, her tension easy to see despite the distance. The score Winn received was pretty meager and Katherine joined the crowd in booing the judges despite it actually being fair for the ride.

Blake went next and Katherine sent evil thoughts his way as she watched him prepare to ride. Now was the time Karma needed to make Blake pay for being a despicable human being. As usual though, Blake did not have to face justice. His ride went well, and he received a score much higher than Winn. The crowd cheered as Blake stood and triumphantly waved his hat in the air.

There's still one more ride to go, you cocky asshole.

Katherine didn't care what happened to the other riders in the bronc competition. All she wanted was for Winn to beat Blake, and maybe for Blake to become crippled. Was that too much to ask from the universe? Her focus wandered while several other cowboys rode. She noticed Trix had secured himself a spot near the chutes, and she watched him joke with Winn and the rodeo staff.

Trix threw his head back with a big laugh she could hear all the way up in the stands. He nudged Winn in the ribs and Katherine noticed some of the tension washed off Winn's face as he caved into Trix's teasing. It was obvious Trix was putting on a show to help soothe Winn's nerves. She smiled and couldn't help but wonder if there wasn't something more to Trix than she'd given him credit for.

The announcer called Winn's name again then said the horse he'd drawn for the second go round was named Haymaker. Katherine and the crowd let out a nervous sigh. That horse was notorious for throwing cowboys quickly and violently. She cracked her knuckles and tried to remind herself she'd forfeited her right to fuss over him. As Winn was trying to get settled on the agitated horse, Katherine looked to Trix again. No longer needing to provide comic relief for Winn's benefit, he looked stern and worried. She'd been right, he'd been putting on an act.

The door to the chute opened and Katherine couln't breathe as she watched Winn masterfully ride the hell out of the infamous horse. After the buzzer sounded the crowd went wild. Winn climbed from the bronc to the back of the pick-up horse. Katherine exhaled, and then cheered when the thrilled announcer's voice cracked as he yelled the high score Winn had received.

Maddie leaned over and shouted to be heard over the excited din in the stands. "That boy is still hot."

Katherine's watched Trix as he bounced up and down punching the air. Then she had to stifle a laugh when he jumped into Winn's arms, wrapping himself around his friend's torso like a baby monkey.

"Yeah, he is," Katherine replied.

Katherine did the math on the men's scores and knew there was still a good chance Blake could beat Winn if he managed to put up even a halfway decent ride. She watched as the man she'd never cared for, but now truly hated, climb onto the back of a little horse in the chute.

Now's your chance, universe.

The gate flew open, and the first part of the ride went fine, then Blake started to slide off center and brought his free arm down to the rope. She smirked as the announcer called out the disqualification, and then sighed when Blake hit the sand well and clear of the flailing hooves of the bronc. Katherine knew better than to cheer Blake falling off, but she looked to the sky and thought, *guess that's close enough.*

Maddie leaned over. "He's going to be a bear to deal with after this."

Katherine nodded. Maddie didn't know half of the behavior Blake was capable of when he wasn't getting what he thought he was owed: in this case an easy victory over Winn.

"Guess we'll steer clear of him tonight," Katherine said.

"Good luck with that." Maddie tipped her head to the ring. Katherine looked down to find Blake sneering at her as he hobbled to the side of the arena. She turned her palms to the sky and shrugged, instantly regretting the sarcastic gesture when his expression went hard. Katherine tried to appear impassive until he was out of sight.

She agreed with Maddie, Blake was most likely going to be unavoidable later.

Great.

CHAPTER 5

With the auction and rodeo finally behind them it was time for a night of kicking back and unwinding in the tent where the band had set up. Trix stood at the makeshift bar and watched Winn dance with Alex. He was glad they had managed to table their crap long enough to get together, but he struggled with how he was feeling. It was a confusing mix of being happy for someone you care about, and at the same time feeling proufoundly jealous. He didn't want to be with Alex—hell she reminded him of his sister—but for the first time in his life he thought he might want what they had. A connection. An other.

Trix noticed the beer he was holding was his fifth of the night. Seemed like lately one or two wasn't enough. He pulled in a deep breath, trying to force himself to be the light happy person he usually was, but it'd become a little less easy lately. He turned back to the dance floor where Alex and Winn only had eyes for each another. They didn't see another soul.

Trix, on the other hand, found one person impossible to ignore. Katherine was two stepping with an older gentleman, who, for sure, was having the best night of his life. Her dark hair moved like it was caught up in a breeze, which seemed to only affect her. Her her green eyes stood out, starkly bright in contrast to her dark eye make-up.

She was wearing a little white sun dress, which flowed around her tan body. Everything about her was unapologetic, and he couldn't look away. Katherine's gaze met his and he willed himself to hold it. The corner of her mouth pulled up a tick. She knew he was watching, but suddenly, he didn't care. She wanted his attention. She wanted all of their attention. And she had it.

He hated himself for watching, but even a cobra had a hypnotic beauty to it...from afar. Something drew Katherine's attention, and she broke their eye contact. He followed her stare and saw Blake had arrived. Quickly Trix checked Winn and Alex who thankfully seemed to have forgotten the rest of the world existed.

After Blake's embarrassing failed attempt at breaking the River Rock mare, and then losing to Winn in the rodeo, Trix presumed Blake's top priority would be to extract his pound of flesh. Trix hoped Blake wouldn't approach Winn and Alex. Trix would intercede even though he was pretty sure the Blacke could kick his ass. He would risk a beating to protect the bubble his friends had constructed around themselves. Instead, Blake's eyes landed on Katherine, and he sneered a greasy non-smile.

Not your problem, Trix told himself, but he couldn't help watch as Blake approached Katherine and her dance partner. Trix moved a little closer to hear their conversation over the band.

"Excuse me, sir," Blake said, laying on a thick layer of unnecessary pleasantry. "If you don't mind, I need a moment of your new friend's time."

The gentleman seemed surprised by the interruption, but quickly schooled his face, saying, "Well, hey there, son. Shame about that second round today."

Blake's facade dropped a fraction. "Yeah. Sure was. Do you mind?"

The ousted man gathered himself. "Oh, right, of course." He tipped his hat toward Katherine. "Thank you for the dance, Miss Grant."

"It was my pleasure, Jack," she said with a practiced smile.

After her dance partner excused himself, Blake scowled at her, and she lifted her chin and said, "That was rude."

"We need to talk." Blake tipped his head toward the tent opening facing the field, which being used as a parking lot.

Katherine's eyes darted over to Trix and his jaw clenched. If she was looking for him to save her from her boyfriend, she'd be disappointed. That was quite literally the bed she'd made, and he saw no reason to rescue her from it.

"Fine," she sighed, sounding annoyed.

Trix watched them leave the tent and after a beat, returned to the bar for another beer. If he couldn't will her image from his mind, then he would drink it away.

***

Katherine and Blake were silent as they made their way past the noise of the band. She drew in a long breath, knowing exactly which version of Blake she was going to come face to face with. He wouldn't be the smooth talker who behaved like someone who grew up knowing which one was the salad fork, the measured man who'd convinced her she shouldn't believe her own instincts about him. No. He was going to be the mercurial, aggressive, overbearing man she had seen unleashed more times than she could count.

When they hit the parking lot, Blake reached down and took her hand, pulling her through several dark rows before he stopped to face her.

"Not a great day for you," Katherine said, letting her bravado lead as she yanked her hand from his.

"I didn't ask for your opinion," he hissed.

"Then what do you want?"

"Where have you been?" he demanded.

"Nowhere."

"But you haven't answered your phone for weeks? I went to your house and your lush mother told me you haven't been around much lately. Her guess was that maybe you were back hanging out with the Crooked crew. So, let me ask you again. Where have you been?"

"It is none of your business. By the way, it's bad strategy to ask a drunk about current events."

"Don't be cute," he said. "You know I want to know if you're staying at the ranch and are back with Winn."

Katherine cursed her mother who wouldn't notice the difference between her daughter being gone overnight or for a month. Briefly, she considered lying and telling Blake she'd been staying at Crooked Brook. Deep down, Blake was intimidated by Winn, and if he thought she was over there he may let it go. On the other hand, with the volatile history between the two men on top of what happened earlier, it could backfire and send Blake into a rage she'd be incapable of handling.

Problem was, she didn't want to tell him the truth either. In the last few weeks, she'd stayed with Maddie here and there, but it was a bad idea to let Blake know all of the places he should look for her. The best course of action was to be vague and let him jump to his own conclusions.

"I'm not staying with Winn."

"Let me guess. He wouldn't let you come crawling back now he's got that hot little redhead?"

Her pride dug in its heels, and she couldn't stop herself from returning the jeer. "You mean the ginger who talked your father into throwing you in the pen with a horse above your pay grade?"

The tick in his jaw told her she'd hit a nerve. An easy thing to do with Blake. He stepped toward her and she fought every instinct and kept her feet planted, her expression hard.

"Watch yourself, Katherine. I'm not one of these chumps who's willing to let your smart mouth run off without any consequences."

She couldn't show an ounce of weakness or he'd pounce. Then, alone with him in a dark parking lot, fifty yards from anyone who could hear them, she'd be in real trouble.

"You have no say over what my smart mouth does. The whole world thinks we had a relationship, but you and I know better, don't we? We were sleeping together. We were taking our frustrations out on one another. You weren't taking me home to momma, and we weren't having date nights. Don't start acting like a jealous boyfriend. It wasn't the job you had when we were screwing, and you certainly don't have that job now that we're not."

His expression was dark. "Who do you think you are? You trailerpark—"

Katherine cut him off. "Don't contact me anymore." She tried to sound convincing before turning to leave, but he grabbed the top of her arm.

"You walk away when I say you can walk away," he said between clenched teeth.

Movement back up at the tent drew her attention and she saw Trix coming into the parking lot and decided to hang her hopes on some form of undeserved gallantry.

"We. Are not. Together," she said loudly, wrenching herself from his grip.

"Don't try me—" he started before getting cut off.

"Hey, youse guys. Don't mine me," Trix slurred loudly as he half stumbled between the cars and trucks. "Didn't mean ta inner-rupt. Juss came out ta pee."

"Get out of here, Trix," Blake said, turning to face him.

"Well now, Blake, only my friends call me that… And you? You're not my friend." Trix seemed to sober up in an instant, making Katherine wonder if the drunk idiot had been an act.

Blake paused, and then must've decided his confrontation with Katherine was sufficiently disrupted. "Later," he growled. Katherine nodded, putting on a dismissive face and he turned and walked away. When she heard the sound of his truck spewing gravel as it left the parking lot, she turned back toward Trix.

"Jacob," she said with a nod.

"Satan."

"What are you doing out here?" she asked, ignoring his insult.

"Wouldn't you and I like to know," he said, splaying his fingers across his hips and cocking a leg out to one side. She could sense his unease at being alone with her.

"Glad you listened to your gut," she smiled.

"What do you know about my gut?"

"I knew you'd follow. You weren't done with me yet."

"Overly confident of your own wares," he accused.

"Am I?" she asked, stepping into his space. "Am I also wrong about what that look from earlier promised?"

When she'd caught him looking at her on the dance floor, she'd been frozen, unable to look away. Usually, Trix's demeanor came with laughs and glib comments, but today his icy gaze was intense, broody. She'd found the combination impossible to ignore. Now that she was alone with him, with those eyes still vivid and harsh, she was unapologetically drawn to him.

His jaw clenched as she stepped even closer. "Well, was I wrong?" she repeated.

"Yep," he said, but his expression told the truth. Under the surface something primal was prowling and she wanted to meet it.

She put a hand on his hip and brought her lips to the base of his jaw, watching his face for a reaction as she pressed her body into his. He stiffened and pulled in a quick breath.

"This about getting back at Blake?" he asked through clenched teeth. His hands balled up at his sides, looking anywhere but at her.

"No," she said, as she kissed his neck and started making her way toward the side of his mouth. When her lips touched his he jerked his head away with a sneer.

"Winn?" he asked, more to himself than to her.

She shook her head. "Is happily moving on."

She reached for him again, and he jumped out of her grip and over several feet. He leaned on the back of a tailgate looking like he was having a hard time getting his bearings.

"You drunk?" he asked.

She sighed. "Haven't had a drop." Then added, "You sober?"

"Mostly."

She approached him cautiously, like a wounded animal. "You can try to find a rationale that suits your narrative, Trix. Why can't this be about mutual attraction?" When she was standing in front of him, she reached out and took his hand, placing his palm on her side. His fierce eyes bore into to hers and the hunger in them made her stomach tighten. Holding his gaze and firmly pressing his hand into her waist, she said, "I want your hands on me."

He narrowed his eyes as she pulled his hand up the length of her body. Never breaking eye contact she steered his hand past the swell of her breast, up her neck and around to her cheek as she turned her face in his palm where she nipped the skin.

***

Trix's entire body was rigid. The feel of her beneath his fingertips was driving him mad. Her boldness shocked him, but also told him she would be the kind of lover he craved: brazen, strong, fearless. How could he have expected anything else? Slowly, he cupped her cheek and then moved his hand to the back of her head, his fingers gliding through her hair. They stopped, holding their breath, staring at each other.

He fisted his hand in her hair and she gasped, her eyes flaring. "We tell no one," he snarled.

The corner of her mouth pulled up and she gave a slight nod. In an instant, he was dragging her to him, and her mouth was quick to open to his harsh kiss. One hand knotted in her hair the other banded around her waist, their bodies pressed into one another as the kiss built up steam. She moved her hands around to his back where she raked her nails down the length of him. He growled into her mouth and deepened the kiss. Leaving one hand in her hair, his other moved to explore down her back and wrench her hips to his.

He released her mouth and tracked his lips down her neck. Her breathing was fast and ragged in his ear as she tipped her head back to give him better access. He devoured her: her scent, her warmth, he pulled all of it into himself and felt frenzied by it.

Her hands busied themselves behind him with something his brain didn't comprehend until he heard the tailgate fall open with a metallic crash. Realizing her intention, he reached down and lifted her by the thighs, turning her to sit on the end of the tailgate. She kept her heels hooked in the small of his back as she pulled his body to her and grabbed his face, dragging his mouth back to hers.

His hands traced down the outside of her thighs and found he could slide his hands all the way down under her ass without encountering a barrier. She had to be the hottest thing he had ever felt beneath him.

He withdrew from her slightly. "Shit, I don't have any protection," he panted, realizing he was ruining something that was promising to be remarkable.

"It's covered," she rasped, bringing her mouth down to bite his neck.

He groaned then tried to regain his bearings. "What?"

"Seriously, Jacob, it's covered. I need you now, please." Then she was reaching down to the button on his jeans. His mind when blank when her hands found him. Violently he pulled her hips toward the edge and she brought her hands behind her to brace herself as she leaned back, face turned to the sky, knees pressing to his waist.

He entered her swiftly, fully and he barely heard her cry out his name over the blood rushing past his ears. For a moment he was lost in the sensation between them, but then some semblance of thought returned, and he worried he'd been too rough. Under normal circumstances he would never take a woman so forcefully. She sat up to drag him into a kiss before tugging him away from her by his hair, her eyes hard and intense when they met his.

"More," she demanded, and his self-doubt vanished along with his self-control.

***

Trix's self-awareness returned after they'd both exploded, and he realized his legs would only hold him up for a few more seconds, if that. He looked to Katherine's flushed and panting face. She seemed to recognize his weakness and slid over, making room for him to sit beside her.

When he sat she turned and bit her lip. "I wasn't wrong about your gut."

"No," he had to agree, forcing his mind to stay in the moment and pretend like there wouldn't be consequences to what had just happened. "But I'm not usually one for being this rash."

"You should try it more often." She shot him a saucy smile. "You're good at it."

"Wasn't really how I was brought up," he confessed, surprised and confused at his own honesty.

"Strict family?"

"More like…regimented. Dad wasn't around a lot since his priorities were more about money than family. When he graced us with his presence, there wasn't a lot of tolerance for rash behavior." Hearing the words come out of his mouth convinced him he had actually lost all of his damn mind.

She watched him for a beat longer and then said, "I get that."

"Listen, Katherine…" Trix started struggling to figure out how to say the rest of the sentence.

"Trix, I know. This stays between us."

He nodded, thankful she'd said it for him.

"We do have at least one other problem though," he said. "I have no idea how we're going to get home. I told Alex they should leave without me."

She chuckled. "What was your plan when you came out here?"

"If I'm honest, I assumed following you and Blake into the parking lot meant I would leave in the back of either an ambulance or cop car."

She tipped her head. Trix guessed she was looking for proof he was joking. When she didn't find it, she gave him a soft smile. "There's a white knight in there after all."

"I don't recall the hero taking the princess against the back of an F-150," he said.

"Heroes come in all shapes and sizes, but don't kid yourself, Trix. I'm no princess."

"I know," he said quickly, then regretted it when her expression flashed hurt before she covered it with apathy.

"I have Maddie's car," she said. "She ditched me to leave with Junior."

They jumped down from the tailgate and she pointed down the line of cars to direct him. Then she drove him home, the entire ride packed with uncomfortable, unending silence.

CHAPTER 6

The next morning Trix stood in front of the mirror trying to work out exactly when he'd become a backstabbing, untrustworthy prick. His reflection defiantly stared back. The infinitesimal part of him that wasn't sorry brazenly sat up in the front row, rubbing its palms together. It was all too ready to replay every gasp and moan, every detail down to her scent, her flavor, her heat, the sharp pain of her nails digging into his back as she came, the strain of every muscle in his body as he followed her.

Enough.

His fist flew out and punched the glass. He barely registered the sound of shards hitting the sink and the burning pain from the little gashes on his knuckles.

He'd had mind-blowing, life-altering sex with Winn's Katherine.

Ex-Katherine.

He was scum, a traitor. He was a drunk who made bad decisions that could never be undone. How could he face Winn today?

He bolted from the bathroom and almost ran into Bishop.

"What happened here?" Bishop asked, gesturing toward the broken mirror.

"Accidentally hit it with the clippers. I'll go grab the dustpan, and I'll snag a new one next time I'm in town," Trix offered.

Bishop sent him a questioning glance and Trix reminded himself to be who everyone expected him to be.

"What you think I hulked out?" he said laughing and giving Bishop a nudge with an elbow as he shoved his bleeding hand into a pocket.

When Trix donned his happy-go-lucky mask his friend's shoulders relaxed. "Nah, course not, man. Must have been a cheap one, eh?"

"Must've." Trix hoisted a reassuring smile, which fell as soon as Bishop turned away.

After cleaning up the evidence of his shame in the bathroom, and tacking his torn skin together with super glue, Trix went to the horse barn where the back of Frank Power's trailer was pulling out. Frank had been one of Winn's good clients until earlier this summer when he'd succumbed to pressure from Ted Martin and taken his horses off the Crooked Brook property to bring them to Blake's training program. After the drama yesterday, and Blake's public humiliation, Frank was justified in bringing his business back. It didn't hurt he was now the owner of the River Rock mare who had put Blake in his place, and then some.

Alex and Winn were leaning on a fence watching the mare and a paint horse walk around the ring. Alex looked up first and did a double take when she saw Trix's face.

"Hey there, sleepy head. Had a rough night?" she teased.

"Could say that," Trix admitted, still unable to bring his eyes to meet Winn's.

"Glad you made it back from the auction," Winn joked. "Thought maybe a cougar had finally taken you hostage."

"Hey, that was one time, and she was only like forty," Trix defended himself trying to force a light tone. Normally he didn't mind the misinformed wide brush which painted him as a manwhore, but at the moment the assertion was gasoline on a guilt fire. He brought his gaze up to meet Winn's. When he did, Winn cocked a brow and watched him for a long tense moment.

"You look sick. You okay, man?" he asked.

"Yeah. You know… A few too many." Trix hoped to dodge any more scrutiny.

"Gotta learn to behave yourself on a school night," Winn scolded lightheartedly before turning his attention back to the horses.

"Behave myself," Trix echoed absently.

Trix looked at Alex who was still looking him over. He forced a large grin, which she eventually returned.

Alex then turned back to Winn. "Okay, thanks to some clever maneuvering by yours truly, Frank Powers is a Crooked Brook client once again. So, you two have some work to do." She gestured to Frank's horses.

"Clever maneuvering? Is that what we're calling your rash gamble with my life?" Winn said in a mock disapproving tone.

"You say tomato, I say placed my faith in you and your abilities." Alex laughed and then added, "Well, I was right, wasn't I?"

"Don't let it go to your head, princess." Winn sent her a grin before turning to Trix. "I want the River Rock mare to have some time to herself before she has to do anything, yesterday was harder for her than any of us. Trix that means you're on the paint. That work?"

Trix nodded, knowing he would lie in front of a train if Winn asked him to right now. Winn returned the quick nod and Alex volunteered to go grab tack from the barn.

"Before this one left a few weeks ago we learned it had a pretty bad spook about machinery and water. We also know it spent the last few weeks over at Blake's, and we can only guess what it had to endure over there," Winn said. "We'll first do some light work without any scary things and build up his confidence."

Incapable of making words that sounded normal, Trix nodded. He watched Winn climb into the arena, and with nothing more than body language, he separated the two horses, convincing the River Rock mare to stand while he caught her and led her out of the ring. Once Winn disappeared around the corner, Trix let out the painful air he was holding and bent over, hands on his knees.

Get your shit together immediately. If you're not going to confess, you need to put on a better show.

Trix righted himself and pulled in a deep breath. He was unwilling to share what he'd done since he was sure the fallout would be too devastating to the life he had here. He needed to pretend everything was sunshine. In theory, he should be good at that.

Alex and Winn returned and Trix tacked up Frank's paint horse then got on it. He warmed up with a little walking and jogging around the arena, then turned to Winn for direction.

"If memory serves, this one's had some serious training hours already put into it. It's got a great spin, a good stop. It's sensitive and attentive," Winn said.

Trix nodded.

"Why don't you run through the reining skills you've learned and see how it feels to put him through his paces?" Winn asked.

"Will try my best." Trix grinned past his clenched teeth, swallowing the extra saliva his queasiness was pumping into his mouth. Winn had been generous with his time and patience these last few years, taking Trix under his wing to teach him how to be a better trainer. Winn's charitable nature only served to widen the guilt pit in Trix's gut.

"You've got this," Alex said from the side of the ring. Trix worried she was being extra supportive because she sensed something was off with him. He didn't want her sensing anything about him.

Following Winn's instructions, Trix loped the horse around trying to get a sense of where and how much pressure it needed to turn, slow down, speed up, and so on. He pulled up in the middle of the ring to try a spin on the haunches. He asked the horse to start the spin, but Trix hadn't set his weight properly so as soon as the horse jerked his front end to the right, Trix immediately fell off the left. The poor gelding immediately stopped to stare down at him while he looked up at it from the dirt.

Winn climbed down from his perch on the fence and slowly started walking out to them. "You're not supposed to fall off them when they do what you asked."

Trix stood, swiping dust from the back of his jeans, gingerly reaching out to retrieve the dangling rein. Automatically, one of his hands went to the horse's neck in an attempt to communicate it was not the animal's fault.

"That was pretty dumb, huh?" Trix asked.

"Yeah," Winn said. "You haven't made that kind of mistake in months."

"Definitely feeling off my game today," Trix confessed.

"The horses don't care if you're having a good or a bad day. They give us their best and we owe them the same. You've got to table your shit when you walk in the barn. Tired? Don't care. Hungover? Don't care. Sad, mad or otherwise? They don't care."

Trix hung his head. He knew Winn was right. The horses deserved better, and him being lost in his own head was going to get him, or someone else hurt.

"You're right. I'm sorry. I'll get it together."

"Okay, do it again. I swear, I must have said this a dozen times: your seat keeps you on the horse. Not your hands. Not your feet.

You can't start a spin like that standing in the stirrups and hope holding the horn will keep you from taking a sand dive."

Trix nodded. Winn was right, he had probably said that same phrase hundreds of times since they started his training.

I don't deserve his tolerance.

Winn turned back toward the fence, and Trix saw Alex watching him, a soft, compassionate smile on her face. She was trying to learn as much as she could about the horses before she went back to Chicago. Trix was glad she could learn a tough lesson by watching his body take a fall. He gave her a mock pained grimace, making her giggle.

When he climbed back on the paint, Trix took a few laps to allow the horse to warm up after their unplanned time out. Then he brought it back into the center of the arena, properly set his weight and put the horse through a spin. After a few more exercises to let the horse show off what it knew, Winn said, "Well, that was better."

"Felt better." Trix popped a self-deprecating grin, cramming his guilt down so it wouldn't show on his face.

Winn hopped down from the fence and stretched his neck to one side and then the other as he said, "That's good for his under-saddle work today. I think what we'll do is take him out to graze by the creek. Maybe we can convince him to walk through the water if it's low pressure and it's about getting a little extra food."

Trix nodded and dismounted. While he was taking off the saddle, Alex joined him in the middle of the ring. "I think Trix and I could try to do that on our own," she said to Winn. "I know you've got some care to administer to the new rehab horse."

Winn took off his hat and ran a hand though his hair, an obvious tell he was uncomfortable. "I don't know. That one has a pretty strong aversion to water. He needs to take it slow and steady."

"We can do slow and steady," Alex pressed.

"I... Uhh..." Winn looked unsure.

"Come on, kid. I'm sure it'll be fine," Trix pushed. "At some point you've got to let go of this one-man-army thing you've got going on and let us help you more." It was a ballsy move considering he'd just proven he was not a stellar horseman. Winn sighed and watched the sky for a moment before relenting. "Fine, but you stay with her the whole time."

"Of course," Trix said quickly.

"Okay, I'll be in the aisle. You guys come get me if things go sideways." Winn leaned over and planted a quick kiss on Alex's mouth, then turned to go.

Alex and Trix looked at each other with excitement having won a head-to-head with Winn. "We will," they both said in unison, like children who were getting away with a second dessert.

***

Alex walked with Trix and the paint horse to the wooded area by the creek on the east side of the property. The lightheartedness she'd felt for their victory over Winn was proving to be short lived. Trix kept his eyes focused straight ahead, and she felt a clouded weight radiating off him. Clearly there was something going on, but she couldn't even guess as to what it could be. Trix wasn't a chest-pounding alpha male who would need to nurse his ego to hide embarrassment after falling off a horse. Maybe his date last night ended poorly. Could this be what a denied and sexually frustrated Trix looked like? All pouty and distant?

Alex stopped walking and broke the silence. "You know, Winn holds the monopoly on mysterious brooding cowboy. I'm not sure he's willing to share that title with you."

"It's a hangover, Red, I'm not about to challenge Winn for his strong silent-type championship belt."

"You sure you're okay?" she pressed, her eyes dropping to his battered knuckles.

"Ah, this?" he asked, holding up his hand. "I banged it working on the tractor the other day. No worries. I'm okay. Played a little too hard last night is all, but it won't happen again. Trust me." He was trying hard to convince her, but she knew he was lying to her about his hand. She decided to let it go. For now.

It took less than an hour to convince the paint horse it could walk through the creek while being led, and Alex felt like it was a big achievement for a training mission without Winn's direct oversight. As they walked back to the barn, Alex looked over at Trix. "Thanks for convincing Winn I could be trusted to do this."

"No problem, Red. Us transplants have to stick together."

She nodded, then a realization struck. "Wait. You're not from Montana?"

"I'm from New York."

She laughed and then realized he was serious. "You're actually from New York? How did I not know this?"

He shrugged his expression winsome. "It's not something I advertise. As you know, you lose a lot of Montana street cred when they find out you're a city slicker."

"Hang on. You're from New York City?"

"Upper East Side."

Her jaw dropped. "Upper East Side Manhattan?"

Trix nodded.

"Super rich people live there," she said, mostly to herself.

"Yep. Lots of rich people," he agreed.

"Who else knows about this?"

He chuckled. "I'm not planning a heist, Red. It's not a secret."

"How on earth did you end up here? Does your family know you're a rancher? Couldn't they buy you a ranch," she joked.

His eyes darkened. This was Trix closing up shop. "You know. Wealthy families, rich problems, I guess."

She allowed him his non-answer, then picked her next words carefully. Definitely Mae's tactics rubbing off on her. "Well, if you ever need to talk urbanite to urbanite, you know where I am."

Trix smiled and squeezed her shoulder. "Noted. You got it from here?" He motioned to the aisle. She nodded, and he left her there.

After returning the paint horse to its stall, Alex ran off to look for Winn. She found him in the wash stall, kneeling down next to one of the rehab horses.

"You knew Trix was from New York and you never told me?" she blurted out.

Winn looked up at her and grinned. It seemed he was starting to get the hang of catching up with her mid-tirade.

"Have you met me? I'm not really the gossiping type," he said.

"That's not gossip, you hick. It's background information."

He shrugged and turned back to wrapping the horse's leg.

"You know why he left New York?" she ventured.

"Now that would be gossip. You know I'm not going to talk about someone else's business."

"Winn, someday this keeping other people's secrets policy is going to come back to haunt you."

He chuckled. "Not gonna work, princess. If Trix wants to tell you his story, he will."

She kicked the other wrap out of his arm's reach. "You're obnoxious."

He grinned as he stretched to snag it. "And you're a brat. Behave."

"No," she challenged.

His hands stopped mid-wrap. "You've got a sixty second head start." His voice was low with a hint of a threat, causing goose bumps to track up her arm.

Alex took off down the aisle and had barely made it into the office before he caught up. He flipped the lock, and the rest of their morning chores were postponed.

CHAPTER 7

That night, as dinner was wrapping up, Mae said, "Bishop, I'll take your clean-up shift today. I think I'd like to spend more time in the kitchen, yet." Bishop glanced up and replied, "All right." Apparently, he wasn't going to question getting out of dish duty.

Trix sighed. Seeing as how she hadn't released him from his duties, she had to be engineering time to speak with him alone. Everyone passed plates toward the front, stacking them in piles, before rising and making their way out of the room. Trix and Mae took the dishes to the sink.

"Something going on with you I should know about?" she asked, not even bothering to put a veil on her intentions.

"Things are good," Trix said while he busied himself scraping plates.

"You need a reminder you've got access to a grizzled old lady brimming with worldly knowledge?"

Trix chuckled and decided partial honesty was his only way forward. "How do you do that, Moms? See right through a man?"

"I've lived a long life with men who couldn't use words. I'm pretty good at hearing what's not said."

"I love it here," he started.

"But?"

"But I'm, you know, trying to work out what's next. This six-week temp job turning into three years wasn't part of my life plan."

"The twenty-two-year-old wanderer I met at that rodeo didn't have a life plan."

Trix shook his head. "No, he didn't. But being here has shown me I need one. I can't be a listless waste my whole life."

"Working here's a waste?" He heard the hurt creep into her voice.

"No. But I can't be a fifty-year-old single man shacked up with ten other old men. What kind of life is that?"

"Honey, this place, this family, we're meant to be your foundation. We give you structure and strength. We help define the footprint you want to leave on this world, but we don't build the walls for you. That's up to you."

"How do I do that?"

"Depends on what kind of house you want to be."

"You're like a pit-bull with a metaphor," he joked, buying himself time before answering.

"When it suits."

"I feel like I don't even know what my options are," he admitted.

"There are a lot of different kinds of men. Ones like Bishop, who want to build a modest life with a woman, and children to pass it on to. Men like Winn, who have a gift to share with the world and will leave a mark on it. Men like Matt who find what's under this roof completely satisfying and fulfilling. Others need wealth," she paused to allow him to mentally conjure his father, which he obliged her by doing, "others need power or fame. What drives a man, and to where is different for everyone."

"What kind of man am I?"

"I'm not sure I can answer that for you."

"I'm worried I'm not a good man," he confessed. His mind jumped to Katherine and his gut twisted with guilt. Mae watched him, not replying, so he continued. "I suppose now is when you tell me bad men don't worry about if they're good?"

"Well, that's not true though, is it? Plenty of men worry about not being good while they're making choices that hurt people. It's possible to have your eyes open to the consequences of a decision and still pick something selfish and wrong."

"Selfish and wrong," he mumbled.

"Not always the same thing," she added worrying him when she appeared to pick up on his conflict. He shook his head. There was no way she knew about what had happened with him and Katherine last night.

"I've made mistakes," he started, but couldn't find more words.

"I know, honey. You wear your guilt on your sleeve. Now I don't know what you're feeling so badly about, but I want you to understand you're not the first man who's wrestled with a screw-up, and you're not alone."

"What if this screw-up isolates me from you?"

"It won't," she replied.

"How can you be sure?"

"Because I know you'd never do something to ruin what you've found here."

That landed somewhere near his heart and made it hard for him to breath. If she only knew. Silence resumed as they continued with the dishes, until Trix broke the quiet. "Why'd you pick me? That day at the auction three years ago there must have been twenty men you could've hired for this job. Why me?"

Mae let out a long breath. "It's a hard thing to explain, but I've been hiring men to work this ranch for almost fifty years. I knew by looking at you, you would fit."

"You just needed someone who could pick up heavy things."

"Honey, we didn't need you. You needed us."

"I didn't know what I needed. How could you have known?"

She shrugged. "There's a fine line between a man who needs a kick in the pants then a hug, and a man that's not worth the effort. Telling the difference is something I've had to get good at."

"Where will I go?" Trix asked sadly.

Mae allowed her rare surprise to show on her face. "You're going to leave? Over whatever's been eating at you?"

"I don't know," he confessed.

"I think you need to take some time. Do some real soul searching. When you're ready to talk about whatever it is, I'm here for you. Until then, promise you won't do anything rash." She paused, then added, "Anything else rash."

"Finding space for soul searching can be hard to do around here sometimes."

After evaluating him for a long moment, she nodded slowly. "You give me some time on that, okay?"

He furrowed his brow, not understanding, but he'd been around Mae enough to know he didn't really need to understand.

"Okay," he agreed, shuffling to his room to be alone until his roommates went to bed.

CHAPTER 8

Each day Trix ignored it, the guilt felt a little farther away. He didn't want to think about what it said about his character, but he was thankful for the reprieve. It'd been less than a week since he'd had sex with Katherine, and like with so many phases of his life before, he went on pretending things were fine. He overfilled his life with forced, lighthearted interactions, and tried not to spend any time in his own head. Gradually, the constant nag of being a traitor was muffled, then distant. With enough hours acting as the easygoing entertainer, he was close to feeling back to normal. Only if he didn't look too deep.

That afternoon he went into town with Junior on a pre-wedding mission for Alex. She was helping Belle with the homemade wedding decorations before she left town, and apparently, making an archway for the ceremony needed to get done three months in advance. He found the whole thing ridiculous. But because Alex was planning on returning to Chicago before the big day, everyone was tiptoeing around the situation, and doing what she asked.

As they entered the hardware store, Alex's voice echoed in Trix's mind. *"It's not that big of a deal. Just your best friend's happily ever after you'd be sabotaging if you don't find everything on this list."* She told them not to return until every item had been hunted and gathered.

Junior glared at the paper and called out over the shelves to the man working the register at the store. "Hey, uh, Fred? You got any of them twinkling lights?"

"What's that you need?" the old man called back.

"White lights… Like for Christmas trees. You have any of those?"

"You soft in the head? It's July."

Junior gave a pained look and Trix laughed as he made his way to the front counter. "Hey there, Fred. How's it going?"

The store owner gave him a suspicious look. "Fine."

"We're on a pretty important quest here. You know Bishop?"

"Yeah."

"He's going to marry that amazing woman, Belle. Not sure that's common knowledge yet." Trix was counting on everyone having a soft spot for Belle. Or the small-town desire to know any scrap of gossip before someone else.

The shopkeeper's face relaxed a bit. "That girl grew up two farms over from me. Sweet as pie, that one."

"She deserves a pretty special wedding, don't you think?"

"You think you're slick, but I'm on to you, Trix."

"But you're still gonna go in the back and look in storage for some of those twinkling lights, aren't you?" Trix asked.

The man muttered, set his glasses on the register, and went down the hall leading to the basement steps.

"Thanks, my friend," Trix called out to his back. "There you have the difference between greatness and mediocrity, not an uncommon disease."

"Steinbeck out of context is blasphemy." A familiar sultry voice had Trix whipping around.

Katherine had come through the open door with Maddie tagging along a few steps behind.

"I was paraphrasing," Trix defended, trying to ignore the yearning in his gut.

"You were misrepresenting a quote," she corrected. "That entire passage is about wanting to be mediocre."

"You surprise me," he said lightly, trying to mask how unnerved he felt at seeing her.

"Because I've read a book?" she asked.

"Because you remember it. I was confident that head of yours only contained devious schemes and make-up tutorials."

"There's other things in there. Like memories of steamy parking lots and—"

He cut her off. "Hey, so, uh…"

Thankfully, an oblivious Maddie said, "You guys are weird," before she saw Junior and let out a squeal. She ran off to jump into his arms and the two of them began making out next to the assorted fasteners clearance bin without a care in the world.

Trix leaned in to Katherine, his voice low. "We had an understanding."

"I'm aware," she said.

"The other night was a mistake. People finding out would have pretty grave consequences for both of us. I thought mutually assured destruction would keep everyone in line."

Katherine turned her emerald eyes to his, making the floor feel instantly unstable, but he held his ground. This was too important.

"Under one condition," she said. Trix narrowed his eyes and waited for her to go on. "No more Katherine-is-an-evil-bitch punch lines," she demanded.

"But, if it quacks like a—"

"Don't finish that sentence, Jacob, or I promise I'll have posters made to describe and rate my sexual encounter with you."

"Jesus, okay. Deal. Keep your damn voice down." Behind him he heard Fred coming back down the hallway.

Katherine smirked then leaned up to breathe into to Trix's ear. "It would be a pretty glowing review, though."

Trix groaned, then cleared his throat to cover the sound. Fred dumped an armful of white Christmas lights on the counter. "I have ten boxes of these and you're going to buy all of them."

Trix nodded, inspecting one of the boxes to divert his attention from Katherine. He was going to have a hard time getting the feel of her whisper out of his mind. Trix glanced over at Junior, still attached to Maddie's face. "Okay, lover boy, what's next on the list?" he asked.

Junior pulled away, putting Maddie down, feet back to the floor.

Katherine said, "We should probably get back to the diner. Break's over."

Maddie nodded, leaned up to put a quick kiss on Junior's cheek, and bounced out the door.

"Nice seeing you, Junior," Katherine said, then her eyes went to Trix and she pulled the corner of her bottom lip in between her teeth before adding, "Trix." He crushed the box he was holding.

Katherine turned to follow her cousin out the door.

"Dummy, give me that," the shopkeeper said, taking the flattened box to scan.

Trix tried to put his head back on straight. "Okay, Fred, so talk to me about ribbon."

"Ribbon? This is a hardware store." Immediately Fred seemed to cave. "I'll get you guys a catalogue, and you can give it to Belle. I'll order whatever she needs."

"You're a good man, Fred." Trix smiled handing over the cash for the lights.

When they got back to the ranch, Trix brought everything they had to the big equipment barn where Alex was waiting to inspect their acquisitions. Winn and fellow rancher, Griz, were also there, using the nail gun to tack together the wooden arch they'd made.

How come I had to go shopping while they got to play with power tools?

"What did you guys do? We only needed a few more lights. And, where's the ribbon?" Alex asked.

"Careful, Red, your city girl is showing," Trix said. "A mom-and-pop hardware store in a thousand-person town doesn't have a huge selection of ribbon. Here's a catalogue of anything on the planet you may want. Fred says he's happy to place an order. Make him a list."

"Why so many boxes of lights?" she pressed.

"Long story," Trix sighed.

Griz and Winn finished with the arch and started heading over. Trix fought his knee-jerk reaction to bail before he had to speak to Winn.

"Nice work," Trix said, forcing his easygoing tone.

Griz nodded then walked off to busy himself with more solitary tasks, as was the big man's preference.

Winn wiped his hands on a handkerchief. "You guys have luck in town?"

"Not as much as we should have according to your high maintenance lady friend," Trix joked, earning him a pretend scowl from Alex.

"How should I know ribbon is a rare commodity around here?" she pouted.

"Takes a while to get used to country life, Red. Wait until someone asks you to pop over to the discount mall because it's only an hour and a half away."

Winn laughed. "After three years you still struggle to remember to fill up with gas before taking off."

Alex's brow pinched. "Wait. You've been here for only three years?"

"Yeah. Why?"

She squinted at him. "That's crazy. It's so hard to picture you anywhere but here."

Trix nodded and bit the inside of his cheek. He had to agree, and it was depressing to consider his recent indiscretions may lead to him leaving this place.

"If you've been riding for only three years," Alex continued, "that makes my progress feel pretty unimpressive."

"I'd ridden before I got here," Trix admitted.

She scrunched up her nose. "How?"

Winn answered for him. "He rode fancy horses in that there New York Cit-*tay*."

"I rode English," Trix corrected.

"Sorry," Winn replied. "Fancy horses in swanky clothes with delightful little saddles."

Alex laughed. "Oh my. You wore breeches. Didn't you?"

"I rocked the hell out of breeches, Red." He gave a spin and slapped his Levi's-clad cheek.

Alex shook her head. "I can't get that image out of my head. Make it stop."

"Nightmare fuel," Winn agreed.

"Okay, okay…" Trix nodded. "In all seriousness, show jumping is legit, and it's actually really hard."

"I'm not knocking it, man." Winn put his hands up in surrender. "You couldn't pay me to sit on one of those tiny saddles and try to make a horse get airborne."

Alex looked at him incredulously. "You've ridden freaking rodeo broncs."

"Not the same," Trix said. "For sure he'd fall as much as I've fallen off since I set foot on Montana soil."

"Well." Winn furrowed his brow. "Let's not take it too far."

"Dude be real. Ten minutes tops," Trix insisted.

"What? No way."

Trix shrugged. "Your saddle has a handle. It basically has training wheels."

"Training wheels?" Winn's jaw dropped. He turned to Alex for back up, but she was distracted by her phone.

She looked up to meet their stares. "What?"

"Aren't you going to defend your man?" Winn asked.

"Oh. Don't be silly. You can defend yourself when the used English saddle I just bought shows up." Winn looked ready to vomit when she flipped the phone around to show him.

Trix gave Alex a high-five. "Hell, yeah. That's why I love you, Red. It's put up or shut up with you." He leaned over and kissed the top of her head. "Your time is coming, cowboy," he said to Winn. "Oh boy, is your time coming."

Backing from the equipment barn, Trix left the lovers to hash things out, knowing their little spat would soon turn into something adult rated. It felt good to fall back into the old rhythm of lighthearted teasing with his friends. It made it a little easier to stay in denial about his guilt.

Perhaps nothing had to change. So long as he purged Katherine from his mind, and no one ever found out what he'd done.

CHAPTER 9

Deciding to keep Katherine out of his head, and actually keeping Katherine out of his head turned out to be two entirely different things. Trix found whenever he wasn't actively distracting himself, he was thinking about her. He didn't want to see her. Yeah, he wanted to see her. This uninvited obsession and rift had created a curious side effect, which was when anyone needed an errand run in town Trix was an instant and enthusiastic volunteer. He'd convinced himself if he didn't seek her out, he shouldn't feel guilty if he bumped into her. Maybe he would see her, but it wouldn't be his fault.

That was exactly how, a week later, he happened to be in town delivering six little jars of homemade jam to some of Mae's friends when he spied Katherine sitting on the bench outside the quiet town hall. There was a book in her lap, but she was gazing off, her eyes unfocused. Watching her from his truck, he was reminded why she was so hard to forget. She was utterly gorgeous. His jaw worked as he also reminded himself she had been the catalyst in a mistake, which could turn his life upside down. Now here he was, fawning over her as if there were no consequences.

How many times do you have to touch a stove to learn what's hot burns?

But it was no use. When she brought her thumb to her mouth and her expression saddened, Trix jumped out of the truck and made his way across the street.

"We meet again, KG," he said as he walked up. Her eyes focused on him, and there was the briefest flash of worry before she replaced it with her practiced indifference.

"Trix," she said.

"Good book?"

"Yes, actually. If you don't mind, I'd like to get back to it." She pretended to start reading.

"That so? 'Cause it seemed like you weren't even looking at it."

She looked up at him. "I think we've established you don't think much about what you read. Consider I was digesting."

He smirked at her throwing his misused Steinbeck line in his face. "That or something's on your mind. Perhaps the book is a prop to get people to leave you alone."

"Obviously it doesn't work," she said.

He was right. Something was on her mind, but getting to the bottom of what it could be was a hazardous endeavor. Katherine was likely to behave like a snared cat: ready to sink teeth in your arm to keep you from helping.

He decided to live dangerously and risk it. "You all right? You seem even more miserable than your normal, cheerless self."

"I'm fine." She closed the book and stood. "You don't have to pretend to care."

"Well, that's a deflection if ever I've heard one."

"Is that what we're doing today? Pretending you're noble?"

Trix frowned. "What's that supposed to mean?"

"Selfless doesn't seem to be your style."

"You don't know a damn thing about me."

"Why would anyone bother to get to know the party clown?"

"Always straight for the jugular, huh?"

"I'm just saying, if you'd stop putting on a show for five minutes, people might see something more than an idiot performer in there."

He shook his head. "Christ, you're a mean woman."

"Because you don't want to hear the truth about yourself?"

"No, because there's something going on with you and you're willing to slit my throat to divert my attention."

"Fine."

"Fine?"

"I'm pregnant."

That stunned him into silence.

"It's not yours," she said so businesslike, it was as if she was telling him a letter had been delivered to the wrong house.

"Who's?" he recovered enough to ask. Her chin dipped. "Blake's," he said so she wouldn't have to.

How could she be so sure? His mind jumped back to the night of the bonfire and how peculiar he'd thought her actions were. A damning thought began to form.

"The night you came to Crooked Brook, you weren't there to get Winn back for good," he started. Her expression confirmed he was right. "You needed him back for one night," Trix leveled his accusation.

"I can't let Blake raise this kid," she said, no touch of remorse in her voice.

"So you'd trick Winn into raising it for him?"

"I don't know what kind of rose-colored planet you grew up on, but in the world of drunk mommas and absent daddies, we don't apologize for being a survivor."

"Last I heard, your pops was still around. Not sure what kind of cliché tragic backstory you're trying to sell me, but no matter where you come from, it doesn't justify being a heartless bitch." He squared his shoulders, hands on his hips.

"I thought you would know a father doesn't have to be gone to be absent," she tossed back quickly.

"Is this your way of trying to tell me we're the same? Throwing something I told you during a temporary moment of insanity back in my face?"

"I'm telling you that I have no shame for doing everything in my power to ensure my child doesn't have a monster for a father."

"Not everything. You shouldn't have slept with a monster in the first place," he snapped, then turned to look up and down the street, making sure they were still alone.

She recoiled. "How dare you judge me?"

"This isn't judgment. I'm not letting you play the victim in a scheme you created," he insisted.

When she didn't refute his point, he pointed back and forth between them, asking, "So, was I your back-up plan? Were you going to talk me into being the runner-up replacement daddy?"

It was a callous thing to say, and he winced as he said it. For a moment she looked hurt, before she replaced it with a steely coolness. Her voice level as she dismissed him. "Please. Don't flatter yourself. You're a ranch lackey and you'll never amount to anything more."

Trix felt gut punched. True to form, she knew exactly how to land a lethal blow.

"God, you really are more trouble than you're worth," he managed. He needed to leave before his emotions got the best of him, or he'd say something even she didn't deserve.

Turning his back on her, he crossed the street, got in his truck and drove away.

CHAPTER 10

As he headed back to the ranch Trix's anger continued to build. His teeth hurt from the tension in his jaw and his palms burned from the twisting grip on the steering wheel. He was furious with Katherine for being exactly who he knew she was. He was even more furious with himself for pretending she wasn't.

When he arrived at the ranch house, he stomped into the front room, Katherine's confession still ricocheting off the inside of his skull.

"What on earth happened to you?" Alex's voice startled him. He hadn't even noticed her on the couch when he came in. When he whipped around to face her, and she recoiled, proving he needed to get a grip. Now.

"Red, sorry to burst in like that. Having a really rough day."

"Do you need to talk about it?"

"No," he said quickly.

"Uh, what can I do?"

"You on the schedule for tomorrow?" ·

"Nope," she half grinned, appearing to already know where his head was going.

"I need to get sideways."

She nodded. "I'm your gal."

Alex hopped up and jogged to the kitchen to grab supplies. Trix went down the basement steps and started racking the pool balls.

When she came downstairs, he asked, "Play a game?"

"Sure," she said and showed him the beers and bottle of Jack she was carrying. "Thought we were going heavy, but I brought beer in case I read the mood wrong."

He gestured toward the whiskey. "You read it right."

Alex laughed, pouring each of them a healthy splash into some Solo cups. As he broke to start the game, he could feel Alex's eyes on him. Eventually, she said, "So, where were you earlier?"

"Nope. Anything else, Red. Pick anything else."

"Fine. Shall we put a wager on the game, then?"

He watched her suspiciously, knowing full well that she was completely capable of annihilating him in a game of pool. "What's the wager?"

"Loser has to tell Winn we drank his Jack." She flipped the bottle around to reveal a masking tape label that read *"Buy your own!"* in Winn's handwriting.

He smiled. "Deal."

They played best out of five and it took her only three games to put him out of his misery. Alex's easy laugh and playful nature took some of the sting out of the defeat and seemed to put some room between him and his anger. In three short games of pool, they'd also put a pretty significant dent in the bottle of booze.

"Okay, I'd like to sit," she said.

"Thank god, I don't need to have my ass handed to me four times in a row." He laughed, allowing himself to bask in the slowed feeling the alcohol created in his previously whirling mind. She walked to the middle of the room, sat on the floor, and lay down.

"You okay, Red? Maybe we should have slowed down on the hard stuff," he said, eyeing the couch she'd decided to ignore.

"I'm okay actually. I like my day drinking to come with a bit of time on the floor. It's humbling."

He shrugged, then grabbed a few cushions, tossing one to her before joining her. They both stared at the ceiling for a few quiet moments then Alex said, "I like it here."

"We like you being here," Trix said.

"It makes me sad to think about going home soon."

"You don't have to go back to Chicago."

"I do."

"Why?"

"It's where my life is. I have to go back. I shouldn't have said anything. It'll make me sad, then angry when I can't explain it."

"Usually when explaining your actions is hard it means maybe they aren't right," he told her, thinking about his own predicament as much as hers.

She let out a heavy sigh. "Maybe."

After a few solemn moments where he lost himself in thought, Alex broke in with, "Why'd you run away from New York so fast you made it all the way to Montana before you slowed down?"

"My father," he answered. She made an annoyed sound, obviously not satisfied with his two-word back story. "Well, actually it was more about my twin sister, Jenny."

Alex flipped over. Her interest piqued.

"Anyway," he went on, "when you come from that kind of money, you're almost like domestic royalty. My father desperately needed my sister to fit the bill of a quintessential socialite, and wanted her to be a debutante."

"What did she want?" Alex asked.

"To kiss girls."

"Ah..."

"Yeah. Walter Doyle's ancestors didn't claw their way over from the old country and bust their ass building an empire, so he could have a lesbian daughter all over the news."

"A quote? I'm assuming."

Trix waived a drunken arm. "I'm paraphrasing."

"What happened?"

"He kicked her out... for a time. When she left, so did I. Came here, looking for something else. A different kind of person, I guess. People with different priorities."

"You found it," she said, and he could hear the smile in her voice.

"In spades."

"Where's your sister now?"

"Still in the city. They reconciled and made an agreement they could live with, but I couldn't."

"What kind of agreement?" she asked.

"One based in denial. When it comes to her love life, he doesn't ask questions, she keeps it quiet and out of his circles. They're back to playing their roles." Trix watched the ceiling thinking about his sister, wondering what she would have to say about his current woman troubles.

"How sad. For both of them."

"They don't seem to mind, but to me, it's further proof in their world, authentic doesn't have much value." He flipped over to face her. "You know, you remind me of her."

"Yeah?"

"Yeah. Bold, strong… somehow also delicate, damaged."

There was a moment when he thought she'd be offended, but then she smiled. "I can live with that assessment."

"Being with Winn seems to make you stronger," he ventured.

"It does."

"I've never understood why people say being with someone doesn't change you, 'cause it does. Not like you're a different person, but sharing the burden of life helps."

"You're so deep and broody when you're drunk. The burden of life?" She laughed.

"Yeah, I suppose that's more dramatic than I was going for."

"Do you have something that feels too heavy for one person?" she asked, watching his face.

He wrestled with how honest he wanted to be, finally deciding he could trust her with what he was feeling.

"Only the loneliness," he said quietly.

***

Alex's heart broke seeing the pain in Trix's eyes after his admission. She reached her hand out to grab his and gave it a little squeeze. Being serious was something he didn't choose often, and she felt lucky to be shown that part of him. She was trying to find some comforting words when a pair of boots started down the stairs. Winn appeared and was visibly surprised to find them there, lying on the floor in the middle of the afternoon.

"What are you guys doing?"

There was general confusion in his voice but no aggression, making Alex appreciate that even though Winn had recently had his heart torn out by a cheating hussy, he didn't ever get jealous. He didn't appear at all alarmed to find them lying on a makeshift floor bed in the middle of the afternoon. This probably said more about the deep trust he had in his best friend than her, but she was glad for it regardless.

It was only when Winn saw the half-empty bottle of Jack, he finally looked upset.

"Trix, you're up." Alex laughed, pointing at the bottle.

"Aw, jeez. Sorry, buddy. See, I was having a bit of a rough day, and Alex here joined me in a bottle to help forget."

"Don't care about that. I care about who's bottle you chose to climb into."

"I'll grab you a new one in town."

"Two, you'll grab two new ones tomorrow," Winn insisted.

"That's unfair," Trix objected.

"One for me to label and have you drink anyway and one for me to hide from you desperate drunks."

"Fine."

The tension eased, and Winn walked over to offer Alex a hand. Standing she looked back at Trix and smiled. "Thanks for the day drinking and for… the good conversation."

***

Trix remained on the ground and decided maybe there was something to Alex's *humility through floor time* concept. His phone vibrated in his pocket, and he pulled it out to look at the caller ID.

Daddy Dearest.

"Crap," he grumbled. It was as if talking about the man had somehow summoned him from whatever circle of hell he was currently overseeing.

Trix swiped to answer. "Walter."

"Jacob."

There was a long pause.

"Is this where I'm supposed to guess why you're calling, or do you want to get on with it?"

"Your cousin Alfred asked me if you're planning to attend his wedding."

Trix rolled his eyes. "No, he didn't. I've already sent him my regrets."

"I wasn't sure you were receiving mail."

"It's not the Western front, Father. It's a prairie state."

Walter cleared his throat.

"What else?" Trix asked.

"I am growing bored with this wild west experiment of yours. Alfred junior is a fine man, and being around someone your own age who's made better life choices may do you some good."

Trix didn't have anything more to say to his father on the matter. The two of them had already logged too many hours circling this same conversation.

"The wedding is two months away yet. I'm sure you're capable of handing over your shit shoveling duties that far in advance."

"I have to go." Trix said.

"I will buy your ticket."

"It's not about the money."

"Your mother would like to see you."

Trix snorted air out his nose. "Right."

There was another uncomfortable pause.

"If there's nothing else, Walter, I would like to skip to the end of… whatever this is."

"You and Alfred used to be close."

"I know." Trix frowned. His father could care less about Alfred's feelings or their relationship. There must be some other reason Walter was leaning on him about the wedding. Regardless of motive, he was right about one thing. Alfred was not only family, but a friend. "I'll think about it."

"Good."

The line disconnected and Trix stared at the phone. *Asshole.*

Trix cracked his neck and sighed. The decision to stay away from New York for the last three years had been about survival. He worried his old life would find a way to wrap around him, trap him, and suffocate him. It wasn't as foolish as it sounded. His father always got what he wanted, and what he wanted was for Trix to return.

He wanted Trix in a suit, in an office, and back under his thumb. Trouble was, taking a leadership role in his father's investment banking firm had sounded like torture when he was twenty-one and fresh out of college. Now that Trix had built a life here, it sounded even worse.

"He's only a man. He cannot force you to stay," Trix said to the ceiling, then pulled out his phone and shot off a text to his cousin.

AJ if there's still room for me I'd love to celebrate the miracle of you finding a woman who tolerates you.

Hey cuz, of course there's room. Denise has a few friends that will be excited to meet a real-life cowboy LOL.

Does that mean I can wear my shit kickers?

Not unless you want to see me divorced immediately.
Just jeans then.
Very funny.
See you in September.
Looking forward to catching up.

CHAPTER 11

Two weeks after hearing it, Trix was still struggling with what to do about Katherine's confession. With the passage of time, he was feeling calmer but still had no clue as to what, if anything, he should do with the information. She was an adult who could take care of herself. She wasn't his friend, she was his... What? His tormentor? An unwanted specter who had set up shop in his mind? Exactly how much responsibility should anyone feel for the unplanned pregnancy of their personal scary apparition? Despite how front row the problem had been in his mind, he had a much more critical and heartbreaking hurdle to tackle today.

Alex was leaving them.

At the beginning of the summer, she'd shown up broken and angry at the world. Her mother had forced her to come to the ranch tired of watching the train wreck Alex had made of her life in the Chicago. Now the required sentence was coming to an end, and so much had changed. What Alex and Winn had was special. Although Trix didn't know much about love, he did know when you had something that mattered, you hung on to it. Which was why he was baffled by Alex's insistence she had to return to what she called her *real life* in order to repair the damage there.

She talked about going back to the city as a foregone conclusion, something which wasn't up for debate. Her willing return was such a contrast to his own insistence he'd never return to New York. He'd been wracking his brain trying to figure out her motives.

After spending the last week pushing her about her reasoning, he'd come to a depressing conclusion. She was leaving because she didn't believe she deserved the happiness she'd found here. She thought what she had with Winn was too fragile and destined to fail. She was so sure it would crumble. She didn't want to wait around to watch it happen.

Trix saw the obvious flaw in her reasoning, but had been unable to convince her. He'd also been shocked to watch Winn fail to communicate his own feelings over and over again. Trix worried about what would become of both of them if they didn't fight for what they'd found together.

When Trix came down for breakfast the air at the table was depressing and heavy, as if everyone shared his deep sadness. Neither Alex nor Winn had come to eat. Trix suspected they were not together since the tension between them over the last few days had been brutal to watch.

Winn desperately wanted her to stay, but couldn't find words to change her mind. Alex had been frustrated she couldn't make Winn understand her. All around it had been a mess Trix was unable to fix. He looked up and made eye contact with Mae who nodded at him with pinched lips. It was going to be an emotional day.

Around midmorning, it was time for Alex to pack her car, so everyone gathered in the front of the house to see her off. Well, almost everyone. Their farewell was suspiciously short one person. Trix sighed and looked back toward the horse barns.

Damn it, Winn, how can you justify missing this?

Trix watched Alex say her goodbyes. She hugged Belle and Bishop at the same time, and they thanked her again for her help with the proposal. Junior gave her a hug and a pair of cowboy boots Maddie had wanted her to have. Even Griz, their big soft-spoken teddy bear, looked a little choked up as his large frame bent in half to wrap her in his arms.

Alex put on a brave face as she hugged Tiny, Sam, Bud, Harley, Casper, and Sarge. They all smiled and made jokes. When she got to Winn's brother, Matt, her face crumpled completely, and true tears began to fall. Matt pressed his cheek into her hair and whispered something Trix couldn't hear. Mae was next.

Trix worried once she wrapped Alex up, she might refuse to let go, but after a long moment she did. "We love you, kiddo," Mae said and then cleared her throat and wiped her eyes.

Alex got to Trix and wrapped her arms around his neck.

"Last chance to change your mind, Red," he said into her hair.

She leaned back and gave him a scolding smile.

"I'm going to miss you," she said softly.

"Same."

"Tell him…" She trailed off, fresh tears in her eyes.

"I think he knows," Trix said releasing her.

Alex got in her little blue car with Illinois plates and waved one last time through the windshield before she pulled out.

Trix watched her car disappear down the driveway then looked around the group. They all wore the same perplexed expression.

Where in the hell was Winn?

Heading off to find him, Trix searched the entire main house, convinced Winn would've positioned himself to watch Alex leave. When that yielded nothing, he made his way to the barn. No Winn in the arena. No Winn in the aisle. No Winn in the pen working out his denial with a horse. After another ten minutes he finally found Winn's dumb ass in the feed room holding a clip board, pen poised but motionless, eyes unfocused.

"Did you have a stroke I don't know about?" Trix asked.

"What?" Winn's head snapped up, his hard eyes landing on Trix.

"What in the hell are you doing in here while the dust's settling behind your woman? You should know she tore out of here with tears in her eyes."

"Not in the mood for this." Winn brought his attention back to the sacks of grain.

"If not now, when? When she's put fifty miles between you? A thousand?"

"She's made her choice. The least I can do is honor it."

"You're a coward, Winn Taylor," Trix said sharply.

Winn's eyes narrowed. "Don't think I'm too calm to put my knuckles in your teeth."

"Good. Hit me," Trix hollered, shoving Winn around to face him. "Knock out a tooth or two. Whatever it takes to wake you the hell up. It was a mistake to let her leave without telling her how you feel." Trix shoved him again.

Winn swayed from the strike but didn't move to return it. Instead, he said to the ground, "What do you know about how I feel, or what I've told her?"

Trix hard stared at his friend's downturned face. He knew what he'd said was true. Winn was desperately in love with Alex, and if he'd told her so, he wouldn't look like a shame-filled, bottled-up version of a man right now.

"Didn't peg you as a guy who gives up without a fight," Trix accused.

"I fought," Winn said, jerking his gaze to meet Trix's, his mouth set in a firm line.

"Not enough. You had an ace to play, and you choked." Trix pointed a finger toward his friend's face.

"I told her I wanted her to stay."

"But not *why* you want her to stay?" Trix pushed.

"I can't guilt her into staying. I can't guilt her into feeling something more for me."

Trix laughed, and Winn stared back as if he'd suggested keg stands at a funeral. "You think that woman isn't ass over elbows in love with you? Did I say coward? I should have said blind motherfu—"

Winn cut him off. "Did she tell you how she feels about me?"

"No, man, she told you. You weren't listening."

Winn let out a long breath and nodded. "I should've told her."

Trix moved behind Winn and started pushing. "Still can."

"Don't be crazy, she's got maybe an hour head start by now."

"Thirty-two minutes and counting actually, but if you haul ass you should easily catch her." Trix pulled the clipboard from Winn's hands and continued nudging him toward the door.

"What if she's hauling ass?" Winn asked.

"I hear Chicago is nice in the fall."

"Shit, I've… Yeah, okay. But, the horses…"

"I can cover. You're going to catch her, man. It doesn't matter."

They cleared the side of the house and saw Mae standing next to the orange farm truck, keys dangling from an outstretched hand.

"That took too long, Winn," Mae said.

"Well, I'm going now, aren't I?" he said to her as he snagged the keys.

"Late." She hit him with a hard look, but when he appeared sufficiently scolded her face softened and she added, "Be honest."

He nodded, got in, started up the truck and kicked up gravel as he flipped around and tore down the drive.

***

Two hours later Trix was waiting on the porch with Mae and Winn's brother, Matt, when Winn came down the drive. Alone. After parking he hopped out, looking up at them his shoulders sagged.

"Where's Alex?" Matt asked, despite the obvious.

"Not sure," Winn said.

"But you... you caught up to her and told her how you feel?" Trix asked.

Winn pinned a hard stare on him. "I said I was going to do it, and I did it."

Mae broke in. "I'm sure she'll figure out where she belongs. May not be on our preferred timetable, but she will." She nodded toward the house, and she and Matt headed inside. Trix refused her prompt to give Winn some space. When Winn joined Trix on the porch the two of them turned to stare down the empty driveway.

"Details?" Trix asked.

"I went flying down the road, through town like a bat out of hell and out of the corner of my eye I saw her car in the grocery store parking lot. Damn near blew right past."

Trix grinned. "She didn't even make it out of town."

"Doesn't mean she'll come back here though."

"What happened?"

Winn rubbed a palm over his mouth a few times. "I, well, I told her, you know, that I wanted her to come back, stay here, pick me. I don't know what I said Trix, I'm bad at that kind of thing even when there's not this kind of pressure."

Trix crossed his arms and lifted his brows. "There was one big thing you were gonna say though. Did you at least get that right?"

"Well yeah, I said I was in love with her and if she felt the same, she should come home."

"Then?"

"Then I left her standing there in the parking lot."

"I'm sure it was... romantic," Trix lied while shaking his head.

Winn splayed his hands on his hips and dropped his eyes to the ground with a big sigh.

"Think it'll be weird if you're standing here when she pulls in?"

"I think it'll be weird if we're *both* standing here," Winn replied.

Trix put his hands up in surrender. "Okay, okay but think she'll do the run and jump into your arms thing?"

"She's not going to do the run and jump thing," Winn dismissed quickly.

"I want her to do the run and jump thing."

"I'm not even sure she's coming."

"She'll come, man." Trix put his hand on Winn's shoulder.

Winn swallowed hard, bringing his gaze back the road.

"Okay, I'll leave you to it, but I've got a twenty on the run and jump thing," Trix smiled.

"I've got twenty on her yelling at me," Winn countered.

"Equally likely. I don't know a lot about the females, but I don't think *left in a parking lot* is their favorite grand gesture." Trix chuckled before returning to the house.

***

Winn watched Trix leave, full well knowing he wouldn't be going far. He turned back to face the road and allowed himself to hope.

Alex belonged at the ranch. Alex belongs with me. How could I be so sure of something and be wrong?

He narrowed his eyes at what he thought may be a dust trail from someone coming down the long drive. His heart hit the back of his ribs when he saw her blue little Honda come around the bend. There was a hard knock on the window, and he turned to see Trix's stupid smiling face giving an enthusiastic thumbs up.

"Get away from there," Winn yelled, while his insides matched his friend's excited expression.

"Idiot," he mumbled to himself as he strode down the wide steps to meet Alex's car. For a fraction of a second, he considered giving her enough room to run and jump into his arms, but then he saw her expression as she shut off the engine and knew he'd be collecting twenty bucks from Trix later.

Alex climbed out of the car. She planted her feet as he took long determined steps to her, a grin playing at the corner of his mouth.

"Listen up, redneck, if you think this emotional blackmail, playing against my need to have the last word, is going to work for us long term, then you've got—"

He cut off her tirade by cupping the sides of her face and pulling her to him. His mouth found her, and he kissed her deep and slow. He felt the moment the tension in her body went slack, and despite knowing he had an audience, gave serious thought to throwing her over his shoulder and carrying her to his room. She broke from his mouth, the two of them panting the same air back and forth.

"And, I love you too," she breathed.

"I know," he smiled as he pressed his forehead into hers. "Welcome home."

CHAPTER 12

As Alex followed Winn into the house her anxiety ticked up a notch. She wanted to believe him about how the crew would respond, but from the outside looking in it must've appeared like she couldn't make up her mind, and might leave again.

The front room was empty, but the sound of the men gathered for lunch spilled from the dining room. As they rounded the corner a familiar scene greeted her. The room was filled with big bodies, lively energy, and the smell of a hearty homecooked meal. A few men looked up when they came in, then casually nodded and returned to their food and conversation.

"Hey, guys," Trix said nonchalantly.

Alex's eyes narrowed, unsure of how to proceed. The normalcy of it all was not what she'd expected. After a long uncomfortable minute Bishop finally laughed and started off a chain reaction where everyone broke character.

"You should see your face," Bishop snorted.

"Welcome back, Alex." Mae smiled before going back to the business of passing platters around.

The men all began to stand and show their relief at her return, the noise level in the room jumped up with all the teasing.

"'Bout time."

"Did ya miss us, Red?"

"Come here," Trix shouted as he stood with outstretched arms. Alex jogged as she made her way into his open arms for a big bear hug where he whirled her feet off the ground. Trix called out to Winn, "You got yelled at. I got the run and jump thing."

Winn shrugged and laughed. Alex made her way around the table giving all of the crew hugs, acknowledging their playful barbs at her expense. Finally, she made her way to Mae. "Glad you changed your mind," Mae said.

"Winn changed it," Alex confessed as she gave the older woman a hug.

Mae nodded in her slow and knowing way. "Hungry?"

"Famished," Alex admitted taking her regular seat next to Winn. The table settled and resumed normal lunch time behavior.

"So, there's some business to attend to, and we may as well get this sorted now," Mae announced to the table. Alex's gut clenched a little. Perhaps her unplanned return was throwing a bigger wrench in things than she'd anticipated.

"Seems a few of you are coming into a part of your life where you need a change in order to explore your next chapter," Mae started.

Some men nodded. A few looked quizzical.

"Bishop and Belle are buying a hundred acres of the northeast pasture from Crooked Brook and they plan on building a home there."

Everyone looked to Bishop who smiled sheepishly. Those closest to him patted his back and offered congratulations.

"Thanks again for that, Moms," Bishop said. "Means the world to me."

Mae nodded as if selling off part of her legacy was just another Tuesday. "While they're building, I told Belle she can move into the house and live with Bishop in the first-floor bedroom. That means Trix and Tiny will need to move out of there. I've had an eye on the loft in the stables. It used to be a studio apartment, so I think it can be converted back into a living space. Seeing as how Trix has recently expressed an interest in having some space, he'll move out there."

Alex glanced at Trix, but couldn't read his expression. What Mae was saying seemed to contradict what Trix had told her about feeling lonely.

Mae continued her human shell game. "Tiny told me he'd rather stay in the house, so he'll take the open bunk on the third floor in Junior and Harley's room. Everyone on board with these changes?" Everyone nodded or spoke their agreement. "Now, to our next set of love birds." She sent a pointed look at Alex and Winn. "I'm not old-fashioned, dumb or deaf..." Alex's cheeks flushed, and Winn's thigh began to bounce under the table. Trix, being Trix, laughed out loud. Others snickered.

"I have a proposal that will alleviate this lack of privacy. Matt turns forty in not too long." Mae paused so the table could give Winn's brother crap for getting old. After everyone ceased their jibes she continued, "I believe that milestone means he'd fit in better with us old farts on the second floor. I plan to move him into Alex's current room and Alex will move down into the basement bedroom with Winn."

"Thanks, Moms," Winn said.

Alex saw past her embarrassment to look up and around the table. No one was looking at her.

Mae continued. "We'll keep the work schedule the same as it was before Alex pretended to move back to Chicago. So whatever shift you worked last week, you'll start working again tomorrow. All clear?"

Everyone nodded again, and the meal resumed like any other day.

Alex felt a weight lift from her shoulders as she realized the monumental decision she'd made was actually right because instead of worry, she felt hope for the first time in maybe ever.

CHAPTER 13

Three days after the move, Trix went up to the loft and took a deep breath. He was thankful Mae had found a way to give him some space. His paranoia made his move out of the house and into the loft essential. As it did so often, his mind looped in anxious circles around the secrets he was holding. He'd slept with the woman who cheated on his best friend. That betrayed not only the trust Winn had placed in him, but the trust everyone here had placed in him. Now he was guarding the secret about her pregnancy from them too. He shook his head wishing he could delete her from his mind. How tranquil his life had felt at the beginning of the summer, and now it was only August and he had rocked the boat so much, all he could see was waves.

His phone rang, it was his father. Again. Walter had barely contacted him since Trix moved to Montana. Now he was calling less than a month after their last conversation.

Trix answered the phone. "I guess it's a slow time of year for screwing people out of money if you're finding time to call again."

"Must ignorance always be the first thing out of your mouth?"

Trix shook his head at the barb, but responded coolly. "To what do I owe the pleasure, Father?"

"Alfred told me you've had a change of heart and will be attending his wedding."

"Alfred is my friend, and I should be there to support him. That's the first thing you and I have agreed on in a long time."

"I am glad to hear it. I've purchased a ticket for you, and I assume we can send for your things at a later date."

Trix's brow crimped n confusion. "What?"

"You must have amassed some belongings in the years you've been playing cowboy. We will have them packed up and sent back to New York along with your car if it's still running."

"I am only coming back for that weekend."

"Jacob, I understand the need to sow some oats, so to speak, but enough of this nonsense. You will come back for the wedding and you will stay. You will resume your life, and we will all begin to move past this ridiculous charade you've put us through over the last few years."

"You don't understand a damn thing. This is my life and I plan on living it. Here. In Montana."

"I will not tolerate this any longer."

"You say that as though you've been tolerant to this point."

"If you refuse to do the right thing, you will force my hand."

"A threat without a punchline has no teeth, Walter. I believe it was you who taught me that."

"If you do not return, I will remove the assets from your trust and purge your name from my will."

"I haven't taken a dime from you for three years."

"Yes, I imagine expenses are low when you live in a hostel slash labor camp." Trix made an offended sound his father spoke over. "That kind of lifestyle suits when you're young and dumb, but it will not last. When it ends, which it will, you will require security from the job I offer and the life you were born into. I am telling you now, if you do not return to New York and take the job at Williams and Doyle after the wedding, those options cease to exist."

"This life doesn't have an expiration date on it. I am choosing this, and it will not end."

His father chuckled dryly. "It will end. Of course, it will end. You've never been capable of staying the course long enough to make something permanent. Why would your foray into ranching be any different?"

Trix's hold on the phone clinched like a vice, but he kept his tone light. "Walter, so salty today. Have you been in the scotch?"

"Damn it, boy, hear me when I say, make better choices, or you will have nowhere to turn when this Montana experiment ends."

"So much wisdom crammed into one ultimatum. Trust me, my decision remains unchanged. I live here now, Father. You should start to wrap your mind around that."

"I guess we'll see."

"We'll see what?"

"If you're willing to bet your future on the off chance you won't screw this up. Not a bet I would make, considering your track record," his father said then hung up.

Trix stared at the phone and resisted the urge to throw it.

CHAPTER 14

Katherine waited for Maddie to stop her car at the entrance to the trailerpark then climbed out and shut the door. Leaning into the open window Katherine said, "Thanks. Sorry about wasting the day."

"No worries. Hope you feel better," Maddie said brightly as Katherine stepped back and watched Maddie drive off.

The two had planned to use their day off to grab lunch and do some shopping in Great Falls, the nearest town with a mall, but their plans were cut short when, after only an hour, Katherine had started to feel sick. She hadn't had a lot of symptoms so far in the pregnancy, but it appeared that as the first trimester was ending, her body was starting the process of ruining itself to grow another human. She'd spent all morning fighting the urge to fold over from the discomfort in her lower abdomen and when that got too hard, she'd asked Maddie to take her home. The last thing she needed was for her lovable, but nosy cousin to start asking personal questions that Katherine wouldn't answer. Maddie couldn't help her with this anyway.

Katherine took a steadying breath. Time was running out. Any day now she'd need more than a loose blouse to hide what was going on. She needed to make some decisions. She thought of Trix, then felt guilty. He'd only come to mind because she needed something. She'd already made him an unwitting accomplice in this when she confided in him, a lapse in judgment she still didn't understand. Perhaps it was because she knew Trix's estranged family had money. If anyone had the means to help her it would be him.

You're a heartless calculating bitch, just like he said you were.

She felt bad she'd be using Trix, but it was worth it to save herself and her baby. Now was not the time to get soft.

As she walked down the road toward her house, Katherine heard a car coming up behind her. She stepped to the side to allow them to pass, but no one came around. Turning, Katherine's gut sank when she saw Blake's truck a few feet behind her. He must have been watching the park, waiting for her.

Shit.

"We need to talk," he said as he got out and strode up to her.

"Blake," she sighed. "I don't have time for this."

"Right, like some pressing waitress duties have followed you home."

"Something followed me home," she mumbled.

"At the rodeo I told you our conversation wasn't over. I've been calling and you're blowing me off. People don't get away with that."

"I don't have any interest in seeing you anymore. It's a straightforward conversation, and I thought we'd already had it."

"That's not the line you took a few months ago when you were running your nails down my back," he said with a slimy smirk. Katherine grimaced, she was all too aware that slipping up and slipping back into bed with Blake had been a huge mistake. She didn't need him rubbing her face in it.

"Maybe that mediocre rendezvous was the reminder I needed," she scoffed.

"You think this hot and cold thing you do is cute, but it's a turn off."

"This may come as a shock, but turning you on isn't on today's To-Do list," she countered.

"It should be."

She shook her head at his arrogance. "I know you believe that."

"Look around you. You want to be in this trailerpark forever? You want to end up like your mother who has to chase the bottom of a bottle in order to forget she's attached to a loser?"

"My father is twice the man you'll ever be," she said, her voice rising.

"I know the only things he accomplished in his life were buying a shack and raising his kids to be a drug dealer and a slut."

"Go to hell."

He raised his arm to point at the trailers around them. "I'm already here."

"You condescending asshole," she shouted. "I'd rather rot in this place than suffer another moment as some trophy you wrongly think you deserve."

He puffed up his chest on the next breath of air and quickly made a move toward her. She had to fight the urge to flinch. He'd never hit her, but he frequently lunged at her as if he was going to. She found it so likely he would someday, she always had to wonder if this time would be the time. Not knowing was almost worse than being struck.

Do not show fear.

"What are you going to do?" she challenged. "You think you can bully me into a relationship? You're that desperate?" His brow slammed down, and his hands clenched into fists at his side. She kept pushing. "When we got together it was about you winning something from Winn. The point's been made. There's nothing more here. What words are required to convince you we don't need to have this conversation ever again?" His eyes stayed hard as his jaw worked. Blake was not good at losing but maybe all he needed was an out that preserved some of his ego. "I know you think you have a lot to offer. I'm saying offer it to someone else."

He snorted. "I've never been the guy who has to chase a skirt. I'm done with you and all the trouble that comes with you."

"Then we agree," she said, ignoring how he was twisting this into him breaking off a relationship that never existed.

"But that means you don't call me anymore either. I don't care if Winn hurts your feelings, or if your mom needs to get bailed out, or if you have an itch that needs scratching. If I'm gone, I'm long gone." Blake looked at her as if those words would somehow magically cause her to see the error of her ways. She had to hide the relief from her expression.

"I can live with that," she said.

He watched her for a long moment, and then cursed at the ground as he turned back to his truck. She held her breath as she watched him leave. As soon as his truck was out of view, she folded over banding an arm around her waist. A wave of nausea flowed up from her gut to form a pool of saliva in her mouth. She bent, prepared to vomit but nothing came.

She had no way of knowing if that would be the end of it with Blake. He was unpredictable at best. If Blake were to see her when the pregnancy started showing would he put it together, or would he assume, like most did, that she bounced between several beds, and someone else was the father? His family had enough power and wealth, they could easily take the baby from her if they were so inclined. The only thing she could imagine that would be worse than raising a child in her home, would be a child growing up in Blake's household.

In that moment it became clear to her what she needed to do. No amount of scheming was going to get her out of this. No amount of plotting would guarantee that the Martin's never knew they were grandparents.

She needed to leave town.

As another round of cramping struck, she looked down the road wondering if she could make it to her house. Should she even go home? She couldn't tell her mother what was going on. Maybe she needed to sit down. The cramping became worse, and she looked up to the property management office housed in the trailer at the entrance. It was only one-hundred yards away. When she made it up the steps, she came through the door so hard, Debbie Jo behind the desk gasped.

"Sorry. Sick. Can I use your bathroom?" Katherine managed.

Debbie Jo watched her suspiciously for a moment, but then nodded. Katherine made it down the hall and locked herself in the bathroom.

I need help.

Only one person came to mind.

***

Trix and Griz were working on a tractor engine. Or rather Griz was. Trix was there pretending to be helpful and enjoying the fact that his calm and steady friend never forced conversation. His phone rang, and he looked down. Katherine. They hadn't spoken since she told him about the baby. He pulled in a deep breath and walked nonchalantly away from Griz. When he made it into the yard where no one could hear him he answered. "What?"

"Trix?" There was tremor in Katherine's voice.

"What's wrong?" he asked softer.

"I'm bleeding."

"What? Are you hurt?" He was confused, but his heart began to race.

"The baby…" she mumbled.

"Where are you?"

"The trailerpark, in the office."

"Twenty minutes."

He surprised himself over the panic he felt. He didn't know much about pregnancy, but her fear magnified his concern. He poked his head into the door of the machine shop and called out, "Griz, something came up. I'm taking off."

"Okay."

Trix jumped into his truck and sped down the backcountry roads. Arriving at the trailerpark he jogged up to the old doublewide that served as the park's office.

"There a girl in here?" he asked the lady behind the desk.

"Restroom," she said tipping her head down a hallway.

Knocking on the bathroom door he called quietly, "Katherine?"

"Trix?"

"You alone?"

"Yes," she replied, and he heard the lock disengage.

He pushed the door open and found her in the little room bent over and bracing herself on the sink. When she looked up at him, the fear in her eyes made him want to punch a wall.

"You okay?" he asked stupidly.

She shook her head. "I need a ride. Can you take me to the doctor?"

"Of course."

She nodded, and he went to help her, but she shooed his hand away. "I'm okay."

They walked to the parking lot and he watched her gingerly climb in, unsure if he should offer to help again. As he drove, she curled up on the passenger side, and when she cried out in pain, he floored it.

They skidded to a stop in front of the small local Emergency Room, and he ran around the front of the truck. Trix slid his arm under her knees and pulled her to his chest, hoisting her off the seat. She leaned her head against his shoulder as he carried her through the doors.

"I need help here," he called to the woman at reception.

She rose and spoke into a radio on her shoulder. "Need a bed in triage." Two nurses came rushing out from the double doors pushing a gurney. Helping Katherine onto the bed, they disappeared, leaving him alone in the waiting area.

His heart was pounding a mile a minute, and he was unsure of what to do next.

Should I leave?

Leaving her felt wrong, but witnessing something this personal felt intrusive. He realized he didn't know how to contact any of her people. Perhaps he could call Junior for Maddie's number? Junior would ask why he needed it. What would he tell him? When no solution came to mind, he went out and moved his truck then walked back to the waiting room. He was still sitting there three hours later when a doctor came out and found him.

"Are you here for Ms. Grant?"

"I... Yes. I guess I am," Trix replied.

If the doctor found his response strange, she didn't let it show. "You can come back now. Are you the father?"

"No. Is she going to be all right?"

"Well... I can't share much with you, but she's resting comfortably, and you can see her."

Trix followed the doctor through to where Katherine had been taken. Again, he was torn. She had called him and needed a ride, but did that mean she wanted him here now? Surely there must be someone else who knew about her situation that she would prefer to see.

He pulled back the curtain and found her propped up in bed, face turned to the opposite wall. She looked so small with a hospital gown swimming around her, and the big blocky bed on all sides. Her pale arm lay next to her side, a tube fixed to the top of her hand. Monitors quietly chimed above her head.

"Katherine," he said quietly.

She turned to him. Her eyes dull.

"You stayed." Her voice was hoarse, the tone hard to read.

"I didn't know, if uh... I wasn't sure if I should. Do you want me to leave?"

She closed her eyes for a long moment and shook her head. "The baby is gone."

"Katherine, I'm sorry. That's... Jesus Christ." He stepped into the room, closing the curtain behind him. "Do you want me to call anyone?"

"No one knows," she said.

"That you're here?"

She pinned a hard stare on him like he was being dense. "About the baby."

"Oh."

Not knowing what else to do, he sat down on the bed next to her and she leaned over to lie on his chest and began to cry. His heart cracked. Trix was unsure how to comfort her, so decided his only job at this moment was to shut up and wait for her to tell him what to do next. They sat silently for what must've been an hour before the doctor returned.

"Ms. Grant, your paperwork has been processed and you're free to go. You've made your follow up appointment with your regular physician?"

"Yes," Katherine said quietly.

"You're going to want to take a few days to recover. You may still have some residual bleeding and discomfort for the next forty-eight hours. Can you take some time off work?"

"Yes," Katherine repeated.

The doctor left and Trix turned to Katherine. She looked up and met his stare.

"I can't go home. Not like this." Her voice sounded small and more unsure than he had ever heard it. He understood, but didn't have any answers. He couldn't take her to Crooked Brook. Where else could they go?

"Maybe we can get you a hotel room. I could run a few errands. Get you set up before I head home." She watched him silently. "Or, uh... I'm off tomorrow," he continued, "and could maybe swap shifts with one of the guys for the day after." When again she didn't speak, he stood awkwardly and went to leave. "I'll go pull the truck around. Meet you outside, okay?"

She nodded. "Thank you," she said as he stepped through the curtain.

CHAPTER 15

Trix and Katherine spent the entire forty-five-minute ride to the motel in silence. He'd decided to take them to a place out of town, off the interstate. There, the chances of them seeing anyone they knew, was almost zero. When they arrived, he parked and left Katherine in the car while he went into the office to rent a room, and then he called Tiny to swap days off. When he returned to the truck Katherine was facing out the window and didn't move when he got in and drove them around to park in front of their room.

"Do you need help walking?" he asked.

Katherine shook her head and climbed out of the cab. The room looked like every other run-down motel in the middle of nowhere. Everything was rust colored, from the walls to the carpet, to the frayed comforters on the two double beds. Katherine didn't seem to mind. Instead, she was looking down at her crumpled clothes.

"I know I'm in no position to ask a favor," she said, "but if I gave you some cash would you run to the store and grab me something more comfortable to sleep in?"

"Sure."

Trix was thankful for a reason to leave, to give himself a break from the current version of her, which threw him for a loop. Katherine Grant being vulnerable was hard to come to terms with. He took the cash she offered without any intention of using it, and drove to the clothing store the next town over. Trix wandered aimlessly. Apparently, women's clothing came with numbers, which was confusing. He did his best, then grabbed some groceries.

When he got back to the room a few hours later, Katherine was sitting on the bed watching the wall while mindlessly picking at the remnants of the adhesive on the back of her hand. She gave him a weak smile as he handed her the clothing bag and went to unpack the food and drinks.

"What the hell?" she asked.

He turned to see her holding up one of the outfits. She held up a boys' pajama top that had an excavator and the phrase "Sleeping Is Tough Business" on it. It came with a matching pair of fleece camo bottoms.

"I didn't understand the women sizes, so I guessed."

He watched her face to determine exactly how much trouble he was in, and to his surprise she started giggling. He let out a relieved chuckle.

"God, you're an idiot," she finally got out.

"I know," he smiled. "Will they fit?"

She wiped her eyes, then nodded. The light-hearted moment passed. "I'm going to take a shower."

"I'll hold down the fort."

Katherine took the pajamas and went into the bathroom. A few moments later he heard the water come on. He kicked off his boots and busied himself by flipping through the handful of channels on the TV. After what seemed like a long time, he glanced at the clock on the nightstand. She'd been in there for almost an hour and the water was still running. Trix knew girls took longer to bathe than his customary five-minute shower, but he was starting to worry. He understood she'd lost a lot of blood. Could she have passed out? Would he have heard? Should he check?

He put his ear to the door, but all he could hear was the sound of the water hitting the tub. He knocked lightly. "Katherine are you okay?"

No answer.

"If you don't say something, I'm coming in," he called.

Still no answer.

He turned the knob and opened the door a crack. Through the steam he saw Katherine sitting on the floor, still dressed, her head resting on crossed arms propped up by bent knees. Her shoulders shook as she cried.

"Hey, hey," he said, squatting down in front of her, his hands going to hers. Her eyes rose up to meet his, swollen and red.

"Katherine, you don't have to hide in here. It's okay to be sad." He leaned over and shut off the water before sitting down next to her. She tipped slightly to lean into his shoulder, and used her fists to wipe tears away from her face as she drew stuttered breaths. Several long silent moments passed as they sat leaning against the wall before she finally spoke.

"It must seem crazy for me to be this upset about a baby I didn't want to have," she said quietly.

"You've had an awful experience. It doesn't seem crazy to be upset."

"I don't need you to feel sorry for me," she said defensively.

"I don't feel sorry for you. I feel terrible you're going through this."

"You literally defined pity, dimwit, and I don't need your pity."

He smirked at her constant need to insult him.

"It's not pity. My ass is starting to fall asleep and I'm trying to move this along."

The small smile he was shooting for drew across her lips. "Asshole," she mumbled.

"I know," he said, rising and offering a hand. "I'm going to set a timer for fifteen minutes. How about you actually take a shower, then come grab something to eat?"

She took his hand and stood, shaking her head. "I'm not hungry, but I promise to shower this time."

Trix left. She closed the door behind him, and the water started again. He pulled out a few apples and some crackers, munching while he eyed the clock, unsure if he'd make good on his promise to go back in there. He sat on the bed and leaned against the headboard with his legs stretched out in front of him. Thankfully, Katherine emerged shortly after, hair down and wet.

He gestured to the fruit and snacks he'd put out and then patted the bed in front of him. She sat cross legged facing him and grabbed an apple, slowly spinning it by the stem in front of her but not bringing it to her mouth. He watched her for a cue on what to do next.

She let out a deep sigh, and then looked up. "I know what you must think of me."

"Do you?" he asked.

"An accidental pregnancy conjures up a certain stereotype. I'm sure you think I sleep around a lot."

"Not necessarily."

"I had sex with you in a parking lot," she said, a single brow arching up.

"Yeah, you did."

"You don't ask yourself if I do that a lot?"

"The question had crossed my mind," he admitted, "but not for the reason you think. I wondered because…well, that was a pretty exceptional experience for me if I'm honest. I guess I wanted to think it was for you too."

Her gaze searched his, so he tried to keep his expression schooled. He wanted her to believe him, but not read so much into it that he would embarrass himself by showing any wayward sentiment. There was a long pause, and he wondered if he had confessed too much. Finally, she said, "Winn was my first."

Trix was suddenly uncomfortable at the reminder she'd been his best friend's girlfriend. He ran a hand over his hair, dropping his head to stare at the comforter between them. "You don't owe me anything. You're an adult, and what you do with your body is none of my business. I'm sorry if I make you feel you have to defend yourself."

She ignored his discomfort. "Winn was my first, and I know it looks like I left him for Blake." She paused, cocking her head, watching for his reaction. Trix tried not to respond. He was too angry about that part of her history to find words that wouldn't be unkind and inappropriate given the circumstances.

Katherine went on. "I know what it looks like, but I'm not with Blake and haven't been for a long time. Everyone thinking I'm *that girl* doesn't bother me anymore, but I want you to know the truth."

"If you haven't been with Blake for a long time, I don't understand how this happened." He felt guilty for pushing the issue, but he wasn't about to sit here and have her lie to his face either. Her expression changed a little. She appeared to resign herself to confiding in him.

"I was on the pill for a while, then it got hard to find time to get all the way to the free clinic for exams. I went off it. I hadn't been with Blake in months, had no plans to be with him ever again and then, one day a few months ago…" Her eyes dropped. "I shouldn't have given in. I shouldn't have said yes, but he was there, and he was good at making me think he cared about me. I needed someone to give a shit, you know? I stupidly thought, what are the odds? Of course, it takes only one mistake."

"People give a shit about you," he countered.

"They don't though," she said. "When you live like that for long enough, even when it's the bad guy telling you you're worth something, you cling to it."

They watched each other for a long moment. He wanted to believe her so badly he mistrusted his own judgment. "Maybe I know more about that than you think," he said.

"Maybe," she conceded. "Guess that's covered for a while now. The hospital gave me a year's supply of the pill to go. You know, cause I'm *that girl*," she said sadly.

"It's hard to change people's impression of you," he said, speaking from experience.

"Yeah. Don't I know it."

"It's been a long day. Do you want to watch something and forget about life for a while?"

"That would be good."

Without thinking he opened his arm up and she tucked herself into the crook at his shoulder. He clicked on the TV to some random program, and they watched a pod of dolphins playing in the deep. A few moments later her body loosened, and her rhythmic breathing told him she was asleep.

Trix looked down at her face resting on his chest and carefully drew the comforter up to fold around her.

CHAPTER 16

Katherine woke, found her head on Trix's chest and took a moment to orient herself. He was fully clothed, still propped up against the headboard. His scent wrapped around her. A deeply masculine and comforting combination of sandalwood and something woodsy she couldn't quite put her finger on. Daylight streamed through the curtains.

He'd pulled the comforter to cover her, and she found it endearing. Her instincts about the kind of man he was had been right. It felt good to be able to start trusting her own judgment again, given what a mess she'd made following her gut over the past year. She watched his face for a quiet moment. His five o'clock shadow was a tick longer than normal, his lips parted slightly as he pulled in peaceful breaths.

She didn't deserve him to be treating her this way, but she was profoundly thankful regardless. The comfort she took from his presence was surprising, but welcome. She'd let her mind wander to him a lot since the rodeo. But habitually, she was on the lookout for things she could exploit for her benefit, and it was impossible to draw the line between thinking of him as a solution versus just thinking about him.

At the end of the day, her motives didn't matter. He was her ex-boyfriend's best friend. He would help her because he was too good of a human not to, but hoping for anything beyond good Samaritan would be a waste of time.

She was nothing if not a realist.

She slid out from under the comforter trying not to wake him. When she was clear he murmured in his sleep and slid down the headboard, curling up on his side. She covered him with the loose blanket.

Katherine stretched and was brought back to her harsh reality by her lower abdomen aching with the movement. Clenching her teeth, she willed herself to not cry again.

You're not this fragile, she told herself. As if she could convince herself she was tough enough to overcome this huge thing with one cathartic crying night. It wasn't true, she knew she would need to come to terms with what'd happened. But not now.

What she'd told Trix was true. She'd royally screwed up letting Blake back into her bed. She had assumed, like she always did, the consequences wouldn't catch up to her, but she'd been wrong. While no longer being pregnant with Blake's child, no longer needing to leave town, was technically a good thing, the loss was deep, and more than anything, so unexpected she didn't know how to process it. She needed time.

Her gaze found her own reflection in the mirror over the dresser and she narrowed her eyes at herself. *Get through today.*

She turned her attention to Trix's sleeping form and decided to busy herself with getting them some coffee.

She didn't want to chance running into anyone she knew by driving all the way back into town to pick up good coffee, so instead she walked the length of the parking lot and popped into the shabby motel office hoping to find bad coffee there.

Inside the smell of decades of indoor smoking seeped from the sun-faded wood paneling and overly worn carpeting. No one was behind the counter, but beside it sat a small folding tv tray with a coffee pot. She poured two cups, and then sneered when the powdered creamer came out in caked chunks.

When she returned to the room, Trix was still asleep and the clock on the bedside table read 07:30. It was strange for a guy who normally got up with the sun to sleep so late. Yesterday had obviously taken its toll on him. He began to stir.

"Mmm… is that coffee?" he mumbled, eyes still closed.

She chuckled. "It's not good, but it's hot."

"No such thing as bad coffee," he said, opening his eyes.

She put his cup down on the nightstand next to him. "You should try it before you say that," she said.

He sat up and glanced down at the comforter she'd put over him, then popped an arm out to stretch his shoulder. Swinging his feet over the side of the bed, he reached for the cup and brought it to his lips, watching her over the foam brim.

"How are you feeling?" he asked, after taking a sip.

"Actually, I'm not sure." She surprised herself with her honesty.

He nodded, seeming to understand what she meant. "Any pain?"

"Minor, but I'm okay."

He downed the remaining coffee in one gulp. "Okay, so we're going to need more coffee. What do you want to do today?"

"Haven't gotten that far," she confessed.

"Up for a morning walk?"

"That sounds good, actually. I'll change." Katherine grabbed the shopping bag and brought into the bathroom.

With everything going on the night before, she hadn't realized Trix had bought her everything she needed. She smiled looking down at the toothbrush, toothpaste, deodorant and hairbrush. The other outfit he had grabbed was also from the boys clothing section, and included a tank top, pair of running shorts and a hoodie. Dressing she came out of the bathroom and realized Trix hadn't grabbed anything for himself. He was still dressed in his wrinkled shirt and work jeans.

"I feel bad you don't have a change of clothes," she said.

"Nah, it's all right. At some point today, I'll run home to snag a few things. That is, uh, if you still think you'll want company later."

"If you're willing to stay," she ventured.

He nodded. "I am."

A somber beat passed between them and she decided it would be a long day if things were this serious the whole time. "I'm a little disappointed at the lack of construction equipment on this sweatshirt." She smiled at him when he looked a little sheepish.

"I'm never going to live that down, am I?" he asked.

"For sure not."

"Fine. For the record, which arbitrary number on women's clothing are you?"

She laughed. "I'm not telling you."

"Jesus Christ, woman. You're a pain in the ass. Let's go."

She laughed again and walked through the door he held open for her. They stopped at the office to grab more complimentary coffee, then made their way around the back of the property. There wasn't much to see, so they wandered through the dry area near the parking lot and then into a field that was likely private property, which mattered little unless you were causing trouble.

As they walked the conversation was easy and light. Trix was funny and he knew it, always busting out some little quip to make her laugh. They'd been walking about twenty minutes before she started to feel fatigued. Seeing a fallen tree ahead, Katherine motioned to it.

"Do you mind if we sit for a bit? I'm feeling tired."

"Okay. Are you sure you're okay?"

"Umhmmm…you know, weaker than normal."

"Makes sense." Gently he took her elbow as they walked to the tree.

They sat, both facing forward for a few moments. Katherine turned her face to the sky and allowed the morning sun to warm it.

Trix broke into her thoughts. "I think it's going to get annoying if I ask if you're okay as often as I wonder. So, can we agree you'll tell me if you're not, so I don't have to ask every five minutes?"

She smiled at the kind-heartedness of his words. "Yes. I promise to tell you if I'm not okay, so you don't have to ask every five minutes."

"Good. That's good," he said.

"Is that how often you think about it?" she asked, her hands busying themselves by peeling off little pieces of bark.

"What?"

"Do you think about it every five minutes?"

"Maybe. I mean, I obviously don't have any experience with stuff like this, and I worry."

His words exaggerated her guilt for dragging him into this. This situation didn't have anything to do with him, and he had no reason to feel any responsibility toward her at all. Calling him, asking him to stay, all of it was another of her selfish moves.

"It's not really your job to worry, and I'm sorry if pulling you into this is bad for you," she said softly.

His expression made it clear there was something brewing beneath the surface.

"Don't apologize. I'm glad you called me, and I'm glad you trust me with this. But I have to ask, why? Why did you trust me with any of this?"

"It's hard to explain. There's something about you. You make me feel off balance, but also safe. I know that doesn't make sense, but well there it is. I knew I could trust you."

"I guess that's good, but it may be one of the first times in my life someone has thought that about me. Usually, I'm good for a shallow laugh, but I'm not the dependable one." He looked away from her, returning his focus to the horizon.

"You're deeper than you let on." She watched the side of his face as his jaw worked a little, revealing his unease.

He shrugged. "Maybe. I am the clown, after all." He threw her words from their fight back at her.

She winced. "That was a terrible thing for me to say to you."

"It was. But not entirely untrue."

"Hey," she said, leaning to bring her face into his sightline, forcing him to meet her gaze. "It was a terrible and untrue thing to say. I'm sorry."

He pinched in the side of his cheek for a second and then dipped his chin. "It's okay," he said to the ground.

She didn't believe he truly forgave her for the awful things she'd said to him, but it was clear he was through talking about it, so she left it sitting between them.

After a long pause he looked back at her. "Do you feel like you can make it back to the room now?"

"I think so, yes."

He stood, offering her a hand. "I grabbed a few other things to help pass the time. Books, playing cards, stuff like that. Also, you know if you want some time alone or whatever, let me know, and I'll run home for a change of clothes. Maybe some non-Levi pajamas." He smiled at her and she was overwhelmed with real gratitude for who he was.

"Jacob?".

"Yeah?"

"I haven't actually said this yet, but thank you."

He watched her for a long moment, looking a little embarrassed. "Don't mention it."

"Seriously, I don't know what I would—"

He cut her off. "I know."

She exhaled and sent him a tight smile. "Okay."

CHAPTER 17

When they got back to the room Trix was glad to see her eat something for the first time since he'd picked her up.

"Want to relax for a bit?" He held up a copy of *East of Eden* wondering if she would remember. She laughed.

"I thought I could use a refresher," he joked.

"You for sure could."

He sat down leaning against the headboard. He watched her wondering what she would do, and she surprised him when she stretched out on the bed and rested her head on his thigh.

"We should take turns. You start." She closed her eyes.

"Okay." He cracked open the book and started reading. "The Salinas Valley is in Northern California…" Trix read the first two chapters before he noticed she'd fallen asleep. He put the book under the lamp, replacing his thigh with a pillow, scratched a "Ran home. Back soon," note and left it on the nightstand.

He returned a few hours later, having showered and changed, with a bag of burgers and fries from Hank's diner. He found Katherine nose deep in the book. "Late lunch?" he asked, lifting the takeout.

"I'm starving," she said.

They plowed through the huge portions, then she got a mischievous look in her eye and gestured at the leftover fries. "Up for a little Texas hold 'em?" she asked

"You'll be sorry." He grinned.

"Big talk from a big man," she teased as she stood to grab the cards.

Katherine dealt them each two cards and then put three down face up between them as Trix divvied out the fries into equal piles in their Styrofoam containers. She tossed a single fry onto the flattened bag and he followed suit, peeking at his cards.

Katherine took the first three hands.

"I used to be good at poker," Trix joked.

"Must have been a while then, because holding onto that four was a bad call."

"Definitely haven't played since I left New York," he admitted, and dealt another round.

"So, several years."

"Three at least."

She crimped her brow. "Huh. Thought you've been here longer than that. Guess I don't actually know that much about you."

"I was a pretty cliché rich kid. My life was full of expensive cars, vacation homes, and parties, along with crippling insecurities and blinding fear about not being good enough. You know, the usual." He met her gaze and laughed when she did.

"Seriously?" she prodded.

"That was mostly serious. I had more money at my disposal than I should've had, and none of the support from my father I should've had. My behavior followed pretty predictable patterns. Flashy bids for attention I was never going to get."

"You're weirdly adept at talking about it," she said.

Trix shrugged. "I've had a lot of good therapists."

She eyed him for a long time before she said, "Men around here don't see shrinks and wouldn't talk about it if they had."

"Therapy works, I guess." He looked down at his cards and threw a few fries into the pile. "Plus, back home it's way less taboo than it is out here. Your turn. Tell me a deep dark secret. It'll make us even."

Her face darkened. "You already know mine, Trix."

"I'm sorry, that was beyond stupid."

"It's okay. Maybe now we're even," she said then brought her gaze up to meet his, then she added, "I like that we can trust each other."

"Me too."

She asked, "You still call New York home?"

Trix shook his head. "A recent conversation with my father ended that."

"What happened?"

"Well, he's given me a month to 'come to my senses,' then he's rehoming my inheritance."

"What are you going to do?"

"I'm staying here. This is my life now," he said firmly.

She furrowed her brow. "Sounds like that's a lot of money to walk away from."

"Money isn't everything."

"Easy to say when you have it. Less true when you don't."

"Do you want me to move back to New York?"

She studied him for a long moment. "I want you to do what's best for you."

"Crooked Brook is what's best for me," he said a little too harshly.

"Okay," she said softly.

He felt guilty he'd been so sharp. He cleared his throat and eased the tension off his expression. "So, what about you? Katherine Grant in high school. Give me the Cliff Notes."

After a beat, some of the somberness washed off her face and she half smiled. "Well, I guess my high school role was also pretty cliché. I didn't get terrible grades, didn't get great ones either. I was a cheerleader. Everything went like I expected until my brother got arrested peddling drugs. That kind of overshadowed graduation."

Her tone was flippant but Trix saw through it. "You miss him." he said.

"Terribly," she sighed. "Kyle was the only person who knew what it was like growing up in our house with our folks. Now I'm alone with that."

"I'm sorry."

"Don't be. Shit happens right?"

"Right." Trix could tell she wanted to drop it, so he nodded and looked down at their disparate piles of fries. She was kicking his ass. He needed to regain some of his dignity.

Looking at his two pair he decided to bluff and go big, raising a large fistful of fries. Katherine stared at him, examining his expression, and pulled her lower lip in between her teeth. A habit of hers when she was thinking might make him have a stroke someday. He felt like a monster for noticing how beautiful she was when she was in this state. Light and playful. Stunning. She decided he was bluffing and matched his bet.

He flipped over his cards and she grinned before revealing a straight.

"Damn woman," he said as she scooped up her winnings.

"There's a big difference between you and me. When someone talks to you, you assume they're telling the truth, but watch for deceit. I look at someone and know they're lying, but hope to see signs of the truth."

"That's not a great way to go through life," he observed.

"No, it's not," she admitted. "But it does make me better at spotting a bluff."

Trix scooped up the cards to shuffle for the next round. It only took another twenty minutes for her to completely clean him out and he surrendered putting up his palms.

"Don't ever tell him, but I used to let Winn beat me every once in a while."

"I can see why. He's got a pretty serious competitive streak," he said, surprising himself when he didn't flinch at the mention of his friend.

"Too true," she agreed. "I always wondered if he hadn't gotten hurt and lost the scholarship if he would have made it to the big leagues."

"Winn had a baseball scholarship?"

"He didn't tell you?" Katherine looked confused.

"His knee injury happened before I showed up," Trix said.

"Colorado State offered him a full ride his senior year. But when Blake tore up Winn's knee, they revoked it."

Trix didn't try to hide his feelings about Blake. A chance to play ball in college would have been monumental for Winn. Trix realized the scholarship would've represented a chance for Katherine to get out of this small town too. Did she leave Winn when it became clear she couldn't use him to change her own future?

What am I doing here?

He stood. This woman had shredded his best friend and she'd done it right after one of the darkest times in Winn's life.

His mouth tasted dry and bitter. Being here, being with this woman was exactly what his father had predicted he'd do. He was putting everything he had in jeopardy. His friendship with everyone at the ranch was at risk because he was falling for this toxic woman's ruse. If he ruined what he had at Crooked Brook, he would have no choice but to go crawling back to New York. He could sense her looking at him as he pulled on his boots.

"Need some air," he said tersely.

Trix grabbed his keys from the dresser and left without looking back.

***

Katherine winced when Trix slammed the door, knowing mentioning Winn had been a misstep. Still, she was genuinely surprised Winn had never told Trix about the scholarship. The two men hadn't known each other for long, but they were as close as brothers. She'd rarely spoken to Trix, but over the last few days, getting to know him better had felt right. When he'd mentioned the pressure he was getting from his father to move away, her stomach had turned over. She didn't want him to leave. It felt like he was beginning to see her as more than the shrew who'd hurt his best friend. He made her feel like she deserved to be seen. Then she had to go and remind him exactly why she deserved to be ignored.

Katherine watched the clock for two hours. By eight she was starting to believe Trix wasn't going to return when she heard the key in the door. He came in and his face was sullen.

"Hey," she said cautiously.

"Hey," he replied.

"Do you—"

He cut her off. "No. I don't want to talk about it."

"Okay."

"I'm sorry I stormed off."

"You don't need to apologize. We both know you have no duty to be here."

"I told you I would stay," he said sharply.

"And I told you I don't need your pity," she said, matching his tone.

"My word matters to me."

"Okay," she said, hiding the hurt.

They watched one another: the undercurrent of longing was tangible. Wasn't it? God, could she really be imagining this?

Trix walked past the TV and kicked off his boots. If there was actually a connection forming between them, he didn't seem to embrace it. She decided to wait for him to show her how the rest of the night would go.

He snagged his bag and walked into the bathroom. She heard the sink run for a few minutes and then he came back out in a white t-shirt and gray sweatpants. She decided to follow his lead and went into the bathroom to brush her teeth, wash her face, and change into pajamas. She came out and found him sitting on the other bed. His shoulders were slumped, and he was looking at his hands hanging between his knees. He didn't move when she sat across from him. "Talk to me," she said.

Slowly he shook his head. "This isn't about me. We're here because you needed help and I wanted to help you. That's all this is."

"This is about you too. You've been here for me, and I can't tell you how grateful I am."

Unsure how to proceed, she knew it was wrong to pretend she didn't know what his conflict was. It was obvious. He felt guilty. Like he was betraying Winn. But there wasn't a good way to open up that conversation. Would he be capable of truly hearing her side of the story? Maybe she didn't deserve the consideration. If nothing else, she owed him an out, one where she wouldn't add more guilt to the pile he clearly already had.

"How about tomorrow you drive me home and we go on like this never happened?" His eyes narrowed. "Your white knight duties are officially concluded," she added.

Trix swallowed hard. "Probably for the best."

Katherine nodded and began to settle herself under the covers. She turned away from him and curled up facing the wall. She listened for him to move, but he didn't, not for a long time. Finally, she heard his bed rustle and he clicked off the light.

CHAPTER 18

The next morning Katherine and Trix woke, packed, and dressed in awkward silence. They hardly exchanged a word as they prepared to leave the motel. Katherine wanted to clear the air, but found when she looked for the right thing to say, there wasn't anything that hadn't already been said. Trix wanted, or needed, to pretend he didn't know her. How could she argue against something he believed so strongly?

The silence between them in the car ride was uncomfortable and thick. She wondered what was going on in his head as she watched the blood drain from his knuckles over and over again as his hands repeatedly tensed and then relaxed on the wheel. Maybe he was more conflicted and less sure of his convictions than she presumed.

After what felt like the longest forty-minutes in history, they finally pulled into the trailerpark. Trix stopped inside the entrance and turned to her but didn't speak.

Eventually she said, "I want to say even though the circumstances were…terrible, it was nice getting to know you better."

His face tightened, and she instantly read his mood. He was preparing to get back to reality. The reality where she was the villain of the story.

"You're Winn's best friend, and you won't ever forgive me, will you?"

She thought he was going to stay silent, but then he said, "I want to forgive you, but it's not my place. I'm not the one you cheated on. I'm not the one you hurt."

"I broke up with your friend, and that makes me a lost cause?" she pushed.

"You didn't just break up with him. You used him. You wanted out of this place and Winn's scholarship was your ticket to Colorado."

"That's not true." She shook her head. "I loved Winn with everything a young girl has to give. He was handsome, funny, smart, and, god, he loved me. There was something about him I was always drawn to. He had a pride I craved. He was proud of what he did, proud of where he came from."

She watched his face and could tell he didn't understand.

"Do you see this place? These trailers?" She gestured at the cramped rows. "Weeds, tires, broken and rusted lawn furniture, burn pits, garbage... These people have given up." Trix looked from yard to yard as she spoke.

"Then there's Mr. and Mrs. Kent." She pointed to a standout trailer, which was as tiny and boxy as the others, but the property was clear of debris and had a crisp American flag hanging at the door. "Look at their house. Clean paint, flowers in the windows... I wasn't looking for Winn to be my ticket out of Montana, he was my ticket to—"

"Flowerpots," Trix supplied.

"Yes," she said with a sad chuckle. "What I mean is, Winn was a different kind of person. I needed that. I needed to get away from the apathy, from the resignation these people have to live the same tired, filthy, redneck life generation after generation. I was captivated by the ambition in him. His drive to make his life better. Not so I could leave town, but so I could learn how to escape indifference."

She wondered if her words made any sense. He didn't move so she kept going. "After he got hurt, all that pride and passion went out of him. I watched it fade away, and I couldn't see that man anymore. I had been so in love with him for so long, I didn't know how to be around him. Didn't even know how to look at him when I wasn't in love with him. I knew it was only a matter of time before he noticed, and we would be one more thing he had which was being taken away. You know Winn, he'd rather be angry than hurt, so I—"

"Ran to Blake." Trix sighed.

"I made him hate me, so he wouldn't have to mourn me. I know Winn and I weren't meant to last. I'm not sorry we're not together. The way I ended it was foolish and cruel. He deserved better. I wouldn't have survived this place without him, and that broken little girl will always love him for it. I miss the person I was when I was with him, and ruining that, becoming someone I didn't want to be, was the biggest mistake of my life."

"I understand," he said quietly.

"It's okay if you don't," she said, knowing it was unlikely her explanation would change his mind. "There's nothing you can think about me, I don't already think about myself. I'm selfish and vapid. The only thing I have going for me is the way I look. That puts me about fifteen years and a couple of kids away from being my momma. Unskilled. No future. Ordinary ex-beauty queen who goes from having a few too many every weekend to having a few too many every night. Weak and destined to be born, live, and rot in this shitty trailerpark."

Trix pulled in a deep breath. "A lot of things come to mind when I think about you, but ordinary and weak aren't on the list. You're right when you say you shouldn't have to apologize for doing what it takes to survive, but you don't need to be with someone to be a good person. You have to look at the version of yourself you don't like and try to change it."

"I'm trying," she murmured.

"I know," he said. They watched each other for a long moment before he shook his head and sighed. He reached into the back seat and handed her the shopping bag.

The gesture felt like a dismissal. "But still, after hearing my side... " She took the bag.

Trix rubbed a hand up and down the stubble on his cheek. "I guess what I'm saying is, this feels too complicated."

She tried not to flinch. "I understand," she lied and climbed from the cab to save face. "Take care, Jacob."

She shut the door. Through the window she saw him nod, and then he was gone.

***

When he saw the sign for the ranch Trix realized he couldn't remember the drive from the trailerpark. Katherine's description of the end of her relationship with Winn was knocking around his head, searching for the right place to be categorized. Truth? Lie? Right? Wrong? He'd wanted to tell her exactly why he understood her desperate need to escape. Hadn't he said to Alex he'd come to Montana in search of a different kind of human? Trix understood what Katherine felt, and he'd refused to tell her. He'd been so uncomfortable with the the situation between Katherine and Winn, and it was more multifaceted than he knew: it was more than he wanted to hear.

He turned in and parked the truck halfway up the drive. He wasn't ready to go into the house. He wasn't ready to see his family and to live in close quarters with the guilt of lying to them. He'd been lying since the rodeo, keeping from them what he'd done. He was going to lie to them again about where he'd spent the last few days.

These people were more important to him than his bio family and he was betraying them, betraying the code they lived by. The rules in Mae's family were straightforward. You take care of your people, and they take care of you. There wasn't room for dishonesty in that arrangement. If he was found out, everything about his life here would change. If he no longer enjoyed the trust and love of the people here, why would he stay?

Trix slung an arm out the open window and closed his eyes as the breeze blew the scent of the land over him. When had this place, this peace, become so complicated? Katherine. She'd erased the black and white from his life. The last few days had forced him to see her as a person. Someone worthy of consideration and compassion. There was more to her than the heartless narcissist they all thought she was. How uncomfortable it was when someone tried to leave the pigeonhole you'd put them in.

As a man who was desperate for people to look at him and see more than his face value, it felt wrong that he was resisting any amendment to her role in this story. Why was it so hard for him to see Katherine in a different light?

Because you're a hypocrite. No, because you love Winn as if he was your brother, and it's not your place to forgive the woman who crushed him.

He'd never been so polarized in his own thoughts, which served as further proof that allowing Katherine to be a real, but flawed person instead of an evil phantom, was twisting his mind. He needed to stop. Stop thinking of her. Stop thinking about her sadness, her strength, her wit. Forget her intelligence, her passion, her beauty—

Trix slammed his fists on the wheel. *Stop.*

He threw the truck into gear and kicked up gravel as he tore up the rest of the drive.

CHAPTER 19

Katherine looked at the clock. Between one and four was the slowest part of the day at the diner. This was a little blue-collar town where every soul had a job, which meant there weren't a lot of mouths to feed between lunch and dinner. At the moment, her only customer was Hope, the sweet girl who left her daughter with her grandpa one afternoon a week so she could sit at the diner counter reading a dime store romance novel and nurse a single cup of tea. Since that tea had been poured and Hope was now nose deep in her book, Katherine went to busy herself in the backroom doing inventory.

She was starting to feel comfortable again in these slow and quiet times. The breathing room which invited introspection no longer felt like a void that would suffocate her. A couple of weeks had passed since she'd lost the baby, and she was feeling physically and emotionally better each day. She still had bouts of startling sorrow, and it was near impossible to comprehend how having a weight lifted could feel so heavy. She'd been unprepared to navigate a life with a child. This simple truth forced her to come to terms with a previously foreign concept: some bad things happen for a reason, and that reason didn't always have to be that the universe was cruel and vindictive.

In a shift away from her norm, she'd decided she needed to be kinder to herself. Kinder about the mistake which had led to the pregnancy. Kinder about losing the baby, and kinder about what felt like an irrational response to that loss.

Allowing herself forgiveness turned out to be work. It was hard, and she had to constantly remind herself of the arrangement. Since she'd never been so gracious with herself, the only thing she could think to credit for the change was Trix's behavior.

He had been kind to her about the unplanned pregnancy. *He* had been kind to her about losing the baby. *He* had been kind to her about processing the loss. If a man who had no responsibility to her, and no reason to be charitable, could manage compassion, then so could she.

She hadn't spoken to him since he'd dropped her off at the trailerpark. He'd texted her a few times to *check her status*, which felt clinical and detached. Especially when compared with the image of him sleeping sitting up in order to not wake her during her most vulnerable hours.

She ticked off the condiment count on her clipboard and allowed her mind to stay with the mystery that was Trix. She began to wonder if in her damaged state she'd simply imagined the fragile link between them. Maybe she read more into the way they'd gotten along. Maybe she exaggerated the intensity of his stares. Maybe she was reaching for a connection, a desperate outstretched hand he was not straining to grasp in return. As he'd said, it was too complicated.

You don't deserve to enjoy tenderness from a man like that anyway, she scolded herself.

As she finished counting the buns and was writing off her feelings for Trix, the door chimed. She walked out to the dining room and there he was. Trix and Griz had come in and were scanning the diner. When his gaze landed on hers, he watched her for a long moment, and and an almost sad smile pulled at the corner of his mouth. He seemed to remember himself and blinked a few times.

"Hey, KG" He made his tone sound as carefree as ever.

"Trix. Griz. Y'all have been pretty scarce for regulars lately," she said.

"Do we get kicked out of the cholesterol club if we don't show up at least once a week?" Trix joked.

"You might," she answered, trying to match his light tone.

"We missed lunch at home," Trix explained. "Had to come down to buy parts."

Griz nodded in agreement then headed to a booth. She didn't bother to grab menus as she followed them to their seats, pulling her notepad and pen from her apron as she went.

"So?" she asked.

"Burger, fries, and iced tea, please." Griz pulled two sugar packets from the dish and began to align the corners.

"I'll do the club and a coffee, please," Trix said.

She jotted down the order and turned to fetch their drinks. The men started talking, and in the empty diner she could still hear their conversation from the nearby drink fountain.

"Should only take one or two days to build, so like...what? Working version by Sunday?" Trix was saying.

"Yeah," Griz mumbled.

"You think we need to draw out some plans, or you're solid on what goes where?" Trix asked.

"I've got it. Only need an extra pair of hands." It was possibly the most Katherine had ever heard Griz say.

"That I can do," Trix answered.

She walked back with the drinks and tried a smile. She was relieved when Trix returned it without hesitation.

"You guys working on a project?" she asked.

Griz nodded, leaving Trix to reply for him. "Griz has designed a fake cow for Winn to use while training the cutting horses."

"A fake cow?" she asked, then remembered how Winn had bolted horns to an oil drum and mounted it on a long spinning arm in the middle of one of the arenas.

"The setup Winn uses now only goes in a predictable circle. All of the horses are pretty bored with it. It doesn't teach them much other than not to spook at a rusty monstrosity."

She nodded. Rusty monstrosity was a pretty accurate description.

"We're going to call it the Bogus Bovine," Trix said.

"No, we're not," Griz said flatly.

"The Hoax Heifer?" Trix continued.

"No," Griz grumbled.

"The Equine Educator three thousand?"

Griz shook his head.

Katherine relaxed a little, feeling like some of the awkwardness was receding. "How does it work?"

"You won't be getting details out of him," Trix answered. "All I know is it involves every pulley in a hundred-mile radius."

Hank slapped the bell.

"Well, good luck," she said and went to fetch their food. After that she busied herself behind the counter allowing their one-sided conversation to continue. She had to smile when Trix asked if they would have enough left-over cable to build a trebuchet and Griz silently stared him down. After a while she went back with the iced tea pitcher in hand. While she refilled Griz's drink he stood and murmured, "Bathroom," and then left. She took the opportunity to slide into the empty bench across from Trix.

"How've you been?" she asked.

"Not too bad. How about you?"

"I'm…better." She gave him a small smile.

He nodded. "Good. That's really good."

"I'm not sure you've ever gone so long without popping in here. I was starting to wonder if you were avoiding me."

"A lot of changes going on at home lately."

She noticed he hadn't addressed the accusation he was avoiding her. While searching for something else to say, she saw Griz had returned from the bathroom and had taken a seat at the counter next to Hope. They weren't speaking but were slightly turned toward one another.

"That could be cute," Katherine whispered. Trix followed her gaze to the counter.

"Griz and country mouse?" Trix whispered back.

"Be nice," she scolded through a grin. Keeping her voice low so it wouldn't carry she said, "Hope is painfully shy, but she's very sweet."

"If they dated, the silence would be deafening." Trix smirked.

"Maybe they'd work out how to blink in Morse code," she said and they both chuckled.

"I don't know much about Griz's taste in women. Verbose he's not. But he's solidly a good person."

"So's she."

Trix nodded. "I helped Hope's dad out during the flooding last summer. As a thank you she made me the best chocolate cake I've ever had. Come to think of it, Griz was there, too."

"The flash floods last year?" Katherine asked. She remembered that as a scary time for a lot of the property owners in the area. Several people had been seriously hurt trying to save their land and livestock.

"Everything was buttoned up at Mae's, so we ran over there to help him throw down some sandbags and dig drainage trenches."

"Seriously, you're a good guy."

His far away expression got tight, and his eyes snapped to hers. "You shouldn't think so."

"Why?" Her brow crinkled, surprised at his seriousness.

"Because I'm not."

"What evidence supports that?" she asked.

"I love the people at Crooked Brook more than I love my own family." He looked down at the table, slowly rotating the mug between his hands. "Yet, all I've done for the last few weeks is lie and hide things from them."

Her gut sank. "So, it's me. Knowing me makes you a bad guy."

"No," he said, his eyes jumping to hers. "Wanting you does."

"Trix."

He shook his head.

"I think we should talk about this," she pressed.

"I don't see how it would help."

"So, we pretend like nothing happens when we're together?"

"That's my plan."

Katherine stood and threw their lunch ticket on the table in front of him, no longer worried if Griz or Hope heard them. "Then screw you for bringing it up in the first place."

Trix looked up and she saw regret and shame in his eyes, but no doubt.

She waited for him to say something, to stop her, to placate her battered feelings, but he didn't.

All she could do was turn and walk away.

CHAPTER 20

Five long, guilt-filled days had passed since Trix had dented the indominable Katherine Grant by telling her he was willing and able to pretend there was nothing between them. Unfortunately, his mind was rejecting the endeavor wholeheartedly. There was only one woman in Montana he should consider off limits, and yet she haunted him like no other woman ever had. Thoughts of her were as inescapable as his shadow cast by the midday sun now glaring down on him as he paced the yard.

Dozens of random times in the last few days her face had flashed into his mind's eye. A calf was born, and he thought about if she'd want to hold it. The sky opened up with a tantrum of a lightning storm, and he pictured her standing in the grass with the static and wind whipping around her.

The smell of coffee brought him back to the roadside motel where a vulnerable woman had trusted him with her pain. All of these torturous mental breaks ended with him seeing hurt in her eyes that day in the diner. He hated knowing he'd wounded her. He hated he wanted to see her again, knowing he shouldn't. The pull to be near her was powerful, it took away reason and the concept of consequence. He needed to be around her. How could he do it without the people at the ranch finding out he was enthralled with the enemy? There was one place they could go where no one would be the wiser. They could go to New York.

An hour later Trix's foot tapped against the truck's floor as he sat in town waiting for Katherine to leave the diner following her morning shift. He shoved aside the awkward feelings about knowing her work schedule by heart.

This is a bad idea.

When she appeared right on time at two o'clock, Trix put the truck in drive and pulled up alongside her as she walked, leaning an arm out the window as the truck kept pace.

"Hey, KG" he said lightly.

Katherine glanced up, a suspicious look on her face. "Trix."

"You off work?" he asked, full well knowing she was.

"Just finished a brutal shift." She cocked her head at him. "You off today?"

He nodded, and his stomach tightened as he forced himself to move forward with his seriously misguided plan. "You want to go for a drive?"

A lone dark brow peaked on her face. "A drive?"

"Yeah, it's beautiful out. I felt like a drive, saw you, thought you'd maybe want to tag along."

She looked down at her pale-yellow uniform dress, then back at him. "What happened to pretending we don't know each other?"

"I'm not sure. Maybe I'm a masochist, but I know I want you to come with me," he replied honestly hoping it would be enough.

He watched her face and could tell that she was tempted but reluctant. If he were her, he wouldn't trust this abrupt change of face either. After a tense few moments she smiled slowly and said, "This feels like maybe you're asking me on a date."

Her smile deepened when he allowed his discomfort to show while his gaze bounced to the empty street to check for witnesses.

"Maybe. Well, it's not really, but something like that," he sputtered.

She laughed. "Always thought you were a little smoother than this."

Trix tried to recover. She was right, he was normally much better at this. "Well, it's not quite a regular situation, but I've got a free afternoon and appears you do to. I'd like to spend it with you if you're interested."

After watching him for moment longer, she nodded. "I am."

He let out a relieved breath, again scanning the sidewalk. "Hop in." He leaned over and popped the passenger side door ajar as she made her way around the front of the truck.

As she was settling in, he turned to her. "Was the shift brutal enough we should grab some adult provisions?"

She slipped off one of her shoes and rubbed the bottom of her foot. "Oh yeah, it was that kind of shift."

He nodded and made a quick pit stop at the gas station. In the aisle he had to smile at the generically named wines on offer. The two options included "White" or "Red" and they both had screw off caps. *Well, that's convenient.*

He returned to the truck, and they headed out of town with the windows down and the music turned up. He watched as she floated her arm out the window and trailed her fingers along the breeze. Even though she had her face turned away, her mood seemed relaxed, and maybe even happy.

Katherine seemed to feel his gaze. She turned and when she did her loose hair caught in the breeze. The stunning smile she gave him as the wind whipped her locks around her face was his undoing. It was settled, today was already his best worst idea yet.

After about a half an hour he turned off a blacktop onto a service path, hopped out to let them through a gate and then drove about a mile in before stopping the truck at the base of a grassy hill.

"Where are we exactly?" Katherine asked, eyes scanning the land.

"Technically Crooked Brook, but this swath right here is now in the loving hands of Bishop and Belle."

"Oh," Katherine smiled softly, "Maddie told me they'd bought some acreage from Mae. It's lovely."

"Shall we?" he asked, reaching into the backseat to grab the convenience store wine.

She nodded and jumped from the truck, making her way up the hill to a large flat area begging for some sitting. She plunked down in the grass and he followed suit. They both spent a moment to take in the reaching green fields stretching to meet with the horizon for as far as the eye could see.

"This is nice," she sighed.

He smiled at her as he untwisted the top to the wine and handed it to her. "Hope you don't need a glass."

"I think you know me better than that," she smirked and took a swig from the bottle before returning it to him.

"Yeah, I suppose I do." He smiled and took a sip.

After a moment she pulled in an extra deep breath and exhaled. "It's so relaxing here."

"It really is. There's something about the absolute quiet of the open land that really allows your mind to shut off. The only other time I feel that is when I'm on the horses. It's almost impossible to have crap bouncing around in your head while you're riding."

"I know what you mean. When I was in high school, I used to dance, and I felt the same way. The outside world stopped existing when the music was playing. I think it's why I loved it so much."

"Yeah?" he asked, tilting his head and slightly narrowing his eyes. "I can picture that. Would love to see that actually."

She shyly smiled at him. "Feels like a long time ago now."

"A handful of years barely," he pushed. "Come on, would you dance for me?"

"What? Here?"

"Why not?"

"I'd be too rusty." She shook her head.

"Please?"

After a long pause her expression softened slightly. "You'd have to be kind."

"I promise."

"You have any Chris Stapleton on your phone?"

"I'm sure I do," he said digging his phone from his pocket.

"Tennessee Whiskey?"

"Uhhh," he scrolled, "yup."

She watched him for a long moment and then pulled her lower lip between her teeth. Trix's eyes were glued to the movement, and he had to fight the urge to reach out to touch her. Katherine stood, saving him from himself, and she popped off her little white tennis shoes before wriggling her toes in the grass.

"I can try to remember my senior recital. It was choreographed to that song."

She stretched her neck to the side and then gave him a grin and a slight nod.

He hit play and the slow bluesy beat started right away. Katherine began to sway. Her arm arced away from her body and he was captivated by the unhurried perfect grace of her fingers. A single knee reached up followed by the rest of a long tan leg that stretched out above her head.

Her body moved so effortlessly with the rolling rhythm, she belonged to the flowing pasture surrounding them. The sun caught in her hair and the slightest hint of gold materialized in the dark waves. When the breeze picked up, it brought her warm and spicy scent to him and blew the hem of her dress against her thighs.

She closed her eyes, getting lost in the music as she started a slow sensual spin. She was mesmerizing perfection. She was freedom itself. His fingers dug into the grass at his sides hoping it would keep him grounded.

She leapt into the air landing without a sound and then arched her body, both arms unfolding above her head as she bent back, face turned to the sky. All of the air left his lungs and refused to return. He rose, allowing her gravity to pull him in, his gaze riveted to a throbbing pulse at the base of her long neck. When he stopped in front of her, her eyes snapped open, and her rapid breathing fanned his flames.

"I don't want you to stop, but if I can't touch you right now, I think it'll kill me," he confessed.

"Trix," she sighed, her gaze stopping short of meeting his. "You're a sucker for pretty things."

"You're not just pretty. you're a goddamn marvel," he said as he brought a hand up to her chin to gently direct her gaze to him.

When her eyes rose to meet his, there was a fragility in them that made him want to barricade her from the world, to prevent whatever had made this amazing woman afraid to be amazing from ever reaching her again. His other hand rose to brush against her shoulder and they both turned to watch his fingertips as they leisurely traced down her arm.

"I need to kiss you and if you don't want me to, or if you're not ready, you've got to tell me now," he said.

Both of their gazes were still trained on his fingers, now gently toying with and interlacing hers. "I want you to," she whispered.

"Thank God," he exhaled as his other hand cupped the side of her face.

She turned up her face to his, her eyes closed, long dark lashes splayed across the tops of her cheekbones. Slowly he bent down to her. His lips brushed hers gently, barely allowing himself a feel of the soft fullness of them before partially drawing away. He came back again, with a little more pressure. He needed her to open, to soften, to give him permission to possess her mouth. When her lips parted, he gently pulled her bottom lip between his own, grazing it with his teeth. She whimpered, and her body swayed into his.

He tilted his head to deepen the kiss and she met him with her building fervor. Her hands roamed to either side of his waist and balled his shirt in her fists, pulling their bodies closer. The urgency in the kiss began to build as her taste, light and sweet, filled his senses spurring him to deepen their connection.

His body was vibrating with the need to have her, but his mind was struggling. His demand for her was so strong, it defied precedence for what it meant to him to want a woman. He needed to understand better. He needed her to understand. They needed words, space, and time, not this explosive desire. As he fought to rein himself in, she began to pull away. He followed her lead but pressed his forehead to hers as they both worked to draw air.

"Trix, I'm sorry, I don't think I'm ready for anything more"

"Don't apologize. Honestly, I don't think I am either," he admitted.

"That doesn't mean I don't want you to do that again someday," she smiled up at him.

"Maybe even later today," he matched her grin before pressing his lips to hers briefly.

"I'd like that," she sighed.

The song looped and started again. He interwove his fingers with hers and curled their hands against his chest between them. He pulled her closer with the other arm around her waist and they started to sway together.

"You're an amazing dancer," he said.

"I told you I loved to dance."

"That wasn't what I was expecting."

"What did you expect, 'rah-rah, go team go' and a kick?" she looked up, smirking at him.

"I didn't expect to be unable to breath," he said, holding her gaze.

She smiled softly. "Maybe you're as smooth as I thought after all."

She rested her head against his shoulder and slowly they danced as the sun began to get low in the sky. The rightness of her in his arms snaked its way through his chest, weaving around his ribs until it wrapped around his heart, and he felt like there were no consequences he wouldn't endure to buy this moment from the universe.

***

Trix drove Katherine home and stopped the truck inside the entrance to the trailerpark. He turned to her, knowing this was where she'd insist on getting out. It was time to move forward with the rest of his plan, even if it would damn them both.

"So, I'm going back to New York."

"You're moving back?" she asked in shock.

"What? No. I have a family thing. A wedding."

"Jesus Christ, Trix. We need to work on your delivery."

"My cousin's getting married, and I thought, well, maybe you'd, um, want to go?"

"With you? To New York?"

He ran a hand over the top of his head, avoiding looking at her. "I mean, you don't have to. I thought, maybe—"

She cut him off, saving him from his panicked backtracking. "That sounds amazing. Honestly it does, but you know I can't afford to take time off, let alone a plane ticket."

"I've already thought of that. It's only for Saturday and Sunday. I'm sure you can finagle shifts so that it's not actually time off. Plus, my father has already purchased a plane ticket to make sure I attend, and because he's a rich asshole who has forgotten coach even exists, it's first class. I think I can convert it to two regular people tickets and, voila, it's Katherine Grant versus the Big Apple."

She watched him for a long time, then she smiled. "Okay."

"Okay?"

"Yeah, it sounds like fun. When?"

"Not this weekend, but next."

"All right, I'll work on moving shifts," she said, her smile deepening. "We're going to New York," she laughed.

"We're going to New York," he echoed, returning her smile.

This is a bad idea, his conscience told him.

Trix shook his head. He'd picked denial and he was sticking with it.

He could spend time with Katherine and maintain his relationships with those at the ranch who hated her. All he needed to do was keep those two parts of his life separate.

How hard could that be?

CHAPTER 21

Everyone had finished their chores early in order to enjoy an afternoon off for a Labor Day party at Crooked Brook. Music poured from a little portable speaker and the outdoor tables were overflowing with food and friendly conversation between all of the ranch employees and several additional invited guests. Trix sat across from Alex and Winn and began to eat way more ribs than someone who cared about body fat should. Junior and Maddie joined him on his side of the table, and they joked about the amount of food he'd managed to balance on his plate. Then Maddie turned to Junior, seeming to jump off in the middle of a sentence that started elsewhere. "Of course, I was like you totally have to borrow my proposal dress next weekend. 'Cause, you know, Katherine and I are basically the same size and it would be a tragedy to be in New York and not have something amazing to go out in."

Trix choked on his food. His denial game was imploding sooner than he'd thought and all because of an unwitting wrecking ball named Maddie.

Trix watched as Alex did a double take. "Did you just say that Katherine is going to New York next weekend?" she asked.

Maddie looked over to her and cautiously nodded. "Yes?"

In a flash Alex's eyes shot to Trix, and he jumped to his feet, bolting toward the house. When he turned back, he saw Alex had risen to pursue him, and he kicked himself for not planning for this eventuality. Of course, Katherine had told her cousin she was going away. She'd probably had to in order to convince Maddie to work a few shifts for her. It was obvious Maddie didn't know Katherine was going with him, but Alex knew about his trip and now she knew Katherine was going too. *Shit.*

"Jesus Christ, Trix." Alex didn't waste any time once she'd caught up with him near the back steps. "Do you think we're stupid? That we wouldn't figure it out?"

When Trix didn't immediately respond she pushed, "Are you sleeping with the woman who absolutely broke your best friend?"

"Alex, it's hard to explain."

"Answer the question."

"Yes."

Alex's gaze traveled the hundred feet across the yard to where Winn was still seated at the table. "Winn and I have our troubles, but lying to each another is not one of them. So, unless you give me a good reason why I shouldn't tell him you're screwing his ex, then I'm going—"

"I love her," Trix spat out.

"What?" she gasped.

"God help me, I think I'm in love with her, Red. Like chest hurts, can't breathe, every minute I'm not with her hurts." He rubbed his palm into his sternum.

"It's Katherine," she said, wide-eyed.

"She's a goddess."

"She's the devil."

"Maybe," he conceded.

"What am I supposed to do with this information?"

His shoulders sagged as he watched the ground. "Sneaking around is killing me. I know I should come clean, but I don't know how."

"You tell them all that you lost your damn mind, temporarily, but you've broken it off and you'll do dishes for a year as penance for your stupidity."

"I can't do that, Alex. I… I need her."

"What has she done to you? How has she convinced you she's worthy of you? Because she absolutely is not. You deserve so much better."

"Doesn't exist. Not for me," Trix insisted.

They both looked up to find Winn approaching.

"Goddamn it," she sighed.

"Yeah."

"You have twenty-four hours to figure out how to tell him. If you don't, I will."

***

Katherine was working Maddie's shift on Labor Day as part of her trade off to get the New York weekend free. The diner was busy, but everyone was loitering, so most of the work involved refilling cups and mugs. Her phone vibrated in her apron pocket and she couldn't stop the grin when she saw it was a text from Trix.

We've been made.

The smile fell from her face as she struggled to identify her feelings. She knew this was probably scary and tough for him since there wasn't exactly a Katherine Grant fan club at Crooked Brook these days. She didn't like knowing he was upset. On the other hand, she was pleased the news was out in the open. She was through pretending she didn't want Trix.

The danger was the very real possibility he would decide he was unwilling to endure any backlash to be with her. He'd already proven once he was willing to walk away for the sake of his family at the ranch. She wanted to believe she was ready to accept either outcome, but that wasn't true. She took a deep breath and replied.

We've been made.
Who?
For now, only Alex.
Not great. Are you ok?
Call me?

Katherine's stomach twisted. She made a quick sweep of the diner with a coffee pot in one hand and a pitcher of pop in the other. Once she was sure no one would miss her for a few minutes, she went out the back.

Trix picked up on the first ring. "Hey." He sounded out of breath.

"Hey."

When he didn't say more, she reached for empty words. "It's going to be okay," she said, although she had no idea if it would. Again, he didn't respond. "Tell me what happened."

"That twit Maddie and her big mouth—"

"Hey," she cut him off, because he was talking about her cousin, but also because she was taken aback by his rare use of unkind words.

"I'm sorry, but you know how she gets. She started babbling about lending you a dress to go to New York and it took Alex all of two point five seconds to figure it out."

"Oh," Katherine exhaled.

"Yeah, and now Alex has given me a twenty-four hours to tell Winn or she rats me out."

"Fairly generous of her given the circumstances," Katherine said.

"Doesn't feel like it from where I'm standing."

"What are you going to do?" she asked, worried what his answer would be.

"I don't know."

"I guess you could tell Alex you won't see me anymore. Maybe she'll let it go." The words pained her to say, but she'd always known it was likely he'd have to pick.

"Not going to happen," he said.

"Okay." She exhaled her relief.

"How do you think it will go?" he asked.

"Well, he cares about you and hates me, so my guess is not well."

"Shit."

"I'm really sorry."

"I'm not. Well, I'm sorry I lied to everyone, and I'm sorry this is going to hurt Winn. I hope to god it doesn't tank our friendship. I can't be sorry about feeling close to you. Not anymore."

The back of her eyes stung with his admission. The most likely outcome of this news spreading at the ranch was an ultimatum, and she wasn't going to let him give up his family for her. She wasn't worth it.

She cleared her throat. "Thank you for saying that."

"It's true, Katherine, I need you to—"

"Let's focus on one thing at a time, okay?" She cut him off. She didn't want to hear words he'd regret after he chose his family over her. "Think about how you're going to tell Winn and then get it over with."

"Okay, but—"

"I have to get back into the diner now."

After a long pause he said, "Okay," and then disconnected.

Katherine sagged against the wall in the alley, then rearranged her expression and headed back to work.

CHAPTER 22

The next morning Katherine caught sight of Crooked Brook's orange farm truck in the parking lot at the feed store and couldn't stop her pulse from quickening at the thought Trix may be inside it. She walked over, then noticed that the truck was backing with the trailer cocked off to the side, dangerously close to hitting the truck in the next spot over. She could only think of one person who could be driving that truck who wouldn't be able to park a trailer. Her suspicions were confirmed when she heard Alex yell, "Goddamn it." from inside the cab.

Katherine stepped in front of the truck and waited for Alex to look up. When she did, she muttered something to herself, then threw the truck into park, still half in, half out of a spot. Alex leaned out the window.

"Something I can help you with?" Alex asked with ice in her tone.

"Appears I'm not the one who needs a hand."

"Yeah, yeah, everyone loves to get in a jab at the city girl. I need to pull forward. You can move, or I get to hit you with a truck."

Katherine debated leaving her to her own devices, but this ridiculous girl was important to Trix, and Trix was important to Katherine. If there was even the smallest chance she could be with Trix, a truce was going to be necessary.

"I'm not poking fun. It can be hard. Can I help you?" Katherine offered.

Alex watched her with hard eyes. "Yes, fine," she said between clenched teeth.

Katherine approached the driver's side door and motioned for Alex to scoot over into the passenger seat. "I'm guessing before you left, Winn and Trix gave you some crap advice about parking, like: 'You've got to feel where the trailer wants to go'?"

"They told me to 'become one with the trailer.'" Alex made air quotes with her fingers as she recalled the woefully unhelpful advice.

"Idiots," Katherine said as she pulled the truck forward. "It's physics, not magic. They want to pretend they have some mystical connection with all things machine, but, like almost everything they do, it's simpler than they let on."

Katherine put the truck in reverse. "You need to use the side view mirrors not the rearview. If you're pulling a stock trailer instead of a flatbed, you won't be able to see out the back. Step one, get lined up as straight as possible. That's done going forward. Step two, back up and watch the trailer in the mirror. If the ass end goes the way you don't want, pull forward and turn the wheel the other way when you start again. Make small moves, small corrections and go slow. It takes practice, but it's not rocket science." As she spoke, she looked out the window and rotated the wheel slightly back and forth a few times as she seamlessly backed the trailer and truck into the spot.

"Thanks for the tutorial," Alex said, but couldn't stop herself from adding, "If you think a small favor like this is going to change my mind about what you're doing to Trix, you're delusional."

"That's pretty big talk from the woman who thinks she's sleeping with the love of my life," Katherine floated.

"Winn isn't the love of your life," Alex hissed.

Katherine's eyes narrowed a fraction, but she half smiled at Alex. "So confident. I'm surprised you're more worried about Trix than you are about my history with Winn."

"Winn isn't in love with you."

Katherine's stomach flipped. "That implies Trix is."

"Trix is confused," Alex corrected. "I know you're taking advantage of him. I don't know what your end goal is, but I'm sure you're working him over. If you break him with your games, you'll have to answer to me."

"Don't threaten me. Besides, from where I stand, I'm not the one who needs a warning about letting a cowboy fall too hard. If you hurt Winn, I will ruin you. And that's trailerpark talking, not city bluster," Katherine promised.

"You don't get to think, let alone worry about, Winn anymore. He *is* the love of *my* life and I would never do anything to hurt him."

"Aside from driving off the property like you were going to leave him for good."

"You're out of bounds, bitch."

"And you're in a glass house, princess."

"Get out of my truck," Alex ordered.

Katherine paused to drive home her point. "Tell the boys I said hello," she said and left a seething Alex alone in her truck.

That could've gone better. Katherine made her way back toward the diner. She supposed it didn't actually matter that Alex hated her a tiny bit more now. Today Trix would confess, and Katherine was confident Winn would tell him he needed to stop seeing her or risk trashing the relationships he'd built over the last three years. Regardless of what Trix thought he wanted, she wasn't going to let him blow up his life. She wasn't worth the sacrifice which alienated him from his family at Crooked Brook.

It was going to be a tough day.

***

Trix had been putting off coming clean to Winn all day, but it was now late afternoon, and his twenty-four-hour deadline was fast approaching. Trix was headed to the horse barn when Winn and Alex came flying around the side of the equipment barn in his favorite John Deere Gator. It was the fast sporty one you could get into some trouble in. Trix grinned before he reminded himself this conversation probably wasn't going to end with them tearing around the fields like idiots.

"Hey," Winn called to him. "We're going to go run doughnuts out by the creek, want to come?"

"Uh, no, thanks," Trix said after they'd stopped alongside him.

Winn watched him suspiciously. "You basically invented Dukes of Hazzard Gator Edition, and now you're saying you don't want to go play in the mud?"

Alex turned to Trix, eyes wide and expectant, expression basically screaming: *Tell him right now.*

"Actually, man, I need to talk to you. You got a minute?" Trix asked.

Winn looked worried as he turned to Alex, who shrugged.

"All right," Winn said. He got out from behind the steering wheel and Alex followed.

"What's up?" Winn asked.

Trix rubbed the back of his neck and stared a hole into the ground. "Winn, see the thing is, uh… I've been seeing Katherine… and, well…"

"That's a bad idea," Winn interrupted.

"Look, man, I know you hate her—"

"I don't hate her."

Trix and Alex whipped their heads around and asked. "What?" in unison.

"I think it's complicated, but I don't hate her," Winn repeated.

"I can't believe you'd say that," Alex demanded.

"There were redeeming things about Katherine, then, and maybe even still. Now that I've had distance from our break-up, it's easier for me to remember she wasn't always a conniving harpy."

"She broke your heart," Alex insisted.

"Yeah, but now we're together. Should I still be hung up on that?" Winn replied. "In what world does it make sense for you to want that?"

"What we have and what she did to you are two separate things," Alex said.

"There was a time when I cared about her," Winn continued. "Do you think I was stupid enough to be with someone truly awful?"

"Maybe," Alex was close to shouting.

Trix bit his cheek and stood there looking back and forth between them as they continued to argue.

Winn went on. "There were things about her that were good, and now that I've had some space to get over how things ended, I don't know…it feels different now."

"She cheated on you," Alex pushed.

"I haven't forgotten," Winn deadpanned.

"I cannot believe this is how this conversation is going," she said. Trix had to agree. Alex and Winn talking more than he did was not an outcome he'd expected.

Winn opened his mouth maybe to refute Alex's skepticism, but then seemed to change tactics and turned to Trix. "How long has this been going on?"

"I guess, maybe you could say since the night of the rodeo," Trix said with a flinch.

Winn's mouth gaped. "Months? For months you've been running around with Katherine?"

"I...man...kind of. Yeah. There's something about her..." Trix trailed off.

"I can't believe this," Winn murmured.

"You're not the only one," Alex agreed, then turned and stormed off toward the house.

Trix watched Alex leave, then turned to Winn saying, "I've got to tell you I saw this going a lot of ways in my head. But you and her fighting while you and I are fine wasn't one of them."

"You and I aren't fine, Trix," Winn said.

"It sounded like you understood why I'd want to be with her."

"You've been lying to me for months, man. We are not fine."

Winn climbed back into the Gator and drove off, leaving Trix standing in the yard. He decided since the new problem between Alex and Winn was all his fault, he may as well start there and try to get some wounds patched.

He found Alex in the kitchen, proving it was possible to shuck corn angrily.

"Hey," he called to her back. He watched her shoulders tense at his voice, but she didn't speak or turn around. "Look, I never meant for this to cause trouble between you and Winn. I'm sorry it has."

She turned around to face him. He expected her to still be angry, but instead found her eyes filled with tears. "I need him to hate her," she confessed.

"He doesn't have to hate her to love you."

"What if not hating her leads to feeling something for her again?"

"Then he'd have to fight me for her," Trix joked and then instantly regretted trying to make light of the situation when her eyes flared. "Alex," he started, "Winn is very much in love with *you*. That's not going to change. I can tell you that with the confidence of someone who's seen him with her, without her, and with you. I know what it's like to care for someone like that, I know you and Winn..." He stopped when Alex rolled her eyes.

"You better not be trying to compare whatever it is you guys are doing with what Winn and I have. They couldn't be more different. She's not a good person."

"There's no part of you that is happy for me?" he pushed.

"I'm...I want to look out for you. You know why she was with Winn. She wanted out of this town. She left him as soon as he wasn't leaving. She thought she traded up when she got with Blake. All of the decisions she's made are about her own self-interest."

"I'm not in denial about who she was or what she's done."

"You think it's a coincidence that you're a rich kid from Manhattan and now she's set her sights on you? You represent her next ticket out of Montana." He flinched, but she continued. "I'm sorry, but why you don't see what's actually happening here."

"I want to say the same to you," he countered.

They watched each other for a long moment before he sighed. "Look, you and I aren't going to end up on the same side of the fence on this one, at least not right now. I can honestly say your friendship is deeply important to me, and if we need to table this discussion for a while to preserve that friendship, then that's what I want to do."

She studied him, and he began to squirm. She exhaled deeply and nodded, "Fine," she paused to point a finger at him, "for now."

"So about Winn..." he started.

"I'll talk to him," Alex said.

"You think he'll ever forgive me, Red?" he asked.

"I think he's shocked and hurt you could lie to him for so long."

"They always say it's not the crime but the cover up," he chuckled.

"Don't do that. It's not a joke. I know you're gutted he's upset."

She gave him a long scolding look which finally broke him. He nodded. "Put in a good word for me, okay?"

She gave him a sad smile. "Even if he comes around about the deception, you have to know you seeing Katherine may actually be bad for him, and he's not telling you so."

He nodded, and she left him standing there alone in the kitchen.

CHAPTER 23

Trix was feeling raw. He kicked himself when his first instinct was to call Katherine. This was about his family, but he needed to talk to someone else. He took off to find an ear before he admitted his lapse to Mae, which he needed to do sooner rather than later.

He found a great warm-up confessor when he came across Griz working in the shop on a small dresser he was refurbishing.

"Hey, man, mind if I hang out in here for a bit? I need to lay low for a few minutes."

Griz made a low non-committal murmur and began to hand plane the top of the dresser.

"I've really stepped in it this time," Trix said.

Griz didn't respond, the only sound was the metronomic rasping of the tool. Scrape. Pause. Scrape. Pause.

"I've been, well, I've kind of been seeing Katherine," Trix blurted out.

Griz looked up and watched Trix for a few long moments, then he returned his gaze back to his hands. Scrape. Pause. Scrape. Pause.

"You knew?" Trix asked.

Griz gave a slight nod. Scrape. Pause.

"I guess you see more when you keep your eyes open and your mouth shut, huh?" Trix chuckled.

Scrape. Pause.

"The problem is, I know all the reasons I shouldn't be with her, but I'm drawn to her. Something about her has wrapped around me and won't let go."

Scrape. Pause. Scrape. Pause. Griz stopped for a moment to run his hand over the surface of the dresser, and bent down to observe from a lower angle before resuming his task. Scrape. Pause.

"Griz, you ever let a woman get her claws in you so much that picking between her and your best friend would even give you a moment's pause?"

Griz looked up and again watched Trix for several beats before exhaling deeply and then resuming his task. Scrape. Pause.

Trix went on, "No, of course not. You're smarter than that."

Griz again stopped to run his fingers over the dresser. He leaned over and blew the wood curls off the surface, then put down the planer. Picking up a piece of sandpaper he started sanding the top.

"Really, the problem is I lied to Winn because I was a coward. When you've done something like that I'm not sure people can ever truly forgive you." The rhythmic sound of grit on lumber continued to fill the pause in Trix's rambling. "This place is my life and it's never going to be the same as it was, is it?"

The silence stretched on and when Trix thought he'd get no response, Griz looked up, his green eyes buried in a sea of his dark full beard and unruly longish dark hair. "It's going to be okay," he said.

Trix let out a deep breath and nodded. "Thanks, man. Good talk." He clapped Griz's shoulder before heading out, hiding he didn't actually believe his friend. He figured the last sword to throw himself on today was talking to Mae. He may as well get it over with.

Trix found her reading a book in the front room. When he came in, she glanced up for a second and then looked back down to her pages.

"You're finally going to tell me what's been eating at you," Mae said, no hint of a question in her voice.

"You're a spooky woman, you know that?" he asked.

"I know you guys think I'm damn near clairvoyant, but the truth is y'all are so transparent."

He chuckled as much as his dread would allow, and then sunk into the chair across from her.

"So, here it is." He drew in one long breath and said, "I've been seeing Katherine behind everyone's back and lying to Winn and everyone else about it for months. I'm terrified of what this means for my future here and my relationship with everyone even if I did stop seeing her, which I don't want to do. I'm afraid I've already ruined everything." There. He said it.

He watched Mae as she closed the book and set it down on the table between them before scratching the side of her cheek and running a hand over her mouth.

"Guess that explains why you thought your recklessness may get you run out of here on a rail," she said, her tone hard to read.

"I feel terrible about hiding it. But I can't say I regret the time I've spent with her. I know she seriously burned a bridge with this family, and I know people hate her, but I can't. I can't hate her, Mae. No matter how much my loyalty to you makes me wish I could." He was scrambling to plead his case.

"I don't expect you to hate her," Mae said.

"I know everyone think she's terrible."

"If she was such an awful person, don't you think I would've kicked and hollered through her entire relationship with Winn?"

"Of course you would have, but she really hurt Winn."

Mae nodded. "She did."

"So?"

"So, what? Are you looking for my opinion or my blessing?"

"Both?"

"Katherine is a confused, insecure, trouble magnet. She's selfish and tempestuous—"

Trix cut her off. "Sounds like you think she's a terrible person." The deep flash of resentment he felt when Mae insulted Katherine was instantaneous, and he didn't do a great job of hiding it.

"Boy, you said you wanted my opinion. Now you can either shut up and hear it, or you can get defensive and deaf. What's it going to be?" Mae stared him down.

"Shutting up," he said, preparing to hear Mae deliver *give up Katherine or give up Crooked Brook ultimatum* he'd expected to come from Winn.

Mae went on. "Katherine is all of those things, and if you're pretending she's not, you're opening yourself up to a world of hurt. That said, I've only ever come across two souls walking this Earth I didn't think deserved a chance at redemption, and she's not one of them."

Trix's heart skipped a beat. Maybe she'd be okay with him staying with Katherine and keeping the ranch in his life. "You think she deserves a second chance?"

Her gaze snapped to his. "You're doing the shutting up part right now."

"Yes, ma'am."

"When it comes to my blessing, you don't need it. You're a grown man. You're free to do what you want to do regardless of my approval. I don't fire men because of choices they make in their love life." Trix couldn't hide the hope on his face, and Mae shook her head. "But, I'm not the one who could be hurt if that girl's presence is felt on this ranch again, so I can't guarantee you'll still want to work here if you continue to pursue a relationship with her. I know you guys don't tell me everything that happens in your lives, and I don't expect you to, but there are men here who thought the kind of friendship they had with you required being open and honest, and you betrayed them."

She stopped to watch him for a moment and his stomach clenched knowing how right she was. "This place is what it is because we trust, love, and respect each other. If you no longer have that with the others, it won't feel the same for you."

When she paused, she looked at him and raised her brows, confirming he was allowed to speak again, but he couldn't find any words. Mae had given credence to his biggest fear.

"Lastly, you need to consider if that girl is good for you, regardless of how the people here feel about it."

"You think she's bad for me?" Trix asked, confident he wouldn't like the answer.

"I'm not sure I can answer that. I know Katherine's selfishness stems from not having anyone she can count on. She's had to learn to look out for herself no matter how many bodies she had to leave in her wake."

"She had Winn," Trix said.

"I imagine the girl she was when they were together was better for it. But she's a woman now. She's trying to find a way in a grown-up world, and now she's more alone than ever."

"Do you think I can be the person she can lean on?"

"Relationships work when you can count on one another. I don't know if either of you has it in you."

Trix looked down at his hands. Having Mae give your character a less than stellar review was painful, regardless of how right you knew she was.

"What do I do?"

"Stop asking people to make your decisions. You need to make one and then live with the consequences."

"I think I'm in love with her," he confessed.

She watched him for a long moment before she sighed. "I know."

Mae's expression made it clear their conversation was over so Trix rose and placed a small peck on the side of her cheek as she reached to pick up her book.

***

After her run-in with Alex in the parking lot, Katherine felt certain the animosity Trix's friends felt toward her was going to be a hurdle they couldn't clear. She'd thought he'd contact her to cancel the trip to New York, but so far radio silence. Wiping down the counter she scanned the darkened diner to make sure everything was buttoned up for the night. Her keys jangled as she pulled them from her jacket. When her phone chimed, she was nervous to check it, but the text was from Maddie.

OMG! Call me!

Maddie was supposed to pick up Katherine at ten, which was now. She dialed her cousin and pinched the phone between her shoulder and cheek as she went out the door and turned to lock it. Trix was leaning against the wall in the shadows, and she jumped from the surprise of anyone being there, let alone him.

"Katherine," Maddie screamed into the phone. Katherine jolted again. Seeing Trix, she'd almost forgotten she was calling her cousin. "Junior told me Trix is going to pick you up. Trix is picking you up because you guys have been freaking dating." Maddie's shrill voice cut through the air, but Katherine had locked eyes with Trix, and she barely heard.

"I have to call you back," she said absently.

"You owe me an explanation."

"Later." She hung up. Trix's face was grim. Katherine's stomach twisted. In an attempt to counteract the hurt she knew was coming, she reminded herself she'd been expecting this.

"Hey," she started.

"Hey."

"How'd it go?"

He took a deep breath and ran a hand over his mouth. "Everyone's pissed."

She wanted to go to him but stayed where she was. "We knew it wouldn't go over well."

"It's all going to be different now."

"Not for forever."

"I lied to them."

"They'll forgive you."

"Why would they?" His broken expression was heartwrenching.

"Because they love you."

"Maybe not anymore." Trix pressed his fingers to his eyes. "Maybe my father is right." He shook his head. "Maybe I'm not built for the long term with people like this. I walked all over their trust and it's never going to be the same between us. How can I stay here?"

Katherine felt her heart pound. "You're thinking about moving back?"

"I don't know what I'm thinking."

She swallowed and cleared her throat. "Maybe when you go back, it will put things in perspective."

"When we go back," he corrected. "You're still coming, aren't you?"

"I thought we wouldn't be seeing each other anymore."

His brow slammed down. "I don't want that."

"Didn't they say you had to cut me out of the picture?"

"No."

"I don't understand. Isn't that what we thought they were going to do?"

"Yes."

"But—"

He stepped to her. "I want you to come to New York. I want us to have time away from this. Together."

She watched him for a moment, relief from the news about New York warring with the panic she felt about Crooked Brook. "Okay," she gave him a soft smile and he wrapped his arms around her.

They stood there on the deserted street, hanging on to one another for a long time before he drove her home.

CHAPTER 24

As Trix feared, and Mae predicted, his relationship with the crew felt altered. After their initial shock wore off, most of the guys were treating him close to normal, but with an undercurrent of unease. Alex had barely spoken to him, and Trix missed her friendship. Winn hadn't spoken to him at all, which took some doing given the overlap their lives had. Trix responded by searching for more solitary duties. He was working alone on a hay trailer with a broken axel when Winn came into the equipment shed to find him.

"You free?" Winn said in a tone that was hard to read. "I could use a hand with the River Rock mare."

"Yeah, sure," Trix said, wiping his hands on a bandana, and then followed Winn as he walked to the round pen where the aggressive mare from the auction was pacing around the sand.

Winn had done a lot of work with the horse to form a truce, but up to that point he'd been the only one handling her. Winn finally turned to Trix and said, "She's getting good with me and now I need someone else to try to work her."

"She'll try to kill me," Trix pointed out.

"Maybe." Winn shrugged.

"I think maybe you want her to kill me," Trix said, an uncomfortable grin pulling at the sides of his mouth.

"I don't want her to kill you," Winn stated dryly. "I need to know if any of the lessons she's learned with me are going to transfer to other people. After me, you've got the best horse instincts in the group."

"Your brother's better with the horses than I am."

Winn nodded. "True, but I know I don't want her to kill my brother." He said it so flatly Trix actually believed him for a moment. Then Winn finally broke and popped a half grin. "Are you gonna help or not?"

"I'll do this if it starts getting me back in your good graces."

"Fine," Winn said. "But stop being so chicken shit. She'll sense your weakness and take advantage of it."

Trix nodded, knowing Winn was right. "What do you want me to do?" he asked.

"Go in there and work her like every other horse. If she comes at you like she's going to bite or kick, I want you to move and slap the rope on your calf to spook her away. Under no circumstances turn your back on her." Trix nodded and Winn added, "It goes without saying not to raise a hand to that horse."

"Yeah. It goes without saying. So why did you?" Trix asked.

"Man, I used to think I knew you, now I'm covering my bases."

The verbal smack left a serious sting.

Steadying his breath, Trix took one last look at Winn and turned to the horse in the pen. Like Winn had taught him, he gave her his undivided attention so neither of them would get hurt. This was River Rock's Red Flag, and in living up to her name, this one had bit, kicked, trampled or maimed every person but Winn who'd stepped into a pen with her. She was an amazing horse to look at. A deep red chestnut, well-built with great movement.

Trix bent and climbed through the rails of the fence, his eyes never leaving the horse. Her movement stopped, and she stood watching him. Every once in a while, her gaze drifted over to Winn.

You're a smart one, aren't you?

He walked to the middle of the round pen and positioned his body so he was slightly tilted toward her hind end. He brought an arm up and clucked at her to try to send her moving forward in a circle. At first, she didn't move, then she turned to face him, challenging him with her posture.

"She's getting ready to come at you," Winn warned.

"I see," Trix said, never breaking eye contact with the mare. "Go on now," he said, stepping at her and bringing his arm up to send her again. She took her chance to charge at him, ears pinned, mouth ready to strike. Trix waited until she was almost on top of him before he stepped to the side and slapped the rope on his leg. "Go on," he said firmly. She veered off and began circling the pen.

Trix took a moment to steady his nerve and took deep breaths to slow his racing heart. He stepped toward the front of the horse and quietly murmured soothing noises until she stopped. When she turned to the center to come at him again, he moved toward her back end and slapped the rope again. Instead of charging, she obeyed his nonverbal commands and went off in the opposite direction.

"That was good," Winn said. "Stop her, turn her, and send her twice more."

Trix did as he was instructed and was pleased with himself and the mare for being able to do what Winn was asking.

"Nice," Winn said. "Now stop her and make her come to you."

Trix nodded. This time he took a few steps back and she turned and took a few steps toward him. Her expression was calm and non-threatening.

"That's good," Winn said. "All right, go to her. Rub on her a bit. Tell her she's a good girl. She likes when you scratch right under her jaw."

Trix nodded and approached the horse. She watched him, but appeared content to stay where she was as he got closer. When he was close enough, he reached out to put a hand on her neck. She flinched, and he murmured more soothing sounds until she relaxed.

"That's a good mare," he said, relieved and feeling proud. Trix scratched under her jaw and she flexed her nose out a little to give him better access. "Good mare," he repeated.

"Next time, we'll have you lead her." Winn said. "For now, kind of back away and climb through the rail right there."

When he was clear of the pen Trix turned to face Winn, waiting for him to dictate the terms of their interactions.

"Good work. Thank you," Winn said.

"You bet," Trix nodded, watching Winn for cues as to what to do next.

"I could use you back at the stables more. I know you've been lying low these last few days, but you still have a job to do here. She's going to need work like that with you every other day or so."

Winn wanted Trix back at the stable to perform his job duties, not because he was interested in fixing their friendship. That hurt, but Trix nodded and decided if Winn was only interested in wearing the boss hat, then Trix may as well remind him he was going to be out of town. "I can do that. A reminder: I'm off this weekend. Tomorrow Katherine and I leave for a wedding in New York."

Winn nodded. "Yeah, I heard that."

"I care about her, man."

"I heard that too," Winn said.

"So?"

"So, have fun I guess." Winn shrugged, looking annoyed.

"That's it?"

"Watch your back," Winn added.

Trix bit back his quick defense. Winn seemed to be watching to see if the conversation would escalate. Because Trix didn't want that, he nodded and sighed. "Roger that."

He left Winn at the stable and went back to the equipment shed. He stared at the busted axel. It needed to be replaced. If he tried to repair it, it would forever have a weak point, which could snap again.

Something like that, something you couldn't depend on, had no purpose here.

CHAPTER 25

The next morning Trix and Katherine left for New York. His spirits started lifting as the distance between them and Montana grew. Flying away from the drama of the last week felt freeing, and he felt like he could draw a deep breath again. His light mood, however, was short lived. A different kind of weight settled on his chest when they arrived at JFK airport, and he spied a limo driver holding a sign with his name. A favor from his father, which wasn't really a favor. Being home wasn't going to be a carefree vacation, and nothing about his family was going to be straightforward. A limo wasn't a nice gesture, it was a reminder of the ultimatum his father had levied. Chose this life, or say goodbye to this for forever.

Trix peeked at Katherine to see if she found anything about the waiting limousine strange, but she bounced her brows as she slid into the soft leather seats. Trix joined her and couldn't help but grin when his work boots left dirt on the perfect black carpet.

As they made their way into Manhattan, Trix studied Katherine's face and swallowed his anxiety about her coming face to face with where he came from. He should've given her some kind of indication as to the moneyed snake pit he was walking her into. As her eyes drew up the sides of the immense buildings, her face was hard to read. She wasn't oozing awe like a cliché small town girl.

You never thought this was impressive. You were hoping she'd be impressed?

The car stopped and let them out at a five-star hotel adjacent to Central Park. If she wasn't already clued into what his previous life was all about, she was about to have a marble and crystal crash course in gratuitous luxury.

As they stepped from the limo, she glanced up at the baroque stone front of the building and turned to him. "The rich kid moniker doesn't exactly paint the whole picture huh?" she asked, seeming more amused than impressed.

"Not really," he confessed. "I maybe should have been clearer?"

"Money is money, Trix. Once you start talking about more than I have, there's a wide range in the category."

"I guess. Unfortunately, the wedding is in a ridiculously pompous venue. Should we shop first?" Trix hoisted their bags from the back before the driver could get there.

"You want to *Pretty Woman* me?" She laughed.

"No, I, uh," he stumbled through his discomfort.

"Are you going to be embarrassed if I wear the wrong thing?" Some of the humor fell from her face.

"No, not at all. I'm worried you may feel uncomfortable. I want to make sure you're comfortable."

"Don't worry about me," she said with confidence, and he worried she still hadn't fully grasped the situation.

You shouldn't have done this to her.

He watched her for a long moment, trying to detect if she was hiding a crack in her façade, but she shrugged and handed the porter her bag like she'd done it every day for her entire life.

The nearly hundred-year-old hotel lobby was a study in opulence with its intricately carved wood, marble floors, and a crystal chandelier the size of a Volkswagen hanging from the high ceiling. Katherine breezed through, barely looking around.

"Checking in for Doyle, Jacob," Trix said to the receptionist.

The woman looked up at him, a glint of recognition flashing over her face as her eyes traveled up and down his frame taking in the jeans and work shirt he was wearing.

"Welcome back, Mr. Doyle. So nice to see you again," she said with a wide grin as she handed him two keys. "You've been booked in a junior executive suit for tonight's stay."

Trix groaned internally. His father had likely thought that was a conservative choice, but Trix would need to come up with over a grand to pay him back. The receptionist continued to look at him with big expectant eyes. He tried to conjure a memory of her. Her nametag said Becky. When nothing sparked, he simply said, "Thank you, take care now."

He caught Katherine's eye and she smirked at him. Trix shrugged, turned to the elevators, and heard Katherine chuckle.

When they entered the suite, Katherine looked mildly impressed as she walked around the room, lightly skimming her hand over the gleaming wood surfaces as she moved from the living room into the bedroom. She eyed the king-sized bed layered with an abundance of fluffy white linens. Trix laughed when she threw herself backwards against the pile of pillows and down comforter.

She turned on her side, propping her head in one hand as the other tucked under the comforter to feel the sheets underneath. "My god, like butter. I'd wager these sheets aren't from the dollar store."

He shook his head as dove in next to her grabbing, and then pulling her to him.

She howled. "You caveman, your boots are getting the bed dirty."

"Good. Let's really wreck it," he said bringing her mouth to his.

She kissed him back, but put her hand between them before things could ramp up. "Didn't you say the ceremony started at four?"

"Mmmmm-hmmm," he said as he threw a leg over her hip.

"That means we have to leave an hour and half from now," she said and pushed his leg back to his side. "I have to get ready." Katherine climbed out of the bed.

"This is my sad face," he said as he pointed to his dramatically pulled down lips.

"Should have booked an earlier flight then." She laughed and went to the window, pulling open the drapes. The park and the skyline came into view and she pulled in a sharp breath.

"It really is something," she said.

"Yeah, it is," he agreed quietly.

She turned to him and their gazes held for a long beat. He thought she may be considering taking him up on his offer to tarnish the bed. Then, she snapped out of it, grabbed her bags and headed into the bathroom. "Holy shit," she shouted. "This shower. I want to live in it."

He smiled to himself before turning on the TV to the financial news, as if he could spend the next ninety minutes catching up on all of the things his father thought were consequential in this world.

After letting current events wash over him for about an hour he stood and started rummaging through his things. Thank god his cousin had put his foot down when others insisted the wedding had to be black tie. Trix had no idea where his formal wear ended up, but he'd held on to one bespoke suit, which cost more than he made in a year working at the ranch.

After he'd washed up and ran a comb through his hair, he put on the crisp white shirt and the charcoal suit, and then looked at himself in the mirror as he knotted his light blue silk tie. His face, tanner and more weathered, was different in other ways. He didn't look the same standing in a luxury hotel suite as he used to. It was his eyes, he decided. His eyes were different. There was knowledge behind them. Knowledge that none of this mattered, even though his entire life, he'd been led to believe it did.

His eyes were no longer a good fit for a well-tailored suit.

He was pulled from his reflections by the sound of the bathroom door opening. When Katherine emerged Trix dropped the remote and forgot to draw air. She looked stunning. The dress she'd borrowed from Maddie was simple, but elegant, and fit every curve perfectly. Sky high heels adorned her slender long legs, which disappeared under the black hem below her knee. Her hair was curled and swept haphazardly away from her face on both sides, she almost looked ethereal.

Her gaze met his and he had to resist every cell in his body crying out to pin her against the door frame.

"Is it okay?" she asked, looking worried as she plucked at the fabric of the borrowed dress.

"You're perfect," he whispered.

She smiled and fidgeted with a tie on her hip.

"I'm less angry with Maddie for getting us busted," he said, and she laughed.

Her gaze traveled up and down his body and she pulled the corner of her lip in between her teeth and pulled in a deep breath.

"You look..." she trailed off.

"Hot?" he joked.

"Yeah," she breathed, and again he gave serious thought to tearing the dress off her body.

Katherine appeared to come to her senses first. "We should go."

"I don't want to," he said, and she sent him a knowing smile.

"I didn't come all the way to New York only to see a fancy hotel."

"Right, we're here to be tormented by my family." He stood, breaking through the haze he was put in from looking at her.

At the mention of his family, his mood dipped. He knew the next few hours were going to be brutal. His father's disapproving everything Trix had ever done was sure to be a constant topic. He worried it would make Katherine think less of him. How could it not? He knew everyone's indictment of his character would be obvious.

"Are you okay?" she asked, startling him.

He shook his head. "Yeah. Shall we?" He offered her his arm and they went downstairs where the limo was waiting. It took them a few blocks to get to the wedding being held in one of the poshest mansions in New York City.

What had he been thinking?

CHAPTER 26

As the limo made its way through creeping traffic, Katherine watched the side of Trix's face while he looked out the window, his jaw working slightly. His unease was palpable and had come on so quickly. She wished she could find words to alleviate it, but that would require he talk to her about its origin, which he seemed unwilling or unable to do. His uncertainty was an unfamiliar sight. She assumed the ultimatum his father had leveled was weighing on Trix's mind given the troubles he was having back at the ranch. She wished he would talk to her.

Her gaze dropped down to Trix's arm. He'd removed his jacket and rolled up the sleeves of his white dress shirt three quarters of the way up to his elbows. There was a fascinating perfection to his forearm. The deeply tanned skin and dark hair stood out starkly against the starched bright fabric. Several lean muscles carved out deep valleys and rippled as he drummed his fingers on his knee, completely unaware of how entranced Katherine was with the gesture.

A few cord-like veins appeared above his wrist and her eyes traced their path to the top of his hand. His long fingers continued their strumming and Katherine could feel the memory of those unyielding hands possessing her, the coarseness of those callouses as they'd toured her body. Suddenly the three feet separating them felt unbearable.

When she moved to bring herself slightly closer to him, he turned to her, his expression wired and intense. His chest expanded on a deep intake of breath, which he held for a long time. She looked down to watch her fingertips graze along a single line of muscle down to the top of his hand. He rotated his palm up and she skimmed the rough patches, which spoke to the punishment they endured for his job.

She pulled her lower lip in between her teeth and looked up to find his attention affixed to her mouth, then his sapphire gaze raked back to hers.

They watched each other, and she felt her heart thudding against her chest as the weight of his stare pressed into her.

His lips parted as a slightly trembling breath moved through them.

She was overwhelmed by the tension from their eye contact alone.

The trance was abruptly broken when the limo door was opened from the outside. Katherine hadn't noticed they'd stopped.

Trix didn't even flinch, he kept his intense unwavering gaze on her. "Katherine, I..." he started but stopped when she shook her head.

"We should go," she prodded.

He swallowed hard and nodded then shifted to step from the car.

Suddenly, he whipped around, grasping both sides of her face to drag her into a kiss that tore the wind from her lungs. Instantly they were drowning, the sounds from outside became muffled. Horns, sirens, traffic all distant, fluid, fleeting. There was no air, no light, no thought. Everything was taken up by him.

The heat from his mouth, the firm impatience of his lips, the low moan rumbling up from the base of his chest. It was as if his only desire was to possess her completely. In that moment he did. Her mind, her body, her heart, were all his. She gave all of herself and more to him, to the kiss, to their connection.

A long shrill horn blast cut through the thick air and he drew away from her slightly while they both panted to draw air. He leaned back, his eyes churning pools, searched her face.

"If I came all the way here so I could live that moment, it was worth it."

"Yeah," she agreed breathlessly.

His gaze stayed on her for a minute longer and she half expected him to make a joke, but instead he gave her a slow pensive smile and then stepped from the car, offering her his hand as she followed.

Standing on the sidewalk, she watched him scan the street as he mindlessly rolled down his sleeves and buttoned his cuffs. He shrugged into his perfectly tailored jacket, tugging it down and straightening it into place in the exact right way before he deftly buttoned the suit jacket with one hand. The moves were so fluid and practiced for the first time she understood exactly how much of this life was in him, a part of him. How, in that moment, how far removed they were from the joking, sweaty, and sweary rancher she knew.

The shift in perception was jarring with the speed at which it shrunk her. She hadn't fully accepted Trix moving back to the city as a possibility, but this version of him fit more than she'd ever considered it could.

Maybe when he was in Montana he was pretending. Pretending this urban life didn't define him, but this version may be who he truly was—a man completely comfortable getting in and out of limousines and expensive suits.

The hard truth was Katherine, dressed to kill and caressing thousand thread count sheets, was the one pretending. The true version of themselves would never meet. It'd been an unnatural act of playing a part which brought them together. When the illusion ended, they would be two-thousand miles, and countless tax brackets apart.

He turned to her, intently watching her face with one eye narrowed. "Ready?"

She had to decide what to do. Should she keep playing her part, or hail a cab and save him the trouble of having to say inevitable words out loud? She looked at his face, so handsome and perfect, and knew she couldn't leave him standing on the street.

Maybe a little more pretending.

"Ready as I'll ever be," she forced a light tone and a smile that swallowed the urge to cry.

He searched her face for a moment longer and then nodded, reaching down to take her hand as he turned to go up the large stone steps of the mansion. Inside the door, a sign with scrolling hand-written letters welcomed them to "The joyous nuptials of Mr. Alfred K. Doyle Jr. and Ms. Denise A. Schultz."

"Guess this is the place," Trix smiled with a bounce of his brows as she tried to contain her awe at the scale of the mansion's grandeur.

She didn't have long to take in her surroundings before an older gentleman broke into her sightline. He was tall and wide through the shoulders with perfectly groomed salt and pepper hair. His eyes were almost gray, but she could tell by looking at him, he was Trix's father. The air around him seemed thicker and he held himself like a man who presumed you were impressed.

He walked up and shook Trix's hand, a move which Katherine found odd since it was her understanding the two hadn't seen each other in over three years.

"Glad you could make it," Mr. Doyle said formally with a hint of sarcasm.

"As it was ordained," Trix countered. A beat of uncomfortable silence hung in the air before Trix turned to her. "May I introduce Katherine Grant. Katherine, meet my father, Walter Doyle."

"It's nice to meet you, sir," Katherine said, extending her hand to him.

"Ms. Grant, pleasure to meet you, dear." Trix's father shook her hand before offering her his arm. "Shall we?"

Katherine placed her hand in Walter's elbow and the three of them walked through the mansion onto the lawn where rows of flower adorned chairs were lined up to face an ornate arch. It was a perfect day for a late summer wedding. The afternoon sun hung low in the sky warming a lazy breeze moving through the estate. Katherine looked to Trix's face to see how he was taking in the scene but found the formal mask he was wearing impossible to see through.

"Where's Mother?" Trix said.

"A headache regrettably kept her home today," Walter responded. The two exchanged a look and Katherine understood something was being communicated but not said.

Most of the guests had already settled into their chairs, but Walter directed them to a pair of empty seats. A woman seated in the row briefly looked up and openly scanned Katherine before she produced a sneer that perhaps was an attempt at a polite smile. Katherine did her best to brush it off and smiled back. After Trix and Katherine sat, Walter excused himself. "I do need to speak with someone before this event begins."

Trix didn't even look up from the program he was flipping through when his father walked away.

"He seems nice," Katherine said, trying to goad Trix into speaking to her about whatever was churning beneath the surface.

"He's not," he answered. Trix looked up and met her gaze, giving her a slow to form smile. "But having you here makes this so much better."

She returned the smile. "I'm glad."

Trix reached over and squeezed her hand.

The music changed, and bridesmaids started making their way down the aisle. The third one to pass was wearing the female version of Trix's face. Her dark hair was mostly up with a few strategic curls set to frame her sharp features. Her eyes the same extraordinary shade of blue as his. When the woman looked over at them, she gave a mock pained grimace, and Trix chuckled.

"That's gotta be your twin sister," Katherine leaned over to whisper into his ear.

"Yup. She's probably über excited to be in that fancy dress," he said sarcastically.

"She's pretty."

Trix turned to her with a pout. "I guess so."

"You're pretty, too," she soothed through a chuckle.

"Thank you. Now I feel better." He laughed.

The wedding march began, and the guests stood and turned for the bride. Katherine noticed Trix continued to face forward.

"What are you doing?"

"I like to watch the groom when he first sees the bride," he confessed.

Katherine lifted a brow and then joined him in keeping eyes on Alfred Junior. She could tell the moment his bride came into view because his smile was filled with the most genuine joy she'd ever seen streak across a man's face.

"That's my favorite part of a wedding," Trix leaned down to whisper without taking his eyes from his cousin.

Katherine now had a new favorite part to a wedding, and for a moment she forgot all the reasons she shouldn't, and let her heart melt a little more for Jacob Doyle.

The ceremony was formal, beautiful, and mercifully short. After the wedding party walked up the aisle, Trix and Katherine followed the other attendees to greet the new Mister and Missus on the steps into the mansion. She watched Trix give the bride a hug and a kiss on the cheek then he shook the groom's hand enthusiastically.

Turning to her, Trix said, "This is A.J., my cousin. A.J. this is my, uh…Katherine."

Katherine smiled at his verbal stumble. "Congratulations. Everything was beautiful."

"Thank you. Very nice to meet you. I've been told the looming photo shoot will require my most sober attention, so please, go have a drink for me." A.J. gave his new wife an exaggerated apologetic look when she playfully slapped his shoulder.

"Will do," Trix promised and the two of them made their way into the mansion's foyer for cocktails and canapés. Trix's sister saw them and came stomping over.

"Took you long enough," she grumbled.

Trix nodded. "My sister, Jenny. Jenny, this is Katherine."

Jenny's eyes narrowed. "You're awfully pretty," she said with an unexpected hint of accusation.

"So are you." Katherine furrowed her brow and matching the other woman's tone.

"You're not some rich Montana oil brat, are you?" Jenny asked bluntly.

Katherine let out a surprised laugh. "The antithesis of that actually."

"That's an oil brat kind of word."

"Well, Maw and Paw did allow learnin' after chorin'," Katherine said with a sarcastic drawl.

Jenny laughed a little, but then quickly pinned a semi-serious stare on Katherine. "Which is better: bagel bites or pizza rolls?"

"Pizza rolls," Katherine quickly answered, now fully amused.

"Good girl. Okay. Can we go get wasted now?"

"Yes, please," Katherine said with a relieved grin, adding, "What would you have done if I'd said bagel bites?"

"The only wrong answer to that question is: What are those?" Jenny beamed and offered her arm to Katherine, who slipped her hand into the crook of Jenny's elbow.

"My sister's trying to steal my girl," Trix joked.

"Better up your game," Katherine teased before reaching her free hand to grab his as they made their way to one of the bars.

As they got in line Katherine made small talk. "Ceremony was beautiful."

"Yeah, you'd never guess A.J. used to pick his nose to the point of gushing blood at every holiday," Jenny said causing the woman in front of them to make a disapproving huffing noise.

"Well, he did, Beth. You were there," Jenny said to the back of the woman's head, causing her to turn around and pinch her face at them.

"Oh, Jennifer, really. Please try to behave," Beth said with a practiced disdain.

"Thanks for that, cousin. My goal is to get at least twenty condescending verbal reprimands before the night is through."

Beth shook her head and moved out of line.

Katherine let out the amused breath she had been holding. "You guys seem to have a lot of cousins."

"Irish," Trix and Jenny replied in unison.

"Ah." Katherine laughed.

Trix made it to the bar and looked at her questioningly.

"White wine. Anything not too sweet," she replied, as if ordering anything other than a shot and a beer was a regular occurrence.

He nodded and turned back to the bartender. When they'd received their drinks, they went to one of the standing tables nearby. Katherine took in the room, trying to not let on she was more than a little dazzled. Carved dark oak was everywhere, and the chandeliers looked like they cost more than all the homes in her neighborhood combined.

Every one of the guests was impeccably dressed. The men's suites all looked as expensive as the masterpiece Trix was wearing, and the women wore gowns from every high-end designer Katherine had ever heard seen online.

Small, jeweled bags on long chains Katherine thought only existed on the glossy pages of magazines were in the heavy majority. The waitstaff was dressed in tuxes and looked better bred than Katherine as they walked around with hors d'oeuvres and champagne. She made a concerted effort to straighten her posture and pull up her chin, trying to look more the part of invited guest instead of lowly wedding crasher.

"Where's Mom?" Trix asked Jenny, breaking Katherine out of her paranoia.

"At home. She and Dad have decided they no longer need to pretend they don't hate each other." It sounded like a serious subject, but Jenny's tone was light as if they were discussing a movie release instead of the disillusion of their parents' marriage.

Trix turned to Katherine. "Guess this wedding won't be the only painful family obligation I put you through this weekend. Can I talk you into breakfast with my mother tomorrow before we go? I think if I came to New York and didn't see her there would be hell to pay."

Katherine opened her mouth to agree, but his sister cut in.

"Better make it brunch," Jenny said.

"That bad?" he asked.

"Halina says it's been months since she got out of bed before ten."

"Do you see her?" Trix asked.

Jenny put her palms up like she could block the underlying accusation in Trix's tone. "I see her every week, and honestly, she's fine. She's bored and detests Walter. She needs a hobby."

"I would be happy to have brunch with your mother," Katherine said when it became apparent Trix wasn't going to respond to Jenny.

"Letting this girl meet the whole clan is a risk," Jenny warned. "How will you maintain your mysteriousness if she sees how the sausage is made? Or more accurately, the childhood trauma?"

Trix smiled again. "She already knows I'm not the posterchild for well-adjusted."

"Well-adjusted is boring," Katherine added.

"Indeed," Jenny laughed, then gestured across the room. "Great Aunt Faith is trying to catch your eye," she said to Trix.

He sighed. "I think I've got to at least say hi really quick. Won't bore you with that one's reminiscing about the old country."

After Trix excused himself, Jenny leaned over. "Here's your chance. What do you want to know?"

Katherine laughed, she really liked Trix's sister. "I don't think I have any burning questions."

"None?" Jenny asked incredulously.

"I know it sounds strange, but I feel like I know Trix. At least, I know who all of who he is now that I'm here, and that's good enough for me," Katherine fibbed, not wanting to invite more mental torment over who Trix was.

Jenny narrowed her eyes. "That's a good answer, and I want to believe you, but here's probably where I insert some veiled threat like if you hurt my brother I will knee-cap you."

"That's not veiled," Katherine smiled, "but your warning is received loud and clear."

Jenny watched her for a long moment with a serious expression. "He's a good person."

"I know." Katherine's gaze landed on Trix as he leaned over to embrace a tiny elderly woman who was laughing at something he'd said. "He is."

"I think now is when I'm supposed to say that no one will ever be good enough for him, but watching your face, I can tell you already know that."

Katherine looked back to Jenny and she nodded. "Yes, I do." Katherine smiled sadly. Both of them glanced up to see Trix walking back to them.

"No need to drag him down with this silly serious talk. Ask me something innocuous," Jenny prompted.

Katherine grinned. "Okay, where did the nickname come from?"

"Trix's nickname? He never told you?"

"No."

Jenny laughed. "It came from a fight he had with our father. They were shouting at the dinner table over something he'd done, and Jacob goes, 'You're in here being Grape Nuts while I'm out there rocking a Trix lifestyle.' It was such a ridiculous thing to say I about passed out trying not to laugh. I started calling him Trix that day and it stuck."

"How old were you guys?" Katherine asked, smiling as she pictured the scene.

"Oh god, probably fourteen, maybe fifteen."

Trix rejoined them and had obviously heard the tailend of their conversation. "Are we already getting into embarrassing stories?" he asked with an easy smile.

"The Trix nickname origin story," Jenny clarified.

"Oh jeez, that was a helluva of a fight," he said, running his fingers through his hair.

"What was that one about again?" Jenny prodded.

"The call girl," Trix said sheepishly.

"What?" Katherine asked through a shocked laugh.

"Oh my god, that's right." Jenny bent over giggling. "I totally forgot about that one."

Trix sighed. "I, uh, I hired a call girl from a bar to show up at every public event my father held for three months. Her only job was to make sure each time she made it into at least one photo with him. Didn't take long for the rumor mill to get started."

"That is...wow...that's diabolical," Katherine said.

"Did not. Go over. Well." Trix said, his eyes darting across the room to his father.

"I can imagine," Katherine chuckled.

"We were pretty unkind to each other back then," he said.

Jenny's face got hard as sucked in her cheek. "That's an understatement."

"Yeah, it is," Trix sighed. "Speak of the devil. Looks like we're being summoned." He nodded toward his father who was looking at them and making a barely restrained version of a get-your-ass-over-here gesture.

"Here's where I leave you for a bit," Jenny said, taking a long swig of her drink and making her way in the opposite direction.

CHAPTER 27

Reluctantly, Trix brought Katherine over to join Walter as the reception moved into the ballroom for dinner. Trix shook his head at the over-the-top pomposity of it all and couldn't keep himself from imagining how many life changing improvements could be made to Mae's property with the money these people spent on a party. The room was filled with ornately decorated tables, while overhead soft lights hung with flowing draped fabric. There was also a twenty-member orchestra and the four-course meal included options for filet mignon and lobster.

During the meal Trix and Katherine sat through a tedious amount of stock market and high society gossip. He looked over at Katherine and sent her an apologetic grimace, but she chuckled and shook her head. Trix's attention strayed to his sister who'd managed to secure herself a spot at the kids' table. She was making exaggerated hand gestures and the children were laughing hysterically. Trix was jealous since it was unlikely hedge funds were the topic of conversation over there.

When the meal was finally over, Walter insisted that Trix and Katherine join him in a saunter around the room. It appeared he had designs on making them interact with every elbow in the place. Trix knew some of the people, but most were strangers. Regardless, each time they spoke with someone, Walter found a way to make a joke or take a swipe at Trix's life choices. There was no obvious benefit to his father parading him around as the failed prodigal son. If he was so embarrassed, why was he insisting on this little shame outing?

Trix looked over at his father and caught him blatantly checking out Katherine while she was chatting with Mr. Palmer, one of his father's old business partners.

Gross. Typical.

It dawned on Trix what this charade was about. Walter was trying to drive a wedge between them by belittling Trix in front of Katherine. Leave it to his womanizing father to believe the only thing keeping Trix in Montana was Katherine and her physical attributes. They approached an older woman who Walter introduced as Mrs. Guthrie and she, in turn, introduced them to her grandson William. *The surgeon*, she stressed.

Walter replied. "If you remember, this is my son Jacob and his friend, Ms. Grant. Jacob is… " He turned to Trix. "What would you call it? On walkabout?" Trix gritted his teeth, not responding to the continued humiliation. "Or are we pretending you're in the cattle business?"

The old woman smiled sweetly, obviously not sure how to respond. "I understand you live in Montana now, is that right?" she asked.

"Yes, Mrs. Guthrie, I moved there a few years ago," Trix answered.

"Ahh," she said with a polite nod. She looked to her grandson perhaps in hope that he would save her from the uncomfortable interaction. He didn't.

Katherine jumped in. "Jacob's an integral part of a cattle ranch. One of the last vestiges of truly rugged life left in these times. Wouldn't you agree, Mr. Doyle?"

"There's no need to try to romanticize it, my dear. He's a farm hand." Walter's eyes were malicious and triumphant as they watched Trix over the rim of his glass.

"With strength and courage that's necessary if you'd like to keep eating those sixty-dollar steaks." Katherine pointed out.

"Soon to be replaced by machinery, I'm sure," Walter scoffed.

Katherine's eyes flared, but her smile remained deep. "I can see why a man such as yourself would choose to replace honest masculinity with robotics."

"Meaning?" Walter cocked his head to the side.

"Soft hands don't always get the job done. Eventually you find yourself looking for an apparatus to perform a task you're no longer equipped to perform."

Despite Katherine's saccharin tone Walter's brow furrowed, obviously trying to untangle if he was being insulted. Katherine leaned over conspiratorially toward Walter and stage whispered, "Bet the missus has a top-of-the-line vibrator."

The surgeon grandson snorted into his drink and began to cough.

"What did she say?" Mrs. Guthrie asked.

"I said the Shultzes must have a divine decorator," Katherine said louder to the old woman and gestured at the ornate wedding arches and striking flower arrangements.

Walter Doyle's knuckles turned white against his highball glass.

Mrs. Guthrie nodded, and after a beat said, "I agree. Absolutely stunning."

"Yes, stunning." Walter said between clenched teeth, while Katherine held his stare.

Trix wanted to laugh at Katherine's verbal victory, but he also felt a deep embarrassment she'd needed to step in to defend him. He looked over at her and she appeared to be searching his face for signs of anger.

Trix waved toward the door. "Would you like to see the terrace?"

"That would be lovely. I'm sure it's…stimulating. If you'll excuse us?"

Trix cupped Katherine's elbow as they walked out of the ballroom and onto the immense stone terrace. Little standing tables had been set up around the perimeter and the cooler night air was filled with the scent of blossoms and chamber music.

The soft glow from the hanging lights cast a bronze shadow across Katherine's face as she looked anywhere but at Trix. He wondered how appalled she was at the spectacle Walter had put on, and Trix's feckless response to it.

"That was rough," Trix said.

"They're not that bad," she countered, her tone remarkably light given the pain of the last few hours. "I'd love to ask the band to play 'Cotton Eyed Joe' just to see these stuffed shirts get the vapors."

He chuckled uneasily. "I fear your sacrifice would be in vain. I doubt the orchestra knows anything composed this century."

"Have you fulfilled enough of your family obligation to this shindig, or do we need to stay for cake and crap?" she asked.

"We are not staying for cake and crap," he answered.

She smiled softly and when he gestured toward the exit, she followed his direction as they made their way out to the street.

***

The short ride back to their hotel was silent and tense. Katherine worried about Trix's mood and suspected her behavior was the driving force. As she had assumed she would, she'd embarrassed him. They didn't speak as they got out of the car, and her inability to read his mind was killing her. She wondered if he was trying to find kinder words than *Look it's been fun, but I'm moving back to New York and you obviously don't fit in.* When they made it halfway through the lobby she stopped, and he halted beside her. She thought about what she could say to invite him to vent at her and was surprised when he reached out to tuck a strand of hair behind her ear.

"You were really something tonight," he breathed.

"Hey, at least I didn't drop the F-bomb." She stared at the ceiling, trying to remember. "I don't think."

"You told my father my mother must have an exciting collection in her nightstand," he pointed out.

Katherine's stomach dropped. "Well, if you didn't want trailer trash at your side, you shouldn't have invited me."

"What? That's not what I'm saying at all. It was—"

"Hey, I get it," she snapped. "I don't fit in here and I didn't try hard to."

"What? No, I thought you were—"

"Out of place and uncouth?" she supplied.

"You were—"

She cut him off again. "Rude? Brash? Tacky?"

"Goddamn it, woman. Will you let me get a word in edgewise?" Trix shouted. Katherine opened her mouth to interject, but he spoke over her. "I'm trying to tell you I'm in love with you, and you won't shut up long enough for me to get the words out."

"You shut up," she snapped, her mind blank. Her eyes scanned the lobby, confirming the few people who were milling about had turned to stare at them. She didn't care and apparently neither did Trix because he yelled, "Did you hear me, you childish infuriating she-devil? I'm in love with you."

"I heard you," she lifted her chin, "and you're being ridiculous."

He slapped a palm to his sternum. "I'm ridiculous? That's got to be the most assinine response to someone pouring their heart out I've ever heard."

"It's foolish."

"It's foolish to be in love with you?"

"It is foolish to let this," she gestured back and forth between them, "get out of hand."

"Let it," Trix shook his head, his expression disbelieving. "You don't want to *let this* get out of hand. What in the hell are you doing here, then?"

"Exactly."

Trix huffed and studied her face for a long moment. She worked hard to keep her expression passive despite the pit forming in her stomach.

"Unbelievable," he said flatly and left her standing in the lobby alone.

Katherine's mind was whirling as she shuffled to sit in one of the hotel's plush chairs. She looked around at the excess of luxury feeling every ounce the substandard outsider. She blinked back tears realizing Trix's emotional confession had startled her because she knew it couldn't possibly be true. He must know deep down, no matter if they were in Montana or New York, there would be forces stronger than her working to tear them apart.

"Here I thought I was the only one who bailed as soon as I thought I wouldn't be missed."

Katherine jumped, spinning around to find Jenny approaching.

"Where's Trix?" Jenny asked.

"If I had to guess? In the room lamenting the day he met me."

"Didn't I already threaten your kneecaps?" Jenny's smile was shallow and didn't reach her eyes.

"You did. You also agreed with me that no one would ever be good enough for him," Katherine said as Jenny sat across from her.

"Oh, Christ, that wasn't supposed to be a directive to break up with him. He's going to kill me." Jenny started removing dozens of bobby pins from her up-do.

"I didn't break up with him." Katherine struggled to find the right words. She gave Jenny a brief rundown of the drama Trix was facing back at the ranch and the crisis of faith she'd had after their ride to the ceremony.

When Katherine was done spewing out her insecurities Jenny reached up and scratched her head. "So, you don't want to let yourself feel anything for him because you think this life, this version of Trix, is the real one, and the one you have back at the ranch is an act? You think all this because he's good at putting on a suit coat and because his cowboy friends are mad at him right now?"

"When you put it that way it sounds ridiculous, but essentially, yes." Katherine dropped her eyes to fidget with a small thread coming loose from the hem of her dress. It appeared even the wardrobe gods wanted to make sure she comprehended her own shabby status.

"Hey. Just because you can teach a bear to ride a bicycle doesn't mean it's right. Sometimes it's downright unnatural."

"What? Is Trix the bear in that analogy?" Katherine asked, her eyes popping back to Jenny.

"Yes, he's the bear," Jenny looked annoyed. "New York is the bike and my father's lifestyle is the circus. I didn't really think it was that convoluted. Maybe my high opinion of your intellect was premature due to your use of the word antithesis."

Katherine narrowed her eyes. "You're lucky your brand of bitch is one I admire."

"I believe you about that."

"So, you're saying what? Trix actually wants and deserves to retire from the circus?"

"That's precisely what I'm saying."

"He'd be giving up so much if he stayed in Montana. What if it's a phase?" Katherine pressed.

"Jacob's not a good actor. If the version of him in Montana seems happy, then that's who he really is. I don't think it's a stretch to say he would give up everything for a chance to be truly happy. If he tells you that you're an important part of that, you have to believe it."

"We're so different."

"Isn't it cliché to be like, he's rich, I'm poor, boo-hoo?"

"Hey."

"I'm not saying you have to get married tomorrow and make a dozen babies, but maybe don't sabotage what you guys have. Maybe believe him when he says he cares about you."

"How do you know what he said?" Katherine asked surprised.

"Must be a twin instinct," Jenny quipped. "Or you know it's obvious to literally everyone, he's fallen for you."

Katherine smiled softly and watched Jenny pat her thighs as she stood up. "Okay, I've got to get out of this frilly dress before the bows permanently scar my psyche."

Jenny made her way to the elevators leaving Katherine to decide what to do.

CHAPTER 28

When Trix answered Katherine's knock he was half-dressed in his tattered jeans, his t-shirt in his hand. His jacket and formal shirt lay discarded on the carpet. The cuffs were still buttoned, the expensive clothes looking as if he'd torn them off in a rage. She saw his jaw clench as he stood there and could sense his barely caged agitation. The jeans rode low on his hips below the ridges of his abdomen and her gaze traced up his sculpted bare chest before gradually rising to meet his raw stare.

"I don't belong here," he whispered.

Katherine bit the inside of her lip and made the decision to believe him. At least for right now. "Neither do I."

Slowly she stepped to him and placed both hands on his chest as his eyes narrowed. Katherine brought her lips to his exposed skin between her hands, placing a delicate kiss to his sternum and then trailed her mouth up to his neck. His hands came up to hold her upper arms. She paused waiting for him to decide if this would continue or if he would throw her out. His light touch continued to climb up her shoulders and then to the sides of her face as he drew her mouth to meet his. His lips were soft and patient as he waited for her to open for him. She tilted her head to allow him to deepen the kiss.

Her fingers traced up his chest to loop around his neck. He dropped his hands to her thighs and lifted her against him. When she wrapped her legs around his waist, he turned to kick the door shut behind them and strode to the bed. He sat and her knees sank into the comforter while she straddled him.

She threw desperation into their kiss, urging him to match her intensity. His hands went to her hips, fingers pressing into her as he pulled her tighter against him. The scent of Trix, sandalwood and masculinity, filled her senses. His skin was hot under her fingertips and her need to possess him became overwhelming. Trix was hers. She would prove it to him, and to herself.

She pushed his chest trying to get him to lie back on the bed. Trix grabbed her wrists, slowing her movements. She resisted and tried again to increase the tempo, but he held her firm.

"Hey," he spoke softly, searching her face. "Can't we take our time?"

"Sorry, I can be bossy in bed. It's my controlling nature." She popped a seductive half smile at him.

"With you, it's not about being controlling, it's a lack of trust."

She made a scoffing noise, trying to blow off his seriousness. "Maybe I prefer it quick and dirty," she quipped.

"Katherine," he whispered. "Trust me. Trust me to show you how I feel."

Her chest constricted, everything in her wanting to believe him, but she couldn't get herself to let go.

"Let me prove it to you now. Please."

His grip on her wrists softened as he watched her face. She wanted to flee from the emotion he seemed to be desperately trying to convey, but she steeled her nerve. His pleading stare wouldn't allow her to move from her spot. When he seemed to realize she'd resolved to stay he wound an arm around her, lifting her from his lap, rotating her to underneath him and moving her up the bed. He rose over her as she lay there feeling exposed. This power he had over her, the power to make her want to believe, to trust, was terrifying.

Her hands moved to touch him, but he gathered her wrists and lightly pinned them to the bed over her head.

"Please," he murmured again before bringing his lips to her neck, his free hand tugging at the dress's sash at her hip. He undid the tie and pulled the fabric open, exposing her body to him. The blatant searing hunger on his face was startling and beautiful. Breathtaking.

He traced his mouth down her body, releasing her hands, which she kept in place, grasping the pillow above her head. Arching she brought her skin to his lips. He worshiped her, slowly, one inch at a time, down the rise of her breast, to the flat plane of her abdomen. His fingers roamed lazily down the sides of her waist, then up and down her legs. There was a tremble in each breath he sighed across her navel, kicking off a tremor in her whole body.

"Jacob," she begged.

"Trust me," he whispered near her hip bone.

"I can't" she admitted quietly, her eyes fixed on the ceiling.

He paused his descent, and she couldn't make herself meet his gaze, embarrassed by her own inability to allow the intimacy he was trying to share with her. After a long moment, he climbed up, his hand grasping her chin, forcing her gaze to meet his own. "Promise me something."

She blinked back tears, and nodded, unable to find words.

"I'll tone it down, but you... You need to stay with me."

Her brows furrowed.

"Stay with me, *here*," he motioned between their eyes. "No rushing, no glossing over, no treating this like I'm some warm body. *You stay with me.*"

"I'll try," she whispered.

He held eye contact for a beat longer before nodding and retaking her mouth. Her hands rose up to run over his body, fingertips sliding over his heated skin, feeling the tension in his shoulders and back as he hovered over her. The heat was returning, and she urged him on as the passion between them began to stir anew. She hooked a heel over his hip and his fingers worked their way to her back to unclasp her bra. He moaned into her mouth as his calloused hand covered her bare breast.

"Jacob," she gasped when he pulled away to bring his mouth to her neck below her ear. "Please."

She worked her way to the waist of his jeans, pulling him free from his pants. He reared back and hooked her thong in his thumbs, slowly pulling it down and over her spikey shoes. His face was intense, his gaze unwavering as he crawled back up her body and lowered himself between her thighs.

"Stay here," he murmured as he began to slowly enter her. She kept her word and held his eye contact, refusing to look away from the emotion churning in his gaze until the sensation of delicious fullness forced her to lean her head back and close her eyes.

She sighed his name as he gently and deliberately worked her body.

Katherine bit her lip as she turned her head to watch his arm muscles bulge and tremble with the strain from his measured pace. He reached up and brought her chin back to center, holding her gaze before he leaned down to again take her mouth. The feeling of his slow but powerful movements inside her and his gentle possession of her lips began to build tension in her body.

His rhythm quickened exactly when she needed it to and she could feel the intensity of his restraint radiating off of him, this fierce, forceful man barely harnessing himself to show her he loved her. In that moment she didn't care where they came from, she only knew reverence for what they had together.

She lifted her knees higher on his waist, pulling him deeper, urging him on, urging him to unleash himself, to take everything she had to give. His self-control broke like a dam. His body was solid and unyielding as he took her with a ferocity that sent her soaring over her peak.

All of him quaked as he followed her, crying out her name.

***

Trix slowly became aware of his surroundings, first noticing the full body tremble that was still washing over him and the flowing aftershocks in Katherine's body below him. He gulped for air, feeling her heart beating against her ribs. He had never had such a powerful experience and he was having a hard time forming thoughts. He lay down next to her and watched the flush fading from her face while she panted, eyes closed. His intention had been to tenderly play her body like a Stradivarius, and somewhere along the way he'd been unable to cage the brutish need that was raging in his gut. Thankfully, judging by her response, she hadn't minded his straying from the plan.

Her eyes opened, and she turned her head to meet his gaze. His instinct was to make some lighthearted joke, but he didn't want to downplay the importance of what had happened between them. He reached up to trace his fingers down the side of her jaw.

"I love you, Katherine," he said softly, and when her brow knit as she opened her mouth to reply, he cut her off. "Leaving a hole where you could say it is better than filling it with a reason why you won't."

"Okay," she said quietly then a sad hush filled the room.

Trix wasn't going to pretend he fully understood the emotional war Katherine was waging, but he could help her understand his own emotional rollercoaster.

"We kind of glossed over a big thing back there and if you want, I'd like to talk to you about it."

Some of the tense concern in her expression softened. "I'd like that."

"I am not going to give in to my father's demand to move back here."

"That's good. I desperately want to believe you're happy in Montana."

"It's so much more than that. I didn't comprehend what happy was until I became a part of Mae's family. I think maybe that's why my fear over putting that in danger was so blinding. I wasn't thinking clearly about what coming back here really meant."

"How can you not blame me for putting that at risk? I'm the one who made a move in the parking lot. I'm the one who brought you into the pregnancy drama."

"You didn't make me lie to my family about those things."

"You wouldn't have had anything to lie about if it weren't for me."

He shook his head. "There's no reality where my choice to be dishonest with people who trust me with their lives is your fault."

She looked like she wanted to argue, but then she sighed and nodded.

"It's like that suit," he said. It's everything I despise. It's a costume, and its sole purpose is to convince others you're more important than they are. Wearing it, I felt like a stranger."

She stayed silent and let him continue.

"I realized something today while I was watching my father at the reception. I've always known my father was commanding and ruthless, but it wasn't until today I realized what truly was going on. He's incapable of forgiveness. For better or worse, I'm a product of my father's world, so when I hurt the people at the ranch, regaining their trust felt insurmountable."

"Mae and her family are better people than your father."

"Yeah, they are. They've always been better at loving me. I have to have faith they'll be better at forgiving me, too."

"They will be." She smiled before her face got sad again.

It took him only a moment to realize where her head had gone. "I think they'll forgive you too."

"They don't love me like they love you."

"They will." Trix was confident although he could see she didn't believe him. "Come here," he said opening his arm to her. When she leaned in to rest her head on his chest, he gently stroked her shoulder.

For now, he was going to block out any further questions on what would happen when they went home. He was going to enjoy having Katherine curled up under the blankets with him.

CHAPTER 29

Katherine stirred early in the morning and relished feeling the warmth of Trix's body pressed against hers. Last night replayed in her mind in flashes. How incredible and caring Trix had been warmed her. His compassionate understanding when she couldn't say what he deserved to hear. Words pounding on the inside of her skull she so desperately wanted to be able to say. Why couldn't she say it?

Because you're a realist and you know what's going to happen.

What they shared was amazing, but amazing things had a short shelflife in Katherine's orbit. She could and would appreciate the wondrousness of this experience, but she would do it without giving over the last little bit of herself she needed to protect herself. She had to hold onto something to help rebuild when it all came crashing down.

Trix pulled in a deep breath behind her, and he threw an arm over her waist, pressing himself more firmly against her back.

Appreciate it while it lasts.

"I'm not going to apologize for wanting you again." Trix's husky voice brushed against her neck as she felt his arousal stir.

"I don't want an apology," she said. "I want you to meet me in that ridiculous shower in ten minutes."

"Five," he growled.

"Deal." Not bothering to cover herself, she strode to the bathroom. She glanced over her shoulder when he groaned, and the wild look in his eye told her he wasn't going to be able to wait five minutes.

When Trix stalked in and joined her in the steamy glass enclosure he was ready for her. Yet, he tortured her with his fingers until she could no longer stand without leaning against the cool tile. Finally, he spun her around and took her until they both shattered.

***

They used the morning to explore and enjoy one another, but the time ticked on and they needed to check out. As he'd warned the day before, Trix had arranged for them to see his mother before leaving New York. Katherine wondered about the woman and was glad they had plans, but was equally glad brunch would need to be short or they'd miss their flight home.

Trix stopped at the concierge on the way out and arranged for them to hold their luggage before they went outside to hail a cab. The ride to some restaurant with a French name was quick, and Katherine marveled at the number of things you could get to in only a few minutes.

Trix wore a pair of slacks with a blue dress shirt, and again she was struck by how odd it was to see him in this place. Still, the dread she'd felt watching him yesterday was mercifully absent. She brushed a nervous hand down the front of her simple sun dress and straightened the bottom of the cardigan. Nervously, she glanced around the restaurant and exhaled when she determined she didn't look out of place.

Trix was scanning the room, and Katherine could tell the moment he found his mother because he pulled in a deep breath and straightened slightly. He flashed her a quick smile before taking her hand to lead her through the dining room. They stopped at a little square table in the corner. The woman sitting there was a tiny sprite with gray hair, Katherine could tell used to be red. She had deep blue eyes, which were flat and dull. When she glanced up at them, there was a pleasantness to her expression, which came across practiced and almost robotic.

"Jacob," the woman said.

"Mother," Trix said as he leaned down and kissed her cheek. Straightening he turned to Katherine. "I'd like to introduce my mother, Eleanor Doyle," he said in the same formal tone he had used to introduce his father.

"Katherine Grant." Katherine reached out and gingerly shook the woman's dainty hand.

"Pleasure to meet you. Please, join me."

Trix came around and pulled out a chair for Katherine before seating himself.

"You look well," Eleanor said coolly, her gaze scanning Trix.

"I am." He replied, accepting menus from the waitress. "How have you been?"

"Splendid," she said, then to Katherine she asked, "Does your family come from Massachusetts?"

"No, ma'am," Katherine answered. "We're several generations deep in Montana."

"I see," Eleanor said. "I know the Grants from Boston. But between you and me, they're an unsavory lot."

Katherine grinned, thinking that her Montana Grants would put the supposed unsavoriness of the Boston Grants to shame. "I'm glad to be unrelated then," she replied smoothly.

She noticed Trix was barely containing a grin by pinching his lower lip between his thumb and forefinger. The waitress returned, and after they'd ordered, an uncomfortable silence fell over the table.

"How was Alfred's wedding?" Eleanor asked.

"Beautiful," Katherine said when Trix didn't respond. "Absolutely lovely."

Eleanor nodded. "I suppose it would have been. The Shultzes always behave like they have something to prove."

"Mom, it was nice," Trix said. "I wish you'd been there. Dad said you were unwell."

She made a little flick of her wrist to brush off his words. "Your father's a bore."

Trix nodded. "Not going to deny that, but I'm asking if you were sick."

"It's rude to ask after a woman's health, dear," she corrected.

Katherine tuned out as Trix and his mother made strained small talk. She was contemplating the puzzle pieces she'd gathered about Trix's origin story. His father was a blown-up pompous airbag, and his mother was a cold void of a human. How could someone as warm and joyful as Trix be a product of these two gargoyles?

Despite how sad for him it made her feel, there was a nagging sensation at the back of her brain that turned out to be relief. These people and this place were not who Trix was. Yes, he came from this, but the strength of his character, his cutting sense of humor, his compassion and deep heart, none of that had been cultivated in this place, and it didn't belong here. Trix belonged at Crooked Brook with the people who loved him in a sometimes messy, but always unconditional, way.

Unfortunately for Katherine, the Crooked Brook crew's love for him meant they'd do anything in their power to protect him from her. An issue which hadn't gone away since Trix decided he wouldn't give in to his father's ultimatum.

She watched him flick food around his plate.

"The staff are increasingly rude, and your sister runs rip-roaring over everything she comes into contact with," Eleanor complained.

"Let's leave Jennifer off your list of grievances."

"Very well. You two always did gang up on me."

Trix put a large piece of ham into his mouth. "If you say so, Mother."

"Oh, Jacob, really? It's not that hard. Chew, swallow, then speak." Eleanor reprimanded.

Trix looked up and without breaking eye contact with his mother shoveled even more food into his gaping mouth, and then spoke past it, "Oh, look at the time."

Katherine cleared her throat to avoid letting the laugh past her lips. She took the napkin off her lap and placed it on the table next to her half-eaten breakfast. "Unfortunately, Jacob is right. We'll miss our plane if we don't leave now."

As they both stood, Katherine took the older woman's hand, giving it a light squeeze. "It was so great to meet you, Mrs. Doyle."

"Yes, same to you. Safe traveling," Eleanor said clinically.

"Mom," Trix said as he gave her a quick repeat kiss on the cheek.

Katherine and Trix bolted for the door, but she had a thought that made her stop abruptly and turn to Trix who stopped with a quizzical look on his face.

"We didn't offer to pay," she said, feeling guilty.

Trix put his hand in the small of her back to get her feet moving again. "She doesn't pay. This place keeps a tab, and they send my father a bill once a week. It's been so long since she's actually seen a restaurant bill, it would probably startle her sensibilities if we'd asked for one."

"Jesus, it's weird here," Katherine said walking out onto the street.

Trix nodded. "Yeah, it is."

Once they were back in a cab, she turned to him and he was already watching her.

"She's nice, but ...restrained," Katherine ventured.

"You can say it. She's an affluent android," Trix said.

Katherine chuckled, thankful she didn't have to pretend his mother was anything else. "I rescind my assumption that she would own a vibrator. But perhaps she could use one."

Trix shuddered and shook his head. "Can we please agree to never talk or think about that again?"

"Sure," she laughed, and they both seemed ready to leave the awkwardness of brunch behind them.

Unfortunately, the light mood lasted only until they reached the hotel. Walter Doyle was waiting at the entrance.

"Why in the hell did I come back here?" Trix said before opening the door.

Walter nodded when he saw them and watched them approach.

"Do you live here now?" Trix asked with derision.

"On occasion," Walter replied. "I understand you saw your mother before leaving town. That was considerate of you."

"It was nice to catch up," Trix said with a hint of sarcasm. "We need to gather our things. We are going to the airport now. It's time I go home."

The two men stared at each other for a long tense minute. This wasn't only Trix putting an end to his visit, this was the moment he was choosing to walk away from his inheritance.

"You're sure of the decision you are making here, Jacob?" Walter's tone was icy.

"Yes."

Walter's jaw worked. "It's a mistake."

"I know you believe money should be important to me, but I don't have any different way of saying it to make you understand I value my home in Montana more."

"I have considered this, and I think *you* should understand if that home no longer existed, you would be lost and without options."

Katherine's stomach tightened. Walter was feeling out something even more drastic than cutting off Trix from his inheritance. Trix's posture became stone. He'd sensed the same.

"What are you trying to insinuate?" Trix asked.

"I've been looking into investments in the cattle business."

"You're not trying to pretend you'd buy Crooked Brook, because that would be ridiculous." Trix shook his head. "Mae would never sell to you, and perhaps the only thing you love more than spite is money. You'd never waste millions to score a pointless victory over me."

Walter cleared his throat. "No, I wouldn't spend tens of millions of dollars on a ranch, but one million on a feedlot, now that has potential for a return on investment."

Katherine's heart began to pound, as she considered the potential consequences if Walter made good on his threat. With enough money he could buy the local feedlot and refuse to do business with Crooked Brook. The overhead costs of traveling farther to an alternate lot, or doing the work to put weight on the cattle while they were at the ranch could easily lead to the end of Crooked Brook. She looked to Trix. He knew the ramifications of what Walter was saying even better than she did.

Trix and his father stared at one another for a long moment as Walter's threat rotted in the air between them. "Well, then, give me a call when you get to Montana. I'll show you around."

Walter's brow slammed down, but he camouflaged his anger with a veil of formality. "I may do that. Now, as you said, there is a flight to catch. I'll get you a cab and keep your lady entertained while you fetch your luggage," Walter said.

Trix's gaze stayed with his father for a beat longer before he turned to her. She gave him a smile and a nod, and he turned and went into the hotel lobby.

As soon as Trix was gone, Katherine turned to his father. "I sense there's something you'd like to say to me, Walter. So out with it before he comes back."

Walter's eyes narrowed but he appeared to also be willing to drop his cloak of pleasantries. "My son comes from a good family and could have a bright future. He's squandering it, but his dalliances with country life and trashy women will come to an end sooner rather than later."

"You're wrong about the kind of man he is, and you're wrong to think you can easily manipulate anything about his life at the ranch." Katherine made her way over to the street to hail their cab herself.

"Your faith in him is as naïve as it is reckless," Walter said, following her. "He's a selfish, impetuous boy. I wouldn't bet the farm he's going to stay that way".

"Trix is none of those things. I don't know how he's done it in this environment, but he's grown into a better man than you'll ever be."

"Ridiculous," Walter scoffed.

"If you think Mae Becker and the home she's built is an easy target, you might have to find out the hard way how wrong you are."

"You're as foolish as he is."

"For a smart man, you don't know shit."

Katherine ducked her head and climbed into the back of the cab she'd flagged down, leaning out to meet Walter's seething gaze. "It was lovely to meet you, Mr. Doyle. Regardless of which one of us is right, I suspect we won't be seeing a lot of each other."

"No, I would think not," he said through his teeth and turned back to the hotel.

Katherine scooted to the far side of the backseat and let out a breath. "Waiting for my boyfriend and the luggage. We're going to JFK," she said to the driver who nodded.

A moment later she heard the trunk open and then close before Trix slid in next to her. She studied his face as they pulled away from the curb. When he turned to her, there was tension in his eyes, but he gave her a little smile. "That was. Well, what do you call that? An epically disastrous visit?"

"You went all-in on a really big pot. Are you that sure he's bluffing?"

Trix sighed and ran a hand through his hair. "Yeah. Maybe. I mean, I think he is, but I don't know. Walter guards his fortune as fiercely as Mae guards her home. I don't think he'd waste money on this, but if he tried, I have to believe the crew would find a way to fight back, and I'm going to be there fighting with them."

Katherine nodded and reached for his hand, giving it a squeeze. "Walter doesn't stand a chance."

Trix chuckled, and then asked, "Are you okay? I'm sure the little sidebar you all had was unpleasant."

She was touched his concern was for her instead of the match he'd just put to his family bridge.

"Don't worry about me, it wasn't too bad, and I'm all right now you're here." She leaned her head to rest on his shoulder as they made their way to the airport and back to something more normal and familiar.

Like his other family's disapproval.

CHAPTER 30

After returning from New York a week ago, Trix's work life returned to normal with a couple of glaring differences. Primarily, Alex remained stalwart that Katherine was the worst human walking the Earth. Also, it appeared during Trix's absence, Winn had decided he would pretend things were completely normal. Problem was, Winn was so incapable of duplicity, it was painful to watch him attempt it. About a week later, Trix was assigned to work with Alex and Winn during the all-hands-on-deck task of administering fall vaccines to the herd. It was the first time the three of them had spent any real time together since his trip, earning Trix a sleepless night beforehand.

The plan for the day was straightforward. The majority of the crew was up in the pastures rounding up and sending cattle back to the front of the ranch. Bishop and Griz were in charge of pulling and administering vaccine doses on one side of the chute while Trix, Alex and Winn worked in the small pen on the other. One mounted rider and one person on foot, along with a few cattle dogs, worked to keep the cows moving, with the third person operating the steel chute, which clamped each cow in place for a quick look over and injection.

The morning progressed as Trix had expected, not quite sullen, but lacking the normal lighthearted fun the three of them used to enjoy. It was lucky they were a good team because exchanging words wasn't necessary to get the job done.

After they'd been at it for a few hours Trix was the one on foot and Alex on horseback, separating the cows and sending them toward the chute while Winn stood on the fencing and operated the gate. Trix looked up at the cattle barn and was shocked to see Blake Martin approaching the pens.

What in the hell is he doing here?

Trix let out a sharp whistle to Winn, then nodded toward the barn. Winn's expression solidified into stone when he put eyes on Blake. Winn let the cow in the chute loose, but didn't allow the next one in. Alex had also noticed their visitor and rode up closer to them.

"Stay on your horse," Winn said to Alex, and when she glared, he added, "Please?" She nodded.

Trix rapped a knuckle against the fence to get Griz and Bishop to look up, and pointed toward Blake. They put down the vaccine materials and walked over, with matching grim expressions.

"You're trespassing," Winn called out as soon as Blake was in earshot. Undeterred, Blake continued approaching them, a smarmy grin on his face.

"Fellas," he said and then he tipped his chin at Alex. "Chicago girl." Blake got to the corner of the pen and lifted a leg to rest a boot on the lower rung as he hung his arms through the middle of the metal fencing.

"I don't think you comprehend how unwelcome you are on this property," Trix started weaving his way through the agitated cattle to get closer to their uninvited guest. On the other side of the fence Griz was also approaching Blake, moving slow and relaxed despite the tension in the air.

"Katherine here?" Blake asked lightly.

"That's none of your business," Trix answered quickly.

"Well now, it is. See, that little bitch thought she could ghost me, and I hear maybe it's because she wasn't done getting passed around this place yet."

Both Trix and Griz jumped toward him, but Blake jerked up on the top rail of the fence section he was holding while also using his foot to lift. The connections at the corner separated and he yanked his panel backwards creating a wide opening for the cattle to run through. Trix was caught in the middle of a stream of cows pushing toward their only exit. He panicked, afraid of losing cattle on the property. He threw his arm up, trying to block their way, when one of the cows kicked out and landed a hoof solidly in Trix's gut.

The harsh pain was instantaneous.

Trix stumbled back to brace himself on the fence, trying to catch the wind forced out of his body.

"Goddamn it," Winn yelled as he jogged over to the outside of the fencing to help Griz push the dislodged section back in place against the herd.

Trix moaned, clutching his side, but managed to climb out of the pen. As soon as the corner was reassembled, Griz charged Blake and tackled him, face first, to the ground. He pulled one of Blake's arms up to twist it behind him, pressing it against his back between his shoulder blades. Griz bent down to lean a forearm into the side of Blake's head, pinning his face in the dirt.

"I am not a violent man," Griz growled into his ear, "but I will break your arm."

Trix tried to ignore the sharp pain radiating from his side. "Griz, it's all right. I'm okay. Let him up. Get him out of here."

Griz looked up and watched Trix's face for a long moment, and he tried to look reassuring as he fought urge to get down on all fours. Finally, Griz relented and stood, pulling a howling Blake to his feet by his arm.

"Leave. Now." Griz released Blake who spit on the ground but had enough self-preservation to take off to the front of the property without looking back.

"Asshole," Bishop called out to his back.

As soon as he was out of sight Trix pulled up his shirt and saw a red welt under his ribs with a dark bruise already forming. "That's going to leave a mark," he joked through clenched teeth, dropping his shirt back into place.

Alex got off her horse and came over, concern written all over her face. "You need to get some ice on that."

Trix felt relief Alex forgave him enough to worry, but he shook his head. "Nah, I'll walk it off. I know you're all thinking it, so I want to say I know it's my fault he was here, and I'm sorry." He waved his arm at the handful of cows that hadn't gone far after escaping and failed to conceal a grimace following the movement. "Let's get them rounded up and get through this."

"No one is trying to place blame." Winn walked over and got on Alex's horse. Bishop let them out of the pen and Winn said, "It'll only take a few minutes to get them back where they belong, why don't you take a break."

Trix tried to force a chuckle, but it intensified the pain. "Gotta tell you, I knew I'd eventually get hurt here. Always thought it'd be a horse."

"Me too." Winn tried a laugh, but his eyes stayed serious.

Trix took a few steadying breaths and then decided he must be overreacting and worked to right himself. "I'm okay, really. It stunned me for a minute. I'm good to go now."

He brought his gaze to Alex, then to Winn and eventually Griz and Bishop, trying to put on his best my-side-is-not-on-fire face.

Winn watched him for a long moment and then nodded. "Maybe we should keep you away from the business end of the cows for a while. Why don't you work the chute?"

"Deal," Trix gritted out through his teeth.

Winn and the cattle dogs had the two dozen loose cows back in the pen in under ten minutes and the vaccination routine was back underway. Griz and Bishop went back to the other side and Trix felt guilty and embarrassed his personal drama had created such a disruption. This was not going to help his case. He climbed up on the fence to work the chute and looked to the pen to watch for the next cow to get funneled in. He took a steadying breath and tried to think beyond the still sharp pain in his side, and shame in his gut.

They managed to get six more cows in, vaccinated and released before he noticed his shoulder was starting to feel sore. He stretched and gave it a good rotation with his elbow out. Trying to block out the piercing ache in his stomach, Trix squinted at the cattle, feeling disoriented.

"You guys?" he called, and Alex and Winn looked up.

"Yeah?" Winn answered.

"Cow time?" Trix managed to get out, his mind now completely foggy.

"What?" Winn answered with his brows knit in confusion.

Trix long blinked, trying to focus.

"Trix?" Winn called.

"Time…" Trix looked up to the sky and his world went black.

CHAPTER 31

Winn watched Trix's eyes roll back in his head before he passed out and fell off his perch on the chute fencing. He ran to him as Alex yelled out. Bishop and Griz climbed over the fencing from the front of the chute, joining him at Trix's side. Winn pulled up Trix's shirt to reveal a large dark purple area along his side. Everyone gasped.

"This is bad," Alex cried. "We need an ambulance."

Winn's mind was whirling. "That could take ages. Go get Mae," he directed Alex. "Griz, go get the backboard from the hayloft. Bishop, get the truck and call Tiny and Junior down from the field."

Everyone bolted away on their tasks. Winn straightened out Trix's limbs and then pulled off his own jacket to ball up and put under his friend's head.

"This is dramatic, even for you man," he whispered to Trix's slack face. "Please be okay."

Alex came running from the back of the house with Mae who had a phone to her ear. When she got to Trix's side she quickly lifted his shirt. Winn watched her face, and for the first time he could remember, Mae Becker looked afraid.

"Twenty-five-year-old male," she spoke into the phone. "Otherwise, healthy. Unconscious after catching a kick. Large dark bruise, left side under his ribs. Spreading rapidly. Happened about...?" She looked to Winn.

"About a half an hour ago. He insisted he was fine, but passed out maybe five minutes ago," he said.

Mae repeated this, then listened to the reply.

Winn sent Alex a questioning look.

"Someone named Trent?" she said.

Winn nodded. *Trent Simmons was the local volunteer EMT. Good. Smart. He'll know what to do.*

The farm truck came bouncing over the grass as Bishop brought it skidding to a stop next to them. Griz appeared moments later holding the old backboard they keep in case there was a bad fall off the horses.

"The guys are coming down to take care of these cattle and horses," Bishop said, Winn nodded barely registering as he watched Mae continue her conversation with Trent.

"No, I don't think he hit his head," Mae said into the phone, her gaze jumping to Winn who shook his head. Mae reached out and held Trix's wrist. "Breathing seems quick, shallow, pulse is...maybe it's a little weak."

Alex brought her fingers to her mouth stifling a whimper.

"Okay," Mae said. "Yes, I think we can safely do that. Okay. How long? Yes." She started motioning to Griz to bring the backboard over. He lay it down next to Trix's inert form. "I'll call you back when we're loaded up." Mae said, hanging up and shoving her phone into her back pocket.

"He's calling in the medevac and thinks they'll intercept us around 43 and SR in about twenty minutes," Mae told them.

Winn's stomach dropped, and Alex's face went stark.

"Oh my god, they're sending a helicopter?" Alex was obviously trying hard to keep it together.

"Carefully, boys. We need to get him strapped down and in the back of the truck." Mae directed. Together they worked to slide Trix onto the board, leaving Alex to fasten the straps across his chest and knees.

Bishop hopped into the bed of the truck and gestured to a few hay bales he'd loaded. "I think we can use these to cushion some of the bounce."

Mae nodded and the four of them hoisted Trix up and onto the bed while Alex pulled tie down straps from the backseat. She fastened one end around a hook in the truck bed and looped it through a handle on the backboard. Winn helped her, and quickly they secured all four corners before Winn jumped into the driver's seat. Mae joined him in the cab while Alex, Bishop, and Griz surrounded Trix in the truck bed.

"Carefully, but quickly," Mae said sternly, and Winn nodded, resisting the adrenaline fueled urge the slam the pedal to the floor.

When they cleared the uneven gravel drive, he accelerated, and kept looking to the rearview to make sure he wasn't losing people out of the back. Mae pulled out her phone and redialed.

"Trent," she said. "We're on our way. Should be at the intersection in maybe fifteen minutes. Yes. Thank you." Mae hung up.

Winn's grip on the wheel tightened until it creaked. He looked in the review and saw Alex was crying as she caressed Trix's pale forehead. Bishop and Griz each pressed down one of Trix's legs, their faces taught and grim.

"Moms?" Winn started.

Mae turned to him her expression serious as she laid one of her hands over his on the wheel. "I know. It's okay. He's going to be okay."

Winn swallowed hard.

Why did that feel like the first time in my life Mae Becker lied to me?

They arrived at the intersection an excruciating twelve minutes later. Trent's 4x4 was already there. When they pulled up, he jumped out and pointed for them to park in the middle of the road.

"Air lift ETA is six minutes," he called as he jumped into their truck bed. Pointing to Alex and Griz, he said, "You two, go to my truck and find the flares. Grab a few and stand there and there." He waved at the two streets not currently blocked by one of their vehicles. "The chopper will land in the middle of the intersection. You need to keep cars from coming through."

As he spoke, he tore open the front of Trix's shirt. The dark bruise had taken over the bottom half of his torso. Winn's pulse pounded as he watched Trent. He looked nervous. This was bad.

Yanking the stethoscope from around his neck Trent started taking Trix's vitals. "You two," he said to Bishop and Winn, "get these tie downs off. We'll keep him on this backboard to move him to their gurney."

Trent pulled a blood pressure cuff out of his bag and secured it around Trix's arm. Winn's fought to undo the straps with hands shaking so badly he had to stop and start a few times.

The distant sound of a helicopter approaching broke through the air. Winn pulled the last strap free and then put a hand up to shield his eyes, searching the sky. The chopper was coming in from the north, flying low and coming in fast. When it was directly overhead it hovered for a moment before landing. The thudding beat of the rotor pounded against Winn's ear drums and he put an arm up to shield Trix's face from the dust and grit being whipped around by the wind.

As soon as the helicopter's skids touched down, two men jumped from the large side door, reaching behind them to pull down a bag and a stretcher with wheels that unfolded down. They ran over, ducking below the whirling blades.

Trent shouted to be heard over the sound of the helicopter and through the men's helmets. "Abdominal trauma left upper quadrant, roughly one hour ago. Patient lost consciousness twenty-five minutes ago and hasn't been coherent since. Signs of significant internal bleeding. BP is 80/46, respiration shallow and elevated at 32 bpm, pulse slow and weak at 26." The men nodded and moved the ranch backboard onto the rolling stretcher. Then they took off running and pushing Trix toward the middle of the intersection. They were loaded and airborne in under three minutes.

Winn watched the helicopter disappear his mind unable to fully comprehend what had happened. He looked down at his shaking hands before his gaze landed on Alex, who, in that moment, dropped a limp arm to her side, allowing the flare to fall and bounce to the ground. She fell to her knees beside it, her face buried in her hands. He ran over to her, kneeling down and wrapping her in his arms as her entire body shook with wracking sobs.

"Shhhh, it's okay. It's going to be okay," he chanted pressing his cheek to the top of her head. Trent and Mae walked over to them and he stared up at them from the ground.

"Where will they take him?" Winn asked.

"Mercy in Great Falls." Trent said. "It's the closest level one trauma center. You all should leave now." Trent told them his face somber.

Mae looked to him, "Trent, is he…? What do you think?"

"Mrs. Becker, it's a serious injury, I know he'll need surgery. I can't guess as to anything else, but you all should head out. It'll take you over an hour from here."

Mae's tone became business as usual. "Can you drive Griz and Bishop back to the ranch? I'll call you guys as soon as I know anything."

"Sure thing," Trent said, and Bishop nodded. Griz didn't acknowledge her and wore a wholly vacant far away expression as the three of them turned toward Trent's 4x4.

Mae stooped down and took Alex's hand. "Okay girl, now that's out of your system, it's time to get up. Trix needs us." Her words were harsh, but softly delivered. Alex looked up and took a deep stuttered breath, and then nodded, wiping her face.

Mae tucked an arm around Alex's waist as they made their way to the farm truck. Winn dug in his pocket and retrieved his phone, knowing Trix would want him to do this, and he had only about twenty seconds to do it.

Katherine answered the phone. "Winn?"

"Katherine."

"Didn't expect you'd ever call me again—"

He cut her off. "Trix got hurt."

"What's happened?"

"It's bad, Katherine. They took him away in a medevac."

"Oh my god. Where are they taking him?"

Winn was at the truck and could see Alex watching him with an anxious expression. He needed to get off the phone.

"Mercy in Great Falls. You should meet us there," he said sharply.

"Winn, what happened?" Katherine shouted.

"Meet us there," he repeated before hanging up and opening the truck door.

CHAPTER 32

Katherine stared at the phone for a long moment before throwing it into her pocket and reaching around to untie her apron. She balled it up and tossed it on the counter next to the discarded coffee pot she'd set down at some point during the upsetting call.

"Hey. Where are you going?" Hank yelled, surprised when she walked past him to grab Maddie's keys.

"It's an emergency," she said as she made her way back to the entrance.

"You're only halfway through your shift," he hollered to her back.

"Fuck off, Hank," she said as she shoved through the door and shot off a text to Maddie to tell her she'd made off with her car.

Katherine's mind sped along with the bald tires on Maddie's little Ford Fiesta as she flew down the interstate. She continuously circled back to worst case scenarios. He'd been thrown from a horse and broken his neck. He'd gotten his arm mangled in machinery. Maybe he'd been accidentally shot? Katherine stared at the sky trying to remember if there were guns on the property. For sure Mae had at least a shotgun stashed somewhere. The horrific possibilities seemed endless.

Trix could be dying.

When she tried calling Winn back over and over again, he never answered. She imagined as soon as she arrived at the hospital, she would find out what was going on, and then castrate Winn for not answering her questions or her calls.

Her vibrating hand came up to pick at a cuticle on the hand on the wheel as she chewed the inside of her lip. Frenetic thoughts jumped to Trix's family. They should know he's been hurt. Would Mae handle that?

Trix had given Katherine his sister's number and the two had been texting back and forth all week. She could call her, but what would she say? She knew how excruciating it was to know he was hospitalized, but nothing beyond that. She decided to hold off.

After an eternity Katherine arrived at the hospital, and as she jogged through the emergency entrance, she saw Alex and Winn were close to the front desk and she marched up to lay into Winn.

Alex's eyes flared. "What in the hell are you doing here?"

Katherine ignored her, squaring up to Winn. "Tell me what happened right now."

Winn drew in a long breath. "We were doing vaccines. He caught a kick. The bruising, I don't understand it was so bad…and then he passed out."

"A cow kick?" Katherine couldn't wrap her mind around what she was hearing. Kicks happened all the time, it shouldn't be serious.

"You have no right to be here," Alex insinuated herself again.

Katherine gave Winn a hard look. He knew what she was capable of if the city girl didn't back off.

Alex turned to Winn with rage in her eyes. "You called her?"

Winn nodded. "You know he'd want her here."

"It's her fault this happened." Alex stepped up into Katherine's face.

"That's ridiculous, and you need to back off before I damage you," Katherine growled.

Alex sneered. "Your other boyfriend showed up, and he's the reason Trix is here."

Katherine looked to Winn. "What?"

Winn's jaw worked. "Blake showed up, talked shit, then he broke open the pen to keep from catching the beating he had coming. Trix, tried to block the cows… " He shook his head. "He should have let them go. I don't know what he was thinking."

"You're the one who's supposed to teach him this stuff. How could you let this happen?" Katherine's nerves made her words nastier than she intended.

Alex stepped between them yelling, "Don't you dare try to make this Winn's fault. We had to load one of our best friends into a medivac because of the toxic bullshit you brought into his life."

Katherine looked down at her hands grasping each other so tightly she wanted to throw a punch to alleviate the tension in them. "Back off," Katherine warned for the last time.

"Enough," Mae's raised voice broke through the tension, and they all whipped around to see her coming down the hallway.

"The doctors?" Winn asked anxiously.

Mae nodded. "I spoke with them. The kick ruptured Trix's spleen. He's in surgery now, but they think they can stop the bleeding."

"They think he's going to be okay?" Alex asked.

"They're optimistic," Mae said.

Winn wrapped Alex up in his arms.

"Mae," Katherine rasped, unsure of what to expect from the older woman. After a tense moment, Mae walked over and wrapped her in a hug. The two women held each other for a minute before Katherine leaned back and Mae released her.

"I'm not going to leave," Katherine said, feeling like it was important to make her intentions known.

"I'm not asking you to," Mae replied.

They watched each other for a moment and then Katherine's gaze traveled to Alex who was still trying to punch a hole through Katherine's chest with her glare.

"*No one* is asking you to," Mae confirmed, despite the obvious hatred on display.

Mae gestured down the hall with her hand. "The surgical waiting room is down the hall. Go sit."

Katherine nodded, and Mae turned toward Alex. Maybe the old woman could talk some sense into the girl so Katherine wouldn't have to beat it into her.

She went down the cold grey hallway and found a small area with a handful of chairs outside a pair of large doors under the Operating Room sign. She sat, boring holes through the doors willing a doctor to come through and tell her Trix was going to be fine. After a few minutes Alex, Winn, and Mae joined her and silently they all sat, lost in their own thoughts and fears, waiting.

Katherine's mind tortured her by rapidly cycling through images and memories of Trix. He was brooding alongside a dance floor, eyes piercing and unrelenting. He was laughing at the diner counter, dimples deep and perfect. He was carrying her with his heart thudding against her ear into an emergency room. He was stalking her in the grass on a hilltop, ready to take her mouth in a way that made her feel like he needed her more than air. He was watching her on a New York sidewalk with soft loving eyes telling her she was cherished.

How could she've let him live one moment without knowing he was everything to her? What kind of woman let a man like that love her without confessing he owned her heart? What if Alex was right, and what Trix felt for her was the reason he was here? She could never make that right.

As they passed the two-hour mark, the tension in the waiting room was nearing suffocating. Everyone looked ready to burst out of their silent fear when a doctor appeared in the doorway. They jumped to attention.

"For Doyle?" the doctor asked as they stood and surrounded him.

"Yes," Mae said.

"We had to remove a large portion of his spleen to stop the bleeding, but the surgery was successful, and with some blood transfusions his vitals are coming back up into normal ranges. They're closing now, and he'll be moved to recovery shortly."

Katherine's knees buckled with relief and she had to steady herself to remain standing.

Collectively, the group let out a long breath, and Katherine heard Mae talking as if she was at the other end of a long tunnel.

"What's the prognosis?" Mae asked.

The doctor told her that barring any complications, a full recovery was expected. Katherine wanted to weep, but clenched her jaw to keep herself together.

"When can we see him?" Mae asked.

"We'll know how he's handling the sedation when he comes off anesthesia and goes to the recovery room. Likely will be at least a few hours before he can have any visitors."

"Thank you," Mae said as the doctor went back through the doors.

When Mae turned to the group her relief was tangible. "We knew he had grit."

Life breathed back into the waiting room and everyone started talking and laughing and hugging. Winn wrapped Alex in his arms and Katherine smiled at the peace she could feel radiating off him. She turned to Mae who smiled and gave her a big hug.

When she released her Mae reached for Alex. Winn and Katherine locked eyes and after a few tense seconds, he gave her a slow smile. "He's going to be okay." Then surprising the hell out of her, he pulled her into a quick but tight hug.

"He's going to be okay," she echoed and couldn't help the relieved laugh that came from her lips.

CHAPTER 33

Once the initial excitement from the good news died down, everyone began going about the business of killing time. Mae went in search of the cafeteria, and Alex and Winn sat down talking amongst themselves, the city girl's gaze bouncing to Katherine more than a time or two.

Katherine decided she could use a break from the judgment on Alex's face, so she went to go call Jenny from outside where there would be more fresh air and less seething disapproval. Katherine took a deep breath and pulled up Trix's sister's number on her phone.

"Hey. I know our connection was undeniable, but Trix is my brother," Jenny answered, chuckling at herself.

"He's been hurt," Katherine blurted out.

"What? Where is he?"

"He was air lifted to the hospital and he's getting out of surgery now. They're saying he's going to be okay."

"Oh my god. What happened?" Jenny whimpered, obviously already losing the battle against tears.

Katherine explained what had happened, and when she finished there was such a long pause, she pulled the phone away from hear ear to see if they were still connected.

Katherine heard Jenny pull in a stuttering breath before she said, "I'm leaving now. How do I get to where you are?"

"We're in a city called Great Falls, there's an airport here. If you get there, I will find a way to get you to the hospital. Text me when you have arrival information."

"Okay. Katherine?

"Yeah?"

"I can't lose him," Jenny said softly.

"He wouldn't do that to us." Katherine said her voice catching in her throat. "Talk soon," she added and then hung up.

She watched the sky for a long beat and prepared herself to go back into battle against the naysayers of Crooked Brook Ranch. They could try to keep her from seeing Trix, but she would make them all sorry if they did.

On her way back to the surgical waiting room, Katherine came around the corner to find Mae leaning against the wall talking on her cell phone.

"I wanted to see how you were holding up," Mae was saying.

There was a pause, and then she said, "Griz, I know it had to've been hard for you. No harm in admitting that. I wouldn't think less of you if you wanted to steer clear of this place."

Mae got quiet and nodded her head as she listened to what Griz was saying. Katherine tipped her head wondering what reason Griz would have to stay away from a hospital.

"Boy, you are not going to out-stubborn me. There's plenty of work needs to be covered at the ranch. I'm going to tell everyone I forced you to stay home."

After another pause Mae sharply said, "I'm hanging up on you now," and then she did.

After ending the call Mae turned around and didn't seem surprised to see Katherine standing within earshot of her private phone call.

Katherine decided there was no reason to pretend she hadn't overheard, so she asked, "What's going on with Griz?"

"His own business," Mae said flatly.

Katherine sighed and sucked in her cheek at the reprimand. "Right, but it sounds like maybe he's not keen on coming here."

Mae narrowed her eyes, but Katherine continued, "I don't know Griz all that well, but if he feels uncomfortable coming here and still wants to help, I may have a solution."

"Which is?" Mae asked while making an annoyed rolling motion with her finger.

"I spoke with Trix's sister, she's going to be flying into Great Falls as soon as she can. Maybe Griz can go pick her up and bring her here? He'll be helping Trix but not logging a lot of hospital hours."

Mae nodded, and Katherine wondered what was going on behind the stone expression.

"Good, get me her flight info and phone number, I'll let him know."

"Okay," Katherine said.

"You get along with his family then?" Mae asked, and it felt like a trap.

"Well, his sister," Katherine said.

"I see."

"You have thoughts about Trix and me that you'd like to share?" Katherine said, not hiding her defensiveness.

"You sure you want to hear what I think about that?" Mae asked with a lifted brow.

Katherine watched Mae's face and wondered the same. She decided that she may as well know what she was up against when it came to Crooked Brook's resistance to her being with Trix. Everything at the ranch began and ended with Mae.

"I guess I do," Katherine said.

Mae watched her for a tick longer. "For what it's worth, I don't blame you for what happened to Trix today. The Martin's have been a problem for my family for a long time, it didn't start with you."

Katherine let out a breath she didn't know she'd been holding.

Mae continued, "I know you're a confused and conflicted girl. You don't have much to keep you grounded at home, and trust me, I have sympathy for that. I see a lot of my younger self in you."

Katherine was surprised to hear her admit that.

Mae nodded. "But here's the thing. Trix is softer than anyone knows, and if you intentionally hurt him—"

Katherine cut her off. "You'll bury me ten feet deep in the south forty and tell my folks I ran off to be a Rockette?"

Now it was Mae's turn to show surprise, and then her gaze trailed up the wall over Katherine's head, most likely trying to put her finger on where she'd heard that before. Katherine decided to help jog her memory.

"It was our graduation day. It's what you said you'd do if I hurt Winn. I've got to tell you, I believed you, and those words had me looking over my shoulder more than a time or two in the last year."

A corner of Mae's mouth turned up as she nodded. "That's right. I was feeling pretty dramatic that day."

"So why didn't you?"

"What?"

"Gut me and let my corpse fertilize the pasture? Actually, you never confronted me about it at all," Katherine pointed out.

She watched Mae search for words. Before she could speak though, it dawned on Katherine why Mae had never pitched a fit about her and Winn splitting up.

"You were relieved." Katherine supplied, the air leaking from her lungs with the hurt of understanding.

Mae watched her in a painfully familiar way.

"I was," Mae simply admitted.

Katherine deflated. The sharpness of those words tore at her chest. Mae, the scion of Crooked Brook Ranch, had taken measure of Katherine and found her wanting.

"Oh," Katherine managed.

"You and Winn were what each other needed at that age, but your relationship was destined to suffocate you both. The small-town love affair wasn't right for either of you. You wouldn't have grown if you'd stayed together. Things that don't grow aren't alive."

"You're not wrong," Katherine had to admit.

"Of course not," Mae half-smiled.

"But with Trix?" Katherine asked with her brows raised.

"You need someone you can depend on, and Trix needs to learn he's dependable. That sounds like a combination that'll maybe work."

Katherine was doubtful. "Sounds like we'd be using each other," she said carefully.

"It's a tricky line between using another person and being your best self because of them," Mae said.

"How do you draw the line?"

"You both have to be better for knowing the other. If one person grows and the other wilts, then that's not love that's, well, parasitic."

"What if I have nothing to bring?" Katherine asked, braced for Mae to confirm she was the parasite in this scenario.

"Loving him, truly loving him, being there and being better, maybe that's enough."

"I don't know if that's in me."

"I don't either, but I'm not ready to give up on you yet."

Katherine decided not receiving a mandate to leave Trix alone was a victory, and she shouldn't push her luck. She nodded and the two of them went back into the waiting room.

While they waited Katherine received a text from Jenny explaining she couldn't get a direct flight, and she would be there in about twelve hours. Katherine leaned over and gave the flight information to Mae who then excused herself to call Griz. After another two hours of waiting, a nurse came out and the group perked up.

"Is there a Mae Becker here?" the nurse asked.

Mae stood. "Yes."

"Jacob is asking for you."

Mae followed the nurse through the doors.

"Well, that's a good sign, right?" Alex asked.

"Seems like," Winn said and reached down to squeeze Alex's hand.

After about thirty minutes Mae came back through the door with a broad smile on her face. "He's doing well," she said before anyone could ask. "He looks ragged but he's in good spirits. His smartass mouth is perfectly intact."

Katherine grinned, picturing Trix giving Mae a hard time from a hospital bed.

"He wants to see you and Alex," Mae told Winn.

Winn briefly looked to Katherine before he gathered himself and stood. When they walked through the door, Katherine tried to hide the hurt she felt.

Mae sat next to her but offered no words of comfort, perhaps sensing nothing she could say would help Katherine's self-doubt about whether she belonged there.

CHAPTER 34

Trix shifted, still feeing groggy. His mind was slow to understand he was lying in a hospital bed, and several hours had passed since the last thing he remembered. He looked up when he heard the door and watched Winn and Alex come into the room. He mustered a smile despite the tension growing in his chest knowing what he was about to ask his best friend to do for him.

Alex rushed to his side, grabbed his hand, and bent down to squish her cheek against his.

"I'm so glad you're okay," she said, leaning back with barely restrained tears.

"I'm all right, Red, or so I've been told. Heard I missed my first helicopter ride, so that sucks." Trix grinned she looked like she was ready to scold him for joking.

Trix looked up to Winn who gave him a half-smile, but he was tired. "Seems you've upped your attention-seeking game," Winn said.

"I'm the star of this show," Trix chuckled.

Winn got serious. "You really scared me, man."

"I know. Thank you for being there," Trix replied, matching the solemnity of Winn's tone.

The two men held eye contact, not needing to say more to make clear how important they were to one another, and how insignificant their troubles before this moment were by comparison. After a beat they both nodded, and Trix winced when the movement hurt a little.

"Are you in a lot of pain?" Alex asked.

"No, they gave me something an hour ago and it's still doing pretty good work. I'm thirsty though, and I think the nurses said I could have ice."

"I'll go grab some," she offered and left to find it.

As soon as she'd left, Trix didn't waste any time. "I know you don't want to hear this, man, but I need to call Katherine."

"She's here," Winn said quickly.

"How?"

"I already called her."

Trix held eye contact with Winn for an emotional moment. "Thank you." Then he couldn't find more words and his chin trembled slightly.

Stupid pain meds.

Winn nodded and had the graciousness to not say anything more.

Alex returned with a small carton of apple juice and a cup of ice shards.

"Trix," Alex said, her expression sad, and she looked like she was going to cry. "I'm so sorry. Ignoring you could have been the last thing…" Her voice broke.

"Hey, hey," he said reaching out and holding her hand. "I'm going to be okay, and I understand why you were upset, but I hope when this all gets sorted that we can talk about how to get back the way it was before."

"Trix, all of this is because of her," Alex said gently.

"It's not, Alex, please. She didn't make me step in front of those cows."

"But—"

Winn cut off her argument. "Not now."

She nodded and wiped her eyes. Trix felt his ability to stay awake begin to dwindle, so he bit the bullet and said, "I need to sleep soon guys. Can you ask her to come in?"

Winn nodded and predictably Alex's face scrunched up, but this time she didn't voice her disapproval. She leaned over and gave him an awkward hug around his head. "We love you, honey, and we're not going far. You ask if you need something, anything."

"Love you guys," Trix said and watched them leave, thankful to his core for his family.

***

Katherine was in the waiting room when Alex and Winn came back through the doors. She schooled her expression to not give Alex the satisfaction of seeing her hurt by how low on the totem pole she appeared to be.

"You're up. He's in room two-twelve," Winn said.

They held eye contact for a brief moment, and she couldn't quite tell what was going on behind his eyes. She rose and went down the hallway and made it to Trix's door, taking a deep breath to steel herself for what was on the other side.

He looked pale, so pale it made her chest ache to imagine his pain.

"How are you?" she asked when he looked up to her.

Trix shrugged, barely. "I think having a whole spleen was overrated," he said and hit her with a thin smile she couldn't get herself to return.

"Trix..." She relented and allowed the tears that were hours overdue. "I was so afraid..."

He raised his hand and motioned for her to join him. She sat next to him careful to not jostle him.

"I'm okay," he whispered pulling her head down to his shoulder with one arm. "I'm okay." He placed a lingering kiss on the top of her head while she cried.

"No one wants me here. Maybe I'm making it worse," she managed.

"I need you to stay," he said.

She looked up and searched his face. He didn't blame her. "I'll stay."

"Good, thank you," he sighed and then his eyes got heavy.

"Why don't you rest," she said.

Trix nodded, and with his lid dropping closed his hand found hers and he held onto her as he drifted off to sleep.

For an hour Katherine watched his face and embraced the warmth that spread through her as she watched his chest rhythmically rise and fall. Trix was okay. He was going to be okay.

She knew she wouldn't allow anyone or anything to take this man away from her. She would find a way to be worthy of his love. She would spend the rest of her life proving to him, his family, and herself she deserved what he offered.

She was going to make Blake pay for hurting Trix. She didn't know how yet, but he was not going to get away without consequences. Not this time.

Trix began to stir and in his sleep his face pinched in pain. She rose to go get a nurse, but his voice stopped her at the door.

"Please don't go," he said, gravel in his voice from sleep.

"I'm not going, I want to find someone to help you."

"I'm fine," he said propping himself up a little in bed wincing slightly.

"Don't move. Don't do that. You'll bust your stitches or something. Hang on. I'm going to make someone help you." She was surprised in how unglued she sounded.

"Katherine, you don't do doting well, and I'm not great at receiving it, so can you please not be weird?"

"I'm not weird," she said, knowing full well she absolutely was.

"I am okay. I promise to tell you if I'm not," he said.

She watched him for a long moment and then nodded and returned to his side.

"Trix..." she started but didn't know what to say.

"I know it must have been scary, or so I've been told. I had the luxury of being passed out for most of it."

"Knowing you were hurt was the worst thing I've ever lived through. I was so afraid you would be gone, and I'd never get to tell you how I feel."

"Which is?" he prompted with a half-smile.

"I love you, Jacob Doyle," she said. "It shouldn't've taken your near-death experience for me to say that out loud."

"I'm glad it worked, because after internal bleeding, I was out of ideas."

She briefly smiled and then drew in a deep breath. "I'm a coward."

"Hey," he said and waited for her gaze to return to his. "You were trying to protect yourself from getting hurt. I get that. I don't blame you for being guarded, but you have to know by now I'm not going anywhere. I'm going to fight for us Katherine. I'm going to fight for you because I know this thing between us is powerful and lasting. I see it clearer than I've ever seen anything in my entire life."

"I can see it too," she admitted.

"You're also going to have to fight," he said and then when she failed to conceal her confusion he added, "whatever self-doubt you have needs to be beaten back." She nodded. "I'm not going to lose an organ every time you need a reminder," he pushed.

She gave him a teasing grin. "I've heard gall bladders aren't all that necessary."

"Stop trying to sell me off for parts, woman."

She laughed.

"Say it again?" he asked his stare locked on hers, his expression serious.

"I love you," she said.

"Leave it to me to almost die when I've found something to live for," he said.

Her heart constricted, and she leaned in to kiss him.

"Now you can go threaten a nurse for some morphine. The part I wanted to be sober for is over."

"Damn it, Trix. I'm going to smack you if you're in pain and delay asking for meds again."

"Don't threaten me with a good time," he said, eyes glinting.

She shook her head, rising. "Infuriating man."

"But you love me anyway."

"I do, god help us, I do," she said and went to find help.

After locating a nurse who she ushered in to assess and help with Trix's pain, Katherine wandered the hallway again. At the nurses' station she stopped and asked if she could borrow a pair of scrubs which luckily they provided so she didn't need to sleep in her diner uniform smelling like grease and her own anxiety.

Before going back to the room, Katherine returned to the waiting area and found only Mae remained. Mae explained she, Winn, and Alex were going to stay in a nearby hotel overnight, and they'd re-group in the morning to determine what was needed. Katherine was surprised but relieved Mae appeared to consider her a part of the Trix team.

After her debrief with Mae, Katherine went back to Trix's room and guessed by his glassy eyes, he'd already had a decent number of drugs pumped into his IV.

"Oh lordy," he mumbled when his eyes were able to focus on her in the scrubs.

"What?" she asked.

"I want to play doctor so badly, but I think there's still a tube in my lad." He lifted the sheets to stare at his lap and then quickly dropped them with a dramatically despondent face. "Yes, that's a tubed laddie."

"One of many reasons it's not play time."

"A pipe in the peen," he said, sounding like his tongue was swollen and then he giggled at himself.

"Please stop," she laughed.

"A straw in the shaft, a duct in my—"

"Trix," she cut him off and his head wobbled, pleased with himself. "You are high as a satellite and need to rest," she insisted.

"You're still so pretty," he drawled.

"Thank you," she said and turned to start spreading extra sheets on the cot like sofa next to his bed.

"I'm going to love you for the rest of my life," he said wistfully to her back.

She stopped what she was doing and let herself internalize those words, even if they were delivered from a doped-up cowboy, they were incredible.

When she turned around to say it back, he was already asleep. She sat down next to him and ran her hand along his forehead and through his hair, allowing the true gratitude she felt for his safety to sink in. God, she loved this man.

CHAPTER 35

The next morning Katherine woke and stretched before rolling over to find Trix watching her. She gave him a faux glare out of the side of her eye.

"I'm not creepy. You're creepy," he said, grinning.

"Only a little, but I like it." She returned his grin before asking, "How are you feeling?"

He ticked his shoulders up, "I don't have a reference point, so I guess as good as can be expected. How'd you sleep? You know in the sixty-minute windows between visits from my adoring fans?"

Katherine laughed. "Those women are trying to keep you alive, not get your phone number you walking ego."

"Some of them may want my phone number. They've seen my naked ass."

"Maybe." She chuckled.

"But they'll have to cope with disappointment. I'm taken."

"Yes, you are," she said as she stood to give him a kiss. Her phone chimed. "Your sister's here."

Genuine happiness came over his face. "Thanks for taking care of that and for keeping her updated last night," he said.

"Of course. Let me go get her before she causes any trouble."

Katherine made it into the hallway and saw Griz and Jenny coming around the corner. When they made eye contact, Jenny jogged over to embrace Katherine.

"He's okay, Jen. He's going to be okay," Katherine reassured her again.

"Can I see him?" Jenny asked. The evidence of how hard the last hours had been obvious in the red rims around her eyes and disheveled clothes.

"Yes." Katherine motioned to the door. "He's in there and expecting you."

Jenny's eyes stayed with her for a long second and then she cleared her throat and straightened her spine before going in. As the door closed Katherine heard Jenny say, "Well, you look like shit."

Smirking at the siblings, Katherine turned to Griz and her smile fell. His face was taut, and she had to lean over to bring her face into the line of his thousand-yard stare.

"Are you okay? Being here, I mean?"

"I'm fine," he said, obviously lying while the tension in his body told the truth.

"I know we're not exactly close, Griz, but if you need to talk, I can listen."

"The story has more words than I have," he said quietly.

"Well, I know Trix would appreciate you facing whatever demon is attached to this place in order to be here, but he wouldn't fault you for taking a break to get some air."

He watched her. His anxiety obvious despite his quiet, calm demeanor. He nodded and turned to leave down the hallway.

Katherine's heart squeezed, his pain was floating below the surface, but she knew so little about him it was impossible for her to imagine what had given him such a strong aversion to being here. She shook her head and decided if he needed to get something off his chest, there were probably a dozen people he'd rather talk to before her.

Plus, she had a cowboy to babysit.

She went to find the cafeteria, maybe feeding him would keep its impudent mouth closed for a while.

***

As Trix expected, his sister insulted him upon her arrival, then quickly allowed her squishy insides to show by ugly crying and cursing at him for scaring her. He let her crawl up next to him and waited for her to calm down. When she stopped actively sobbing, he looked down at her.

"Jen, really, the doctor said I'm going to be fine. Recovery will take time, but he says I should be good as new before Christmas."

Jen drew a stuttered breath. "By Christmas?"

"Before even."

She watched him and sniffed a few times before she seemed to pull herself together.

"When do you get out of here?" she asked.

"He says if everything stays on track, less than a week from now."

"They're going to take out an organ and then let you leave in a few days?" Jen shot him a dubious look.

"They left some of it," he said defensively. "If you don't believe me, go find a health professional to yell at. You're supposed to be nice to me right now."

"Fine," she said tersely then cocked a brow at him. "Will it grow back?"

"What?"

"Your spleen." She nodded at his gut.

"I'm not a freaking starfish, Jen."

"So, no?"

"No," he said firmly, then furrowed his brow. "I don't think so."

Jenny sighed, and her face softened. "I was really scared. Katherine sounded so upset on the phone, I was convinced the worst had happened."

"I know. Everyone was afraid. I'm sorry you all had to go through that."

"I'm sure everyone was afraid, but I could tell she was coming apart, even though she was good at hiding it."

Trix nodded, pulling in a breath as deep as his aching body would allow.

"You told her you're in love with her yet?" Jenny asked.

Trix smiled slowly, meeting her gaze. "Yes, and she finally said it back."

"Why do you look so gloomy then?"

"Well…" He gestured at his abdomen. "I'm not in my best shape here."

"You know what I mean," she countered.

He sighed, knowing he couldn't pull off anything short of the truth or she'd call him on it. "There are still people at the ranch who can't get past her history. They don't want us to be together, and now that this has happened, they're going to think they were right about her."

"Maybe they'll come around? She seems to genuinely care about you."

"She's a good person. Amazing actually, but they refuse to see it. I won't let them ruin it. I won't."

"Simmer down, man-child," Jenny said.

"I prefer childish man," Trix corrected.

"Well don't bust a gut with a tantrum, I'm sure it'll work out. Anyhow, this is not the time to worry about it." She copied his earlier gesture at his stomach.

He smiled at her, but then quietly said, "She's important to me, Jen."

"I know," she patted his hand. "I'm glad you've found something that matters to you."

He nodded, knowing what she was really saying. Trix had never cared about anything enough to fight for it before, so leaving joking apathy behind was new territory.

Katherine peaked her head in the door interrupting his thoughts. "Okay for me to disrupt family bonding time?" she asked.

Trix grinned at her. *This woman loves me back.*

Katherine hitched her thumb toward the hallway. "Mae wants everyone to pow-wow outside to make a plan for the next few days." She walked over and put some fresh fruit and a muffin down in front of him.

"We should do it in here. It's my splenectomy, I should get a say," Trix said.

"Nobody is going to ask you." Katherine laughed. "Plus, the hospital says no more than two people in here at a time."

Trix pouted. "Fine then I make Jen my proxy and my vote is everyone needs to go home and let me get some damn sleep."

Katherine scrunched up her nose. "I don't get the impression people are going to listen. No one wants to leave you, especially if they know I'll be here."

"I want you to stay," he said. "Everyone else moving to Great Falls for a week is stupid. I'll refuse to see them if they don't go home and get back to work."

"What about me?" Jenny asked.

Trix looked to her. "It's up to you sis, but we'd need to get you a hotel and I'm going to be mostly sleeping anyway. Maybe you can go to the ranch and get some rural meditation time in while you get to know my friends. Maybe put in a good word for me and my choices," he said hoping she caught on to what he was actually asking of her.

Katherine rolled her eyes. "Do you actually think that was coded?" She laughed at him and then turned to Jenny. "He wants you to go back to Crooked Brook and convince everyone I'm not teaming up with their nemesis to steal his soul."

"Yeah, I got that." Jenny chuckled. "You're lucky this boy has no talent for deception," she said to Katherine.

"Stop picking on the infirm," Trix scolded, then had to grin at them both. "But yeah, that's the best thing you can do for me right now, Jen."

He could tell the moment his sister decided she would return to the ranch and lobby for the future she knew he wanted.

"You're lucky I love you, dummy," Jen said.

"Yeah, I am," Trix agreed. "All right, my broken ass is already tired. You guys go pow-wow, and make sure everyone comes to say goodbye before they go home. Which is what they all have to do regardless of how much they protest."

Katherine and Jenny nodded before leaving him to fall back asleep.

***

Katherine showed Jenny the way to the courtyard where Winn, Alex, Mae, and Griz had gathered. As they approached, Katherine noticed the crew suddenly got quiet.

"Not the warmest of groups," Jenny mumbled under her breath having noticed the ice forming in the air.

"They're actually good people." Katherine plastered on a sweet smile. "However, they detest me."

"So I've heard," Jenny said.

After quick introductions were made, Mae stood. "Okay, we still have a ranch to run so we need to figure out how this is going to work."

Jenny spoke up, "Trix wants everyone to go home."

"Not going to happen," Alex said firmly, her eyes darting to Katherine.

Jenny held up her hands. "Look I'm relaying a message. He would like Katherine to stay, but he feels like he's disrupted your lives enough. He wants things to get back to normal as quickly as possible."

Alex opened her mouth again, but Mae spoke over her. "I don't see any harm in us going home. I want to make sure he has what he needs, and if he thinks that's covered," she nodded at Katherine, "then I think we take off. It's not that far and we can set up a rotation for visits."

"What are you going to do?" Winn said to Jenny.

"I've also been told my presence isn't necessary." Trix's sister gave them a big Doyle smile. "Trix thought I may be able to go to the ranch, if that's okay with you?" she asked Mae.

"Of course," Mae said.

"Great. I'm kind of excited. I don't have a lot of experience outside of a high rise."

"Not a high rise in sight," Mae said slight amusement.

"I want to rent a car though. I'd like to be mobile just in case," Jenny said.

Mae shrugged. "Up to you. We can drop you off at a rental place on the way out of town. Alex can ride back with you to show you the way."

Alex looked up, but she didn't object. She gave Jenny a polite smile and a nod.

Katherine broke in. "He's insisting that everyone come say goodbye first."

Mae sighed. "That boy thinking he can order us around from his sick bed ends after today. We all clear on that?"

Some of the tension broke and everyone chuckled before deciding who went in first to say their temporary farewells to Trix.

CHAPTER 36

Alex rode with Trix's sister from the car rental place back to the ranch. Despite her earlier sour mood over Katherine staying, Alex was enjoying Jenny's company. She had her brother's quick and cutting sense of humor. There was something about her that made Alex feel a part of her club, which was appealing.

They had covered all of the superficial getting to know you questions and had grown quiet.

"So, you hate my brother's girlfriend?" Jenny asked as if it was another casual part of conversation.

"Yep." Alex decided there wasn't a reason to sugarcoat it. She looked out the window as the flatness of Montana sprawled out before her.

"Because she used to have sex with your boyfriend?" Jenny asked bluntly.

"No, because she's a nasty person who deeply hurt the man I love and is now responsible for putting someone else I care about in the hospital. I think you and I both have good reason to hate her, since it's your brother laying in that hospital room."

"My understanding is that what happened to Trix wasn't her fault."

Alex shook her head. "She's the reason Blake came around to cause trouble."

"Well, this time. Right?"

Alex turned to her and asked sharply. "What's that supposed to mean?"

"I heard this guy has been a problem for you guys before, and it didn't start with Katherine dating Trix."

"Blake's been an asshole for forever, but it is her fault he was there, and she's why Blake pulled that stunt that got Trix hurt."

"I'm not so sure about that. As someone who's seen the way she looks at my brother and the way she defends him, I think you're being too harsh," Jenny said.

"If she did defend him at some point, I'm sure there was something she could gain by doing it." Alex said and looked at Jenny who briefly glanced at Alex before she tipped her head to the side and turned her gaze back out the windshield.

"I heard she challenged and masterfully insulted my father after he tried to humiliate Trix. If she's using my brother to get to his trust fund, going after our father was a poor chess move."

Alex gave a snort of disbelief.

Jenny went on, "Look, maybe you're right, and she's working a nefarious angle, but the way I see it, Trix needs all the strength and support he can get right now. If he's getting strength from her, I'm not going to get in the way, and I won't let you either."

Alex sighed, not wanting to concede the point, but she had to acknowledge there was sound logic there. Regardless of what blame Katherine deserved, she was what Trix wanted right now, and Alex wasn't about to take anything away from him while he was recovering.

Jenny said, "I'll make you a deal. You back off and let him have what he needs from Katherine, and if she turns on him, I'll help dispose of the body."

Alex laughed despite herself. "Agreed."

"Settled." Jenny nodded. "So, what does one do for fun around here?" she asked, officially abandoning the subject, her tone forced Alex to go along.

"It takes some getting used to, but I find people do a lot more sitting around fires and talking to each other than I ever did in the city. It sounds weird, but it's actually really nice."

"I like fire," Jenny said with a mischievous grin. "I'm assuming there's a lot of lite beers and some kind of manly booze?"

"Jack," Alex supplied.

"Yep, that fits my idea of the stereotype." Jenny laughed.

Alex pointed up ahead on the right. "There's the driveway."

"Got it," Jenny said and took them up the long drive. Alex turned to watch Jenny's face when the house and the rest of the ranch came into view.

"Holy shit," Jenny breathed, her expression one of genuine awe.

"Right? Kind of how I felt when I first saw it." Alex confessed letting herself take in the backdrop, which looked like a movie scene with the cloudless sky and endless green grass.

Alex gave Jenny a brief tour of the house and some of the closer buildings on the property before she glanced at her watch. "Almost time for dinner, let's head back in."

"What?" Jenny pulled out her phone and looked at the time. "Okay, dinner at five o'clock, wow."

Alex smiled, it was amusing to watch someone like her take in the routine and lifestyle at the ranch in much the same manner she had when she first arrived.

"Early to bed, early to rise. Yada, yada," Alex explained. "Wait until you get a load of eating every meal with a twelve-person crew, who, most of the time smell like holy hell and are incapable of talking about something unless it has four legs or gears."

"Can't wait." Jenny grinned.

"It's awesome," Alex said and meant it.

***

After dinner wrapped, Alex brought Jenny down to the basement so they could spend some time relaxing with a crew who could use the mental break after the stress of the last few days. Alex and Jenny played pool against Griz and Winn. Griz was quietly saving Winn from a full-blown shellacking, and after he sunk a particularly challenging shot Jenny stood in front of him and cocked her head to the side to study him for an awkward moment.

"If I was straight, I would climb your quiet lumberjack-looking ass like a tree," Jenny said. Griz responded by grunting and turning red across the parts of his cheeks that were visible above his beard.

"Dang, you're not into men?" Tiny let out a cartoonish sigh from the chair he was watching from with Bishop. "I guess I'll have to stop imagining what our kids would look like then."

Everyone laughed.

"Yeah, well, when your twin brother is prettier than you, you start to question your sexuality," Jenny said, and Alex laughed, but the men stared at each other.

Alex broke in, "guys that was a joke. You're allowed to laugh."

They looked to Jenny, who nodded. "It was meant to be funny, fellas."

They all kind of half smiled.

Alex could tell they were still confused, so she prodded, "You all are going to tell me you've never noticed how pretty Trix is?"

After only getting blank stares and shrugs Alex turned to Jenny in frustration.

Jenny shook her head in mock sadness. "Men. You are so predictable."

Winn grabbed her shoulder. "You'll have to forgive us. We don't always know the right way to act. We don't get a lot of folks like you around here."

"Girls who like girls?" Jenny asked brightly.

"No. Family members."

There was a beat of uncomfortable silence as the truth of that landed.

Alex cocked her head saying, "I guess that's true. This little island of misfit toys has a pretty high percentage of black sheep."

"I guess it does," Winn smiled.

"I love that," Jenny said enthusiastically, and the room broke into chatting and laughter again.

***

A few hours later Winn took Jenny out to the horse barn. He wasn't sure why, but she was insisting she stay in Trix's loft. At the base of the stairs, he pointed saying, "It's up these steps. You should have everything you need, and, of course, you can call or come to the house if you need anything."

"Thanks," she said but didn't turn to go.

Winn watched her for a long second and then asked, "You okay?"

"Look, I feel like I know you pretty well, Winn."

"You've been here for twelve hours," he said flatly, despite feeling more than a little amused by her.

"I'm a quick study," she countered.

"Okay." He chuckled. "Your point?"

"You don't strike me as a guy who's made it this far without any regrets."

"That's factual." Winn nodded, now truly wondering where this was going.

"So, you should understand that Katherine has made mistakes, but no one gets to survive this life without making any," Jenny pointed out.

Ah, she's on a mission.

"I've already told Trix, even though I'm worried, I won't object to their relationship. Hell, I'm the one who called Katherine to tell her to meet us at the hospital."

"And you think your responsibility to the situation ends there?" Jenny pushed.

"You disagree?"

"Alex?" she floated.

"Maybe you don't know me as well as you think you do. I would never try to tell Alex how to think or feel."

"I'm not asking you to assert your male dominance, I'm asking you to tell her you're okay. She doesn't have to go all momma-bear, hating Katherine on your behalf."

"Alex knows I've recovered from Katherine. She knows from the moment I met her I stopped pining for a life with anyone else."

Jenny nodded along with his assertions. "She knows all of that, but that's not the whole story. Does she understand the end of your relationship with Katherine? Do you for that matter?"

Winn crinkled his brow, unsure of what she was getting at.

Jenny pressed, "You let Katherine take one-hundred percent responsibility for the end of your relationship, a relationship everyone thinks was a love for the ages until she ruined you. No wonder people think she's the antichrist."

"You do know she cheated on me with a man who's tried multiple times to ruin my life and career. The same man who caused an accident, which almost killed your brother. That's not antichrist level behavior, but she doesn't get a medal for it either."

"So that's a no. You don't really understand the end of your relationship."

"You're trying to rewrite history," Winn accused.

"No. I agree this Blake guy is a gigantic asshole and her sleeping with him was royally screwed up, but that's not really what caused the end of you guys. Things with the two of you weren't supposed to last. Real life is messier and more nuanced than platitudes like: all ex-girlfriends should rot in hell."

"I've said I forgive her. I've said I understand she's trying to be a better person," Winn said, feeling exasperated.

"Have you?" Jenny asked quietly.

Winn opened his mouth to tell her of course he had, until he realized that no, he hadn't.

Jenny smirked at him, raising an eyebrow. "There it is."

Winn pulled in a deep breath and looked up to the sky. "Fine. I need to talk to Katherine about our ending and find us both some closure."

Jenny mimicked her brain exploding and whispered, "Boom."

Winn watched her and tried to digest where the conversation had landed. Her insight was tough to swallow, but not off base. His hands weren't spotless, and no, he hadn't tried to understand any of it from her perspective. It'd been so much easier to hate her. Maybe Jenny was right about the source of Alex's animosity. Winn scanned Jenny's expression and surprised himself when he found her smug grin charming instead of annoying.

He narrowed his eyes. "When do you leave again?"

She threw her head back and laughed. "I'm a spoiled brat, friend. I've got nowhere to

be."

"So, like soon, or...?" he asked, chuckling.

"You know you begrudgingly love me," she said playfully scrunching up her nose at him.

"That's similar to how I feel about Trix."

"Twins," she explained and got up on her toes to kiss him on the cheek before heading up to Trix's loft.

CHAPTER 37

The next morning Katherine was with Trix trying unsuccessfully to convince him to stop fooling around for reasons obvious to her and apparently less obvious to him.

"Fine, you insufferable whining baby," she yelled as she faced him and lifted her shirt to flash him.

His eyes lit up, but when she shot him a frustrated look he laughed. "Now, was that so bad?" he asked.

Her phone chimed, stopping her from saying something crass. She glanced down and was surprised to see it was a text from Winn.

Can we talk?
Sure?
Ok, I'm downstairs.
What?
Meet me in the cafeteria?
Why are you here?
This is a face-to-face kind of thing.
10 mins.

She glanced up at Trix and his brows knit seeing her worried expression.

"Winn's here. He wants me to talk to him."

"Why?" Trix asked.

"He didn't say."

"I don't know if that's a good or a bad sign."

"Maybe your sister burned the place down?"

His eyebrows lifted. "Maybe."

"It's probably about you and me." She sighed.

"Yeah," he said a little absently and then motioned for her to come to him which she did. He palmed the sides of her face and directed her to look at him. "I love you and this wasn't your fault. If I need to butt heads with my family until they understand those two things, I will."

She smiled softly and bent to give him a chaste kiss. "Let's not jump to conclusions. Take a nap, I'll be back soon."

"Okay. Good luck."

"Thanks." She chuckled past the weight in her stomach.

***

Katherine found Winn in the cafeteria. Not a lot of men took up space the way Winn did. Part of it was due to his height, part of it because of his resting do-not-approach-me face, which was working double time at the moment.

"Winn." Sitting down across from him, Katherine waited for him to set the tone.

"Katherine." His tone provided no hints as to his intentions.

"What's this about?" she asked, knowing he detested small talk even under regular circumstances.

"I told Trix I wouldn't stand in the way of his relationship with you, but I know some other folks at the ranch have been...assertive in their opposition."

"Alex," she said. "You mean Alex."

"She cares about him and is worried. She's a good friend," he stated.

"I can understand that." She nodded. "I don't know what I can do about how she feels. She's left no room to change her low opinion of me."

Winn sighed and removed his baseball hat to run his hand through his hair. "It's been brought to my attention maybe that's partially my fault."

Katherine was genuinely shocked to hear Winn talk this way. His stubbornness when it came to admitting fault used to be legendary.

"Okay," she said cautiously.

"Alex hates you because of what you did to me, but there's a possibility the narrative about our break-up doesn't tell the whole story."

Katherine's chest constricted. Revisiting her sins wasn't an area she relished wading into.

"It's a pretty straightforward story," she said, feeling like passing any responsibility would be wrong and prove she was who Alex thought she was.

"Maybe it's not." He watched her for a long intense moment. "Even though I decided to forgive you, that happened in a vacuum. We've never actually talked about it."

Katherine let out a deep breath. Winn saying he forgave her hit her in the gut, and suddenly the prospect of revisiting their break-up felt bigger than the room.

She stood. "Can we walk?"

After a beat, he stood and nodded. In silence they walked out of the cafeteria and followed the long hallway leading to outside.

When they hit fresh air, she swallowed hard and turned to him. "So somehow you think it'll help if we talk about what happened to us."

"Yeah," he said, looking everywhere but at her. "When I think about it there's a lot I don't understand, and a lot I never asked you about."

"Like what?"

"Like, why did my injury kick off a set of events we couldn't recover from, and why didn't I know we were failing until you'd left?"

She took a deep breath, afraid that he was tasking her with excusing the inexcusable. When she turned to him, she was surprised to find his demeanor calm despite the subject matter.

Okay. This is it. Truth time.

"You weren't the same after you got hurt. *We* weren't the same. That's not your fault, and I would never try to shift blame to you, but when things changed, I wasn't what you needed anymore."

"I needed you to be there," he insisted, his eyes intense and uncharacteristically raw.

She shook her head. "No, you didn't. I wasn't in a position to support you, at least not the way you deserved. You needed something I didn't have to give."

"Then we should've broken up. You didn't need to end it like you did."

"You're right."

He looked at his boots, and his shoulders sagged. "Why him?" he asked quietly.

"I was stupid."

He looked up and glared at her, seething the same way as he was the day he confronted her about the rumors she'd cheated on him with Blake. "That's not a good enough answer."

She held his stare for a long moment and knew she owed him a real explanation. "I was so broken, Winn." She sighed shaking her head. "You and I had this thing everyone envied. They wanted to be us. The picture-perfect couple. God, you were so affectionate and attentive, and wonderful, and I didn't want to be with you. I was banging on the glass of the fairytale looking for a way out, and I knew it must've been because something was really wrong with me." She lifted her arm to press a palm against her chest. "Blake was terrible, and terrible was what I thought I deserved."

"You could have told me you felt that way."

"Could I? I knew you felt it, the wrongness of us. You weren't in love with me, but you were so damn complicit in the storyline."

"You should have trusted me to hear you," he insisted.

"If I could go back, I would. I would find the right words to help you see, the honest words I didn't have back then."

"I was so angry with you, so damn angry." He tilted his head back, and he rubbed his palm over his mouth.

"I was screwed up and confused, I thought it was kinder to let you be angry. I thought the truth of what I felt was too hurtful to say out loud."

"Maybe you're right." He let out a long breath and looked at her. "I know I was wrapped up in my own shit back then."

"Rightfully so," she said.

"Not really." He shook his head. "I obsessed over what I'd lost after the scholarship was yanked, and I was blind to a lot going on around me. I guess I didn't realize until now how willfully I closed my eyes to what was going on between us."

She nodded, her eyes stinging as they met his gaze.

"I haven't said this yet, but I'm sorry. Winn, I'm so sorry." A tear spilled over and ran down her face. He wrapped her in his arms, leaning his cheek against the top of her head.

"I'm sorry, too," he breathed.

The held each other for a long time before Katherine felt his body relax as he started to pull away. She swiped a quick hand across her eyes to clear the tears and she stepped back.

"So," she started, not sure what else there was to say, or what Winn would do with a tentative but genuine reconciliation.

"So, you and Trix," he prompted.

"I love him. If the cost of being in his life is I have to prove it to you guys every day, I'm willing to pay that price."

"You don't have to prove anything to me. I want him to be happy, and I want you to be happy. If that happens because you have each other then I'm good."

She was hesitant to ask, "Do you think someday you and I can be friends?"

He shrugged. "We used to like each other, then life got in the way. Just because we're not in love doesn't mean the parts of us that meshed are gone."

"So we can mesh again? Platonically, of course," she smiled.

"Very platonically," he returned her smile.

"Turns out I'm not your type anyway. You've got it bad for redheads," she teased.

"Only one redhead," he countered.

"Sounds like she's the one, period."

He brought his gaze to her and the contentment in them warmed her. "Yeah," he said.

"I'm so happy for you."

"Thanks."

She bit the inside of her cheek as something sprouted in her chest.

Hope. I feel hope.

Winn looked to the door, obviously having hit his emotional conversation limit for the day. "I better go see Trix."

"Please. He's being predictably insufferable," she told him as they went back into the hospital together.

Winn laughed. "No surprises there."

"Thank you for taking such good care of him. I think you guys saved his life, and that's a debt I'll never be able to repay."

Winn nodded slowly, and she could hear the emotional hitch when he said, "He, uh, yeah, watching him, seeing him like that..."

"I know," she said, saving him from having to say more. "But he's okay now thanks to you."

Winn sniffed quickly, then cleared his throat. "Well, as okay as he was before."

"True."

When Katherine and Winn walked into Trix's room she was surprised to find him still awake. His looked to her, and she gave him a soft smile and nod, so he knew she was okay.

"Why aren't you sleeping?" she asked.

"I was worried." He looked at Winn, whose shrug seemed to give Trix permission to be honest. "I was worried you guys were having a battle royale in the hospital basement."

Katherine chuckled. "Nah. I'd say it was more catharsis than cage match." She looked to Winn for confirmation.

"Agreed." he nodded.

"So, what? You guys've hashed out your crap?" Trix asked.

"Yes," she replied.

"Well." He crinkled his brow. "So, we're actually all good then?" he asked looking to Winn.

"We're good," Winn said, but then he held up a finger and pointed it at Trix. "But if you lie to me like that again, you and I are gonna have a scuffle."

"You wouldn't hit a sickly man." Trix grinned.

"From what I understand you're supposed to be right as rain in a few months and when you are, I'm free to pop you one."

Trix laughed. "Brutal, but understood."

"Good." Winn nodded. "Now get some sleep and stop perving out on your girlfriend."

"Hey. You told him?"

"I didn't have to." She laughed. "You're that predictable."

Winn smiled then excused himself. Katherine imagined he was gearing up for the next heavy emotional lift of the day: telling Alex where he'd been.

CHAPTER 38

Alex was having a blast showing Jenny around the ranch. It was like talking to herself several months ago. Jenny had awe for the amazing parts of ranch life, and hysterical disgust for the less than amazing parts. Her running commentary had Alex in stitches.

They climbed into the Gator and Alex took Jenny up in the fields. A large part of the herd came into view and she parked.

"Which one kicked my brother? I want to eat it," Jenny said, and Alex laughed.

"I'm still new to this lifestyle. I've finally mastered telling the horses apart, knowing which cow is which will never happen."

"Pick one."

"If it makes you feel better, my understanding is that all the ones up in this pasture will eventually be a steak," Alex said and then winced when she heard Winn's way of talking about the cattle coming out of her mouth.

Jenny made an exaggerated pouting face. "Actually, that doesn't make me feel better at all."

"I know. Wait until you see the babies. You'll never want red meat again."

"Awwww, baaaa-bies?" Jenny groaned.

"Right? These guys have a totally different way of thinking about animals than us city folk."

Jenny turned to her and rubbed her palms together. "We should go find the cowlets and rescue them."

"Like set them free?" Alex giggled.

Jenny nodded. "Yeah, I guess we can't exactly release them in a stream or something."

Alex laughed. "No."

"Boo."

"Do you want to come help me with some stuff in the barn for a bit? I can't spend all day goofing around or the locals will deem me useless, and I had enough of that when I first got here."

"Let's do it," Jenny said, and Alex brought them back down the hill, driving them over to the stables where she showed Jenny how to muck out a stall.

Not long after, Alex finished the last stall and came out into the aisle where she saw Winn coming through the door and realized she hadn't seen him in hours.

"Hey," Alex called brightly.

"Having fun ladies?" Winn asked as he bent down to give Alex a lingering kiss.

Alex sighed when he released her and then said, "Yes, we're having fun, no thanks to you. Where've you been all day?"

"I went to the hospital."

"What? Why didn't you tell me? I wanted to go," Alex said.

"I went to talk to Katherine."

Alex unceremoniously dropped the pitchfork on the ground, now she was pissed off. "Why?"

"Can we talk?"

Alex's gut dropped. "Winn?"

"I'm okay," he said to her and then he looked to Jenny. "I'm okay," he repeated.

A small smile spread across Jenny's lips and she dusted her hands on her backside. "Well thirty minutes of manual labor is thirty minutes past my limit. Catch up with you guys later."

The door hadn't even closed behind her before Alex was whipping around to face Winn. "Start talking."

He walked up to her and cupped her face in his hands. "Alex, I love you. What we have is the most precious thing I have to my name."

She watched his face, and for the first time in a long time she couldn't tell what was happening beneath the surface. "But?" she asked, terrified of the answer.

"There's no but. That's the truth and it's important you really hear me when I say that."

"I hear you," she said, pulling away from him. "Is this about Trix and Katherine?"

"This isn't about Trix and Katherine. Today was about Katherine and me."

What the fuck? her brain screamed and then tears threatened. Winn held his palms up between them obviously seeing the storm coming.

"Hear me out," he pleaded, and she nodded biting her lip, trying to trust him. "There were things that needed to be cleared up. Things that needed to be said. Things that should have been said years ago."

"Like what?"

"Like admitting that things between her and me were FUBAR before Blake."

"Before she screwed Blake," Alex clarified.

"Yeah, and please don't mistake this for me excusing anything she's done. I'm not. I feel like maybe it's time to better understand her and my actions back then."

"I hate this," Alex confessed, unsure of what else she could say.

"Look, I adore you would probably disappear her Chicago-style to defend my honor," he tucked some hair behind her hair and grinned.

"I know you're making a joke, but..." Alex refused to smile back. "She hurt you and it makes me want to hurt her."

"I know but here's the thing, Katherine and I were young, and we were never meant to last. I know that now more clearly than I ever have, thanks to you."

His soft words chipped away at her angry façade enough she could return his smile.

He went on. "Yeah, she picked an exceptionally shitty exit strategy, but I forgive her."

"So, what? We welcome her back and wait to pick up the pieces of Trix when she's through with him? Haven't we already learned that she is a literal threat to him?"

"I'm not asking you to trust her. I'm asking you to trust me. Trust that I have a handle on this, and that I care about Trix as much as you do."

Alex let out a long breath and looked at the ceiling. She trusted Winn, and she knew he considered Trix to be a part of his family. She needed to take this leap, even if she had no idea what was at the bottom.

"Fine," she said, then looked at him. "She's not going to live here is she?"

Winn shrugged. "I have no idea." When Alex made a face he added, "We're going to let Trix and Katherine decide what happens in their relationship from now on."

"Gross."

Winn tilted his head.

"Okay, okay. I'll try. That's the best I can promise."

"I'll take it," he said and wrapped her in a hug.

When he didn't let go right away and continued to hold her tightly, Alex realized how important this was to him. She decided she would give Katherine a blank slate. She wouldn't judge her for what had happened before, but if that woman stepped out of line again, the gloves were coming off.

***

In the afternoon, Katherine waited in the hallway so Mae could visit with Trix. After she and Winn had waded through their history enough to establish a truce, there was only one thing left on her mind. Revenge. At least in this, her talents could shine.

When Mae left the room, Katherine pushed off the wall and walked into her path. "Blake needs to answer for this," Katherine said, getting right to the point.

Mae nodded slowly and sighed. "Yes, he does. But I don't want my boys running off on some half-cocked vendetta. I know they all want to kick his ass, but stuff like that doesn't come naturally to these men. They're too good."

"I'm not," Katherine said.

A slow grin spread across Mae's face. "What do you have in mind?"

"I heard Blake's father has a rezoning proposal before the town board. They're meeting tomorrow, and it's supposed to be an easy yes vote for him."

Mae squinted. "I can't argue against it with the board. I'll look biased because of the business I have before them."

"Well, I don't have any business before them."

"You think you have enough sway with the five men on that board?"

Now a slow grin spread across Katherine's face. "There are things I know they would rather no one else knows. It's one of the upshots of old men thinking all waitresses are scenery. Plus, I don't need them to vote no, I only need them to delay long enough for Ted Martin to squirm. That's where you come in."

"So, you get the board to delay, I remind Ted how things would run smoother if Blake wasn't causing trouble."

"Exactly."

"Do you think he'd put a leash on that boy for a land deal?"

"I think Ted would ship him to Antarctica for a land deal."

***

The next day Katherine bounced a hip off the door, and with two trays of to-go coffee from Hank's in her hands, she walked into the town board meeting like she owned the place.

"Hello, boys," she said warmly when everyone looked up confused.

"Ms. Grant, so nice to see you, but I don't think we'd placed an order," one of them said.

"Oh, Jack, you didn't. I used these as a prop to walk past your secretary." Katherine set the coffees on the conference table.

"What, uh, what is it then we can do for you? We're in the middle of a meeting," Jack replied.

"I know, I believe one of the issues on the table today is Ted Martin's request to rezone those six-hundred acres of his that butt right up against town."

One of the other members spoke up, it was one of her favorite obese regulars, Chuck. "I don't understand your interest in the matter, and the time for public comment on that has closed anyway."

"I know. This is a slightly less formal way for me to make my request known. I'm asking nicely for you to drag your feet on that one. It would be best for me if you told Ted Martin you didn't vote on it today and that you *might* consider bringing it up again next month."

Chuck's brow dropped, and he shook his head. "Why would we do that?"

"Because I asked you to, and I think things would be better for everyone if you cared about things that were important to me."

"Are you… Is this some kind of threat?"

"Oh, heavens no, Chuck. Absolutely not. I've been serving y'all greasy food since I was a freshman in high school. I love each and every one of you. In fact, I adore you so much I sit on every single secret y'all have."

She paused to make eye contact with each man in turn. "Think about all the clandestine meetings you've had in that corner booth, the gossip you've spread about one another, the hushed fights you've had with your wives at the counter. Hell, one of you had a fight with your girlfriend about you wife. One of you has even had a few whispered exchanges with another member's wife. Wonder what that was about?"

She put on a huge innocent smile as she reached down to pass out the coffees. "Anyway, enjoy the day, boys. I look forward to hearing the board thought it was best to wait on that decision, at least until Ted Martin gets a better handle on that boy of his. I think y'all know the one I'm talking about."

There was a stunned moment of silence before Jack cleared his throat. "That Blake kid has always been a bit of a troublemaker."

"He really is a rascal, isn't he? Would be great if Ted took care of that," Katherine agreed.

"Right," Chuck said through his teeth and the other members nodded.

"Take care now," Katherine said as she breezed out the door.

Standing on the sidewalk, Katherine pulled out her cell and texted Mae.

You're up.

CHAPTER 39

Trix was over being in the hospital. The week-long stay had solidified a few things about himself he hadn't had a reason to know before now. It turned out Trix absolutely hated talking to someone about his bowel movements multiple times a day. Shocker. Other things Trix hated included, but were not limited to, daytime TV, Salisbury steak, young nurses who tried to flirt so they could poke you with needles, old nurses who wouldn't flirt when they poked you with needles, and single ply toilet paper.

At the top of the hatred list was being stuck inside. As soon as they'd let him stand, he'd started pacing the room, then pacing the hallway. It was enough of a problem that Delores—the only nurse who was immune to his charms—had deemed him a menace and threatened to cut off his apple juice supply. Bottom line: Trix needed to be out of this building as soon as possible.

"Here's your discharge paperwork and clothes to go home in," Delores said shoving a pile at him.

"Thank you, and I hope I'm not out of line in saying, but you look absolutely radiant today, Delores." Trix gave her a thousand-watt smile. She turned to him, grumpy dripping off her face along with her jowls. "Nothing, huh?" he asked. She shook her head and looked at him with bored dead eyes. "Even these?" he asked pointing at his dimples as he pulled his smile up to deepen them. "Eh? Eh?"

"Get dressed," she said and then started out the door as Katherine was coming through it.

"Hey Delores," Katherine said with a bright smile.

"Hey honey," Delores said warmly as she left down the hallway.

Trix frowned. "She hates me."

"Leave the woman alone. She's supposed to take care of you, not chair your fan club."

"Everyone else loves me, but she hates me."

"If she hated you she would have overdosed you on opiates the first time you made a joke about her shoes."

"They're orthopedic," he defended.

"They're sensible. Now shut-up and get dressed."

"I'm getting out of this joint." He grinned.

She returned his smile. "You're going home today."

"*We're* going home," he corrected.

She gave him a dubious look. "We'll see how it goes."

They'd talked about Katherine staying with him at Crooked Brook, somewhat under the guise she knew his recovery program, and mostly to prove the group was going to have to accept them as a *them*.

"Alex promised me she's working on the clean slate thing, and everyone else is being open minded," Trix said.

"I'll believe it when I see it," she said with a hitch of her brow.

He grinned and kissed her. He wouldn't allow pessimism to ruin the day.

They were going home and the joy he felt was bulletproof.

***

As they drove onto the property, Trix's shoulders relaxed. Rolling down the window he pulled a long drag off the autumn wind as the scent of the pasture grass hit him and settled his soul.

Welcome home.

As expected, everyone was waiting in the house for their arrival. There were hugs and jokes, the atmosphere welcoming and cheerful. Bishop and Belle cornered him almost immediately, their expressions standing out as the only tense ones.

"What's up, love birds?" Trix asked lightly.

"We think we should reschedule the wedding," Bishop said quickly with worry in his tone.

"What? On my account? Absolutely not," Trix demanded.

"It feels wrong to have so much going on here only a week after you get home," Belle said gently.

"I won't allow you to postpone. Look at me," he said his fingers pointing to his chest. "This is how good I look one-week post-op. Imagine how ready I'll be for a party a week from now."

"You're sure?" Bishop asked.

"I'm sure. I'll be ready to stand up for you like I said I would," Trix confirmed.

"All right," Bishop conceded, reaching out and shaking Trix's hand. "Thanks, man."

After a celebratory welcome home dinner, modified to fit the dietary requirements the hospital staff gave to Katherine who gave to Mae, Trix and Katherine excused themselves to get him settled back in the loft. Jenny had decided that she would make herself at home on the futon in the main house basement, and no one argued with her. Trix thought maybe the other men were a little afraid of his sister, which cracked him up.

"You sure you can do the stairs?" Katherine asked, concern written all over her face as they stood at the entrance to the stable looking up the flight.

He nodded. "It's only a few and I'll go slow."

She watched him and then took his arm and helped him make his way up. The work made him tired but didn't hurt. Turned out all of his caged animal pacing at the hospital paid off.

When they made it into the loft, he again took a deep breath reveling in the smells of the stables, which permeated his apartment. Grass hay and pine shavings, leather, and even the manure went together to create a cocktail which soothed him to his core. The fatigue he had come to expect by the end of the day hit him, and he looked to Katherine. He knew she could tell by looking at him that he was out of gas.

"Good thing you wear sweatpants all the time now," she joked.

"You can say that again." He toed off his shoes and lay down on the bed.

"You need anything?"

"Just you. Here. Tuck into this bed with me." He smiled.

She returned his smile and lay down next to him. He shuffled a little to find the sleeping position he'd discovered worked best and found himself dozing off.

He was home, and Katherine was in his bed.

Despite the twelve-inch incision that was itching like a bastard, life was good.

CHAPTER 40

The day after their homecoming Katherine found Trix a lawn chair to sit in so he could heckle Winn as he went about training the horses. She felt only a little guilty since she knew Winn was happy to have Trix's trash talk back on the property, regardless of how obnoxious it was.

The day had been pretty uneventful, and she'd begun to wonder if her coming to stay with Trix at the ranch was really copacetic with the others. After dinner she was rummaging around in the kitchen to gather supplies necessary to care for Trix's incision and Alex came in.

"Need something," Alex asked coolly. Katherine realized these were the first words the woman had said directly to her since they came back.

Katherine replied, "The tape has fully come off the incision. I want to grab a few things to keep it clean."

"You let his bandage fail?" Alex did not even try to hide the accusation in her tone.

"The tape was supposed to come off." Katherine's eyes narrowed.

"You were too rough with it. It's too soon. You need to put something back on it."

"I thought you'd agreed to stop treating me like I was trying to kill Trix," Katherine said with heat.

"I'm not saying you're trying to kill him. I'm saying your ignorance and neglect will lead to his demise. It's different."

"I'm sure your doctorate from Google University was intensive, but I'm going to stick with the advice I received from the medical staff while *I* was with him in the hospital."

"Don't pretend like your monopoly on Trix's hospital stay was anything other than your desire to separate him from his family. That wasn't our choice."

"That's not what happened at all, you dramatic—" Katherine's voice rose but was cut off.

"Ladies," Mae said casually as she walked into the kitchen. "Do you all want to know what I think about this?"

They both stared at her.

"Of course you do," she said, "I'm the one who knows everything. Don't deny it."

Katherine sighed and looked at her feet. Alex's posture matched.

"You're more alike than either of you care to admit," Mae started. When both women looked up Mae held up a single finger to silence them. "You're both too smart for your own good sometimes. You each have a bull headedness that makes me want to wring your neck more often than not. You've both been forged and tempered by events outside of your control. And let's not forget the big one. You both love the same damn men."

Alex and Katherine stared at one another before Mae went on. "Now there's a lot of ways to love these boys, and there's bound to be a little headbutting now and then. But Alex don't pretend like you wouldn't lay down in traffic for Trix. And Katherine, are you going to try to tell me you wouldn't commit a felony if Winn asked you to?"

"I would," Katherine said.

Alex nodded her agreement.

"Now, the men of this ranch are equally stubborn and fierce, but god help you, if you each have the fortitude to domesticate and love them, then you're more alike than you are different. So, shut-up. Get on the same team and help me keep these idiots in line. I'm not immortal, and it's going to take an army to keep the lights on without me."

Katherine pulled in a deep breath, of course Mae's logic was impenetrable. She looked to Alex who also wore a matching expression of surrender.

Mae nodded with a self-satisfied grin. "Now, use your big girl words to tell each other what's going on."

When neither spoke, Mae made an annoyed hand gesture with her palm up.

"I know that you're trying to look out for Trix because he's your friend and you care about him," Katherine capitulated.

"I want him to be safe and okay," Alex admitted.

"So do I. Can you trust me, and give me the space to do that please?"

"Yes, and I'm sorry. Will you please try to talk to me more so I understand what's happening? I feel helpless and out of the loop."

"I can do that. I'm sorry if I made you feel excluded."

"Thank you," Alex said.

"Do I need to make y'all hug?" Mae asked, chuckling at herself.

"No," Katherine and Alex said in unison.

"Fine, so no hug, but I'm going to insist on something. *I'm* going to go help Trix and you guys are going to take a bottle of wine and sit on the porch together. You're not allowed back in the house until it's gone."

"But the incision—" Katherine started and then stopped when Mae shot her a look.

"Darlin', I have more experience patching up idiot men than a wartime medic. Go away."

Katherine and Alex dragged their feet, but followed Mae's directive and took a bottle of wine and two glasses out to the back porch. There was an uncomfortable moment of silence where Katherine assumed Alex was doing the same thing she was— mentally repeating Mae's words and finding them without fault.

Katherine poured the wine and handed one glass to Alex.

"Thank you."

Katherine looked at the sky as they both slowly and quietly drank for a few minutes.

"Maddie tells me that you're a really good singer," Katherine said, trying to come up with anything that would be common ground.

Alex turned to look at her with a small smile. "That was nice of her. I'm not sure 'really good' is the right description, but I like to sing."

"What you did to help Bishop with the proposal was nice."

"It was so great to be able to help. They're such good people." Alex smiled again.

"They really are," Katherine agreed.

"I, uh, I heard that you're a really good dancer," Alex said, also obviously reaching.

"I like dancing, but like you, I'm not sure 'really good' is accurate."

"What kind of dancing?" Alex asked.

"Mostly contemporary." Katherine picked at a cuticle on the hand holding the wine glass.

"Do you ever watch that dance competition show?"

"The one with the hot guys who can jump like eight feet in the air?"

"Yep. That judge who always screams?" Alex asked.

"I love that show. But my god, that woman needs a slap and a muzzle."

"Right?" Alex laughed.

"I can't stand women like that," Katherine admitted. "I think that's why I have so few girlfriends."

"Me too. I've never been good at female bonding."

Katherine reached over and refilled both of their glasses and watched the last drop come from the bottle. "I don't know why people talk about a bottle of wine like it's so much alcohol. It's really not hard to polish one off."

"Exactly. It's only like four glasses. Who can't put that down?"

"Amateurs," Katherine said and they both laughed.

Alex's looked at the yard, and Katherine followed her gaze to see Belle and Jenny approaching.

"Well, what have we here?" Jenny asked.

"A little back porch sittin'," Alex answered.

"Well, we want in," Jenny said hitching her thumb toward Belle. "I'm appalled. Belle was telling me no one insisted she have the bachelorette party she claims she didn't want."

Alex's jaw dropped. "Oh my god, Belle. We're the worst people."

Katherine felt equally guilty. "We really are. I'm so sorry, honey."

"I'm not the bachelorette party type, and it's not like there wasn't a lot going on," Belle insisted.

"Well, that means Trix owes you a hell of a party down the road to make up for what his little cow kick cost you," Katherine joked.

"Not necessary," Belle insisted. "But I wouldn't mind a glass of wine now with my friends." She nodded at the bottle sitting between Katherine and Alex.

"This one's gone, but I'm sure there must be more somewhere," Katherine said, rising to go to the house as Belle and Jenny sat down.

Katherine started her hunt in the kitchen and saw that another two bottles of wine were already set out on the counter, along with two more glasses and a note in Mae's handwriting that said: "Enjoy ladies."

"Spooky woman," Katherine muttered to herself before snagging the bottles and glasses and going back outside.

It didn't take long for the group to polish off the first of the new bottles and they were in the middle of trading stories involving too much alcohol and bad decisions. Jenny had them crying when she told them she'd taken over a double decker tour bus in Times Square.

"So I'm dramatically pointing up the side of the buildings going, 'The DeWitts own this one. The mister sleeps with his twenty-year old secretary, and the missus sleeps with both the personal trainer and the yoga instructor, but it's okay because their son has a serious coke habit.' Of course, that was quite enough for the actual tour guide lady who made a grab for the microphone, and when I leaned away from her, I went flipping right over the side."

"Christ, how are you not dead?" Katherine asked, still laughing and wiping moisture from her eyes.

"Bounced off a hotdog cart, then a newspaper box before landing in the gutter."

They all roared.

"Snapped my collar bone like a chicken wing," she said rotating her shoulder.

"Oh my god," Alex laughed. "That's the winner. That's got to be the winner."

Belle looked up and quietly said, "I hotwired a car and drove it to California because I wanted to see the ocean."

Everyone stopped, turning silently and disbelievingly to stare at her.

"I was sober though, and I brought the car back," she added with a cute demure shrug.

"Holy shit." Alex chuckled.

"Belle, you have a pair on you, after all," Katherine said lovingly.

"Oh Katherine, hush," Belle said and blushed like the soon to be bride she was.

CHAPTER 41

The next weekend Katherine and Trix sat on the back porch watching crews setting up a dance floor and tables under the huge tent, which had been erected in the middle of the property.

"This is going to be great," Trix said.

"A far cry from a Manhattan mansion," Katherine pointed out cupping a mug and bringing it up to take a deep breath before allowing the perfection that was the first sip of coffee through her lips.

"Thank god."

"You can say that again. This kind of wedding is much more my speed."

"Noted." Trix grinned looking over at her and she had to chuckle.

"What time are you boys getting dressed?"

"Bishop said we don't have to put on the suits until fifteen minutes before the ceremony."

Katherine rolled her eyes.

"I'm going to try to get him to amend that timetable once he's gotten some nerves out with the manual labor of setting up two-hundred chairs." Trix shrugged.

"Well, the girls are getting ready at one o'clock so I'm going to go help them get the center pieces and bouquets made before then," Katherine said, rising and giving him a kiss before she took off to find the female end of the bridal party.

Trix called out to her back, "Okay, I'm going to sit here and supervise like a useless lump."

She whirled around with a loving but scolding look as she wagged a finger at him. "You will rest up. I expect at least one dance with you tonight."

"Fine," he sighed and pulled his feet up to cross his legs and rest them on the railing.

***

The late afternoon weather was perfect for the ceremony, which took place under the homemade arch set among the fruit trees in the center of the property. Katherine was so happy for Belle, who was a vision in a simple flowing white halter dress. The bridesmaids, including Belle's two sisters along with Alex and Maddie, wore simple tea length dresses in varying shades of soft greens. Bishop and the groomsmen wore dark navy suits and every man had taken the time to wash up and remove their hats, which felt like a small victory.

During the ceremony, the pack of cattle dogs came tearing through, running laps around Belle, Bishop, and the wedding party. Cheerful mayhem ensued as they gained speed running through the guests' chairs.

Matt let out a clear sharp whistle, and the pack ran up to him. He made an annoyed downward swipe with his hand, and they all lay down right in front of him. The crowd laughed, and the officiant nodded and continued.

Sitting in the front row with Mae, Katherine caught Trix's eye as he stood chuckling next to Winn, Matt, and the other groomsmen. The smile he gave put butterflies in her stomach.

Finally, Bishop was given permission to kiss his new wife, and everyone hollered making a raucous noise including several not exactly tasteful suggestions. It was a perfect country wedding.

***

The reception was exactly as Trix had predicted. Immediately after the service, the men had taken off all the parts of their suits not required to keep them decent, and more than half had donned a hat, cowboy or baseball. The buffet was set up with a dizzying amount of comfort foods, and the beer coolers were fully stocked alongside a self-serve bar lined with a rainbow of alcoholic colors. It felt like the entire town was at the party. The music was loud and so was the crowd. After standing for the ceremony Trix was taking an involuntary break at one of the tables as ordered by every woman on the property.

The D.J. played "Cotton Eyed Joe" and Trix chuckled to himself, scanning the party to find Katherine. He found her linking arms with Alex and Jenny, the three of them laughing hysterically as Katherine tried to teach the city girls the steps. Winn came up next to him.

"Am I seeing what I think I'm seeing?" Winn asked.

"It's like one of those eye floaties. I'm afraid if I look right at it, it'll disappear." Trix smiled.

"I don't know what Mae did, but she seems to have fixed that," Winn said matching Trix's grin.

From behind them Mae said, "A little common sense and some wine."

Trix jumped, spinning in his seat. "Damn it Mae. We need to put a bell on you. How long have you been there?"

"It's my ranch. I'm allowed to be wherever I want, you unobservant delinquent."

Trix laughed. "Love you, Moms."

She smiled and bent to hug him lightly. "Love you too, kiddo."

When the music changed, he looked up to her. "Do I have permission to get up now, so I can go dance with my woman?"

"Yes." She nodded. "You both need to go wrap those girls up, that's what weddings are about." Her eyes danced to Winn who also nodded.

Trix found Katherine still out of breath on the dance floor, he took her hand and formally asked, "May I have the honor of this dance?"

She smirked at him and then gave him a small curtsey. "It would be my pleasure."

They both looked down at her bare feet and laughed before he wrapped an arm around her waist. The song was slow and swaying, and her body was warm and soft against him. Her light spicy scent drifted up to him when he pressed his cheek to the top of her head.

"Thank you," he breathed on a long quiet exhale.

"For?"

"For this. For you," he said, holding her more tightly. "I'm not sure I can explain."

"Try. I love this side of you, where you get uncomfortable because you're actually more kindhearted than you like to let on."

"All right, well, it's like there's this young bird, perfectly happy to walk around because it doesn't know it can fly. Then one day it takes the right step off the right ledge and suddenly it's soaring. The freedom and the exhilaration it feels: that's what you give me. You're my vast open sky. You saved me from being content on the ground."

She leaned away to flash a perfect soft smile at him. "I'm the one who feels like I could fly."

"So, we sail together," he said, his feet stopping as he bent down to kiss her, a slow, soft, loving brush of the lips that warmed his chest.

CHAPTER 42

The party was still going strong after three hours and despite his best efforts to enjoy the festivities, Trix was feeling fatigued. He locked eyes with his favorite introvert, Griz, who also appeared to need a break from people. He ticked his head toward the front of the property and Griz nodded. The two of them walked around the house and went to hold down some chairs on the front porch. When he was starting to zone out in the quiet comfort of Griz's company, Trix caught sight of Blake's truck coming down the drive.

"This won't be good," Trix said nodding his head toward the road.

"Mmmm," Griz murmured in agreement.

Blake parked, got out, and made his way to them. When he was in earshot Trix called out, "This is a private party on private property, Blake. I'm gonna have to ask you to get back in your truck." Then he slowly brought his beer to his mouth for a long pull.

Griz stood from his chair, crossed his arms, and leaned against one of the large cedars holding up the porch roof.

"Just stopping by to deliver my congratulations." Blake continued his stroll up the steps with a cautious eye on Griz.

"Unnecessary," Trix said flatly. "You know I had almost let myself forget about you with everything that's been going on around here lately."

"Yeah, I heard one of Mae's piss-poor crew of rejects had gotten themselves wounded doing a basic job. That you?"

"Yeah, if memory serves, you might a been there."

Blake spat on the porch, and Trix had to work to keep playing the part of calm and collected.

"You're pretty funny, Trix. You think I don't know you found a way to get the board to delay the vote on my father's rezoning proposal?"

"Not sure I know what you're talking about, Blake. I haven't spoken with anyone on the board. Griz, you talked to the town board?"

"Nope."

Trix shrugged and looked back to Blake. "Although, come to think of it, there are some mighty tough and clever women living under this roof. Now there's a chance you may have pissed off more than one of them."

Blake shook his head. "Not sure what they were hoping to accomplish, but to appease those spineless board members, my father has lined up a training job for me in Connecticut. I'm going to be working with world-class cutting horses."

Griz let out a low whistle.

"That so?" Trix grinned. "I heard it was a working student position at a mediocre farm which does a fraction of the business Winn does."

Blake sneered. "It's a training opportunity of a lifetime."

"Is it now?" Trix tipped his head. "'Cause even though my father is a right bastard, I think if he sent me across the continent to keep me from destroying his business, I might still see through the scheme. What about you Griz?"

"Yup."

"You don't know what you're talking about," Blake hissed.

"Maybe not, but I know I'm not going to miss having you around."

Blake's eyes narrowed.

Trix added, "I also know my friend here looks about done with your company, and he's been itching to break your arm for two weeks now."

Blake's gaze jumped to Griz who slowly nodded.

Trix couldn't help himself, "So unless you'd like a solid taste of the ground again, I suggest you get out of here."

"I'm not afraid of your goon," Blake said.

"You should be," Griz supplied as he pushed away from the timber to stand at his full six-foot four height.

Blake watched him for a moment, but seemed to understand it was time to go. He swore at the ground and then turned to go back down the steps.

"Enjoy your trip," Trix called to his back. Blake went to flip him off, but then turned and kept walking back to his truck. Mae came out of the house, her eyes going to Blake's taillights as he flew down the drive.

"Guessing you handled that?" she asked with a quick hike of her chin.

"Yup. Turns out Blake wasn't interested in participating in Griz's cop-like takedown again." Trix chuckled at himself, but then noticed Griz and Mae made brief eye contact.

"Hang on," Trix said, his brow furrowed. He could tell he'd missed something in the silent communication between them. "Wait. Did you used to be a cop?" he asked Griz.

When the big man shrugged, Trix's incredulous face turned to Mae.

"Christ, Mae, do you ever hire anyone who actually knows how to do this job?" he asked.

Now it was her turn to shrug. "Rarely."

To his disbelieving look she added, "It's easy to teach a man how to work a ranch, but near impossible to teach one to have the character it takes to be a part of my family."

Griz slowly nodded agreement and Trix watched her before allowing a small smirk to pull up the corner of his lip. "Then I'm glad you picked us."

"Me too," she said and bent down to give him a quick hug. "Now get back to the party boys, they're going to throw the bouquet soon."

***

Katherine joined Maddie and Alex who were standing near the dancefloor. Jenny came bouncing up to them. In a singsong voice Jenny said, "Somebody is getting married."

"Yes, our friend Belle. I love you Jen, but sometimes I think maybe we need an intervention." Katherine managed to hit her preferred tone: affectionate and snide at the same time.

"No, you catty bitch. Look what I found hidden in the flower arrangement at the head table." Jenny's eyes gleamed as she whispered, "Looking at this geriatric-leaning hoedown, it's got to be one of your men. So, who do we think this belongs to?"

Everyone stared at the little black box Jenny was clutching between them and when she opened it a gorgeous solitaire diamond engagement ring winked back at them.

The DJ yelled, "Where are my single ladies at?" and the four of them stood there, mouths agape, staring at each other.

Katherine came to her senses. "Okay. This is silly. Jenny put that back. I'm sorry Alex, but Winn is too practical to propose after five months, and Trix knows I'm too practical to get engaged after only a few weeks. So, Maddie? Honey? Maybe it's time you go catch a bouquet."

Maddie squealed and ran toward the dance floor. Alex blinked hard and exhaled with a nod, seeming to agree with Katherine's assessment.

Jenny leaned over and said into Katherine's ear, "You sure about that?"

"Mostly," Katherine replied, but her eyes stayed on the ring until Jenny snapped the box shut.

Next up, *Breaking Silence*
Griz's story

HERE'S A SNEAK PEEK
at
Breaking Country

Breaking Country

Alex took a long look in the mirror. The last four years she'd worked to convince everyone things were okay, even when that was not the case. How hard could it be to fake it for a couple more days?

Immediately her gaze was drawn to the shadow of the remaining bruise around her eye, a screaming reminder of how screwed up things were. With a deep breath, she decided that her new "happy" look required more makeup, so she jogged back to the room to rummage through her bags.

Once back in the bathroom she splashed cold water on her face, ran a brush over her hair and added a quick layer of powder, taking special care to bring her eye back to a normal skin tone. Trying on her best fake smile, she declared that it was time to meet "everyone."

Coming down the stairs, she heard the sound of loud voices bubbling up from the first level, and it ate away at her feigned confidence. As she rounded the corner, the room came into view, and several independent conversations slowly died out. The room was swallowed up by the silence of unapologetic and curious stares. She surveyed the people in the room as they surveyed her. A pack of ranch hands was more intimidating than she ever could have imagined, and God, was it crowded. Cloaking anxiety behind a rehearsed smile, Alex frantically looked for a familiar face. Across the room, she found Matt and abandoned any attempt to hide her angst as she walked hurriedly, eyes trained on the floor.

A moment later, Mae bustled in carrying a large, steaming pot and was followed by two men each with their own hands full of bowls and baskets. The men started to take their seats around the gigantic wooden table.

Mae appeared to notice the awkward quiet in the room and said, "I want everyone to meet Alexandra. She's Becky's daughter."

A murmur moved around the table as the men nodded. Alex was surprised that most of them seemed to at least know of her mother.

She tried to force herself to look up and to acknowledge the eye contact from the men at the table.

"Hi," Alex said dumbly.

"I don't suspect you'll be able to remember this, but here's everyone's names." Mae looked to her left and moved her gaze quickly around the table. "Jacob, Christopher, Sam, Ben, Matt of course, then there's Eli, Nick Bishop, Nick O'Reilly, his brother Jeff, then there's Phillip, Matt's brother Winn, and finally this old man here is James."

While Mae rattled off the names, Alex tried her best to keep up and store the information. Most of the ranchers had shyly smiled when being introduced, and each mumbled something resembling a *hello* or a *ma'am*.

All of them were well built in the way people who work outside tend to be. The majority of them looked like they were in their late twenties, early thirties, with a few exceptions. The man called Sam was older, maybe closer to Mae's age, and the gentleman seated to Mae's right, who she had called James, looked as though he could be ninety.

The one who most caught Alex's attention was the guy Mae had called Matt's brother. He was younger than most at the table and was shockingly good looking.

No way this guy is related to Matt. Even though he hadn't looked up when being introduced—he hadn't acknowledged Alex in any way—she could see the square line of his jaw, the fuzz of a dark five o'clock shadow. The strong width of his shoulders pulled the t-shirt he wore snugly across his muscled chest. Like all of them, his hair looked like a hat had been worn all day and had recently removed. His messy light brown waves had somehow found a way to keep some life and flicked out around the base of his neck and his ears.

Alex found it hard to look away from him, and perhaps sensing this, he finally looked up. She sucked in her breath. His amber eyes were such a light brown they were almost golden. It wasn't the color that startled her though. It was the pure disdain they held.

"How long will she be here?" he asked Mae, without taking his harsh stare off Alex.

Alex narrowed her eyes at the rude question.

"Well, Winn," Mae said with a slight edge in her voice, "Alexandra will be here for as long as she wants to be."

"What will she be doing here?" he asked accusingly, obviously not fazed by Mae's tone.

Others at the table shuffled slightly and began to fidget with their food. Winn had not stopped staring at Alex, and something in her wouldn't allow her to cave and break eye contact first.

"I'm not sure of that yet. But I'm sure it's not one bit your concern." This time the disapproval in Mae's voice was anything but subtle.

Thankfully, her answer seemed stern enough that he finally broke his stare to turn to Mae, opening his mouth to speak again.

Mae spoke over him with a firm, even tone. "Winn, enough of this."

At that he finally dropped his stare to his plate and people at the table released their breath. Alex followed suit, finding it much easier to take in air now that he was no longer staring at her. Slowly movement and life came back to the table, and in a matter of moments, the noise of conversation, clinking plates, and men eating filled the room.

Matt leaned over to her, speaking quietly. "No mind that. He's a little rough around the edges, and he's been pretty stressed lately. Nothing personal, okay?"

"Yeah, sure," Alex mumbled, more for his benefit than out of any sense of forgiveness.

"Everyone here really is nice. It's a great group of guys." Matt carried on. "Trouble is, pretty much everyone has a nickname or two, but we'll let you try to get real names down before we throw too much at you." He winked at her, and Alex found it awkward but slightly endearing.

PLAYLIST

Alice Merton "No Roots"

Maren Morris "My Church"

KALEO "No Good"

Bryce Fox "Horns"

Barns Courtney "Sinners"

AWOLNATION "Sail"

Chris Stapleton "Broken Halos"

Rihanna "Stay (featuring Mikky Ekko)"

Screaming Trees "Look At You"

Chris Stapleton "Tennessee Whiskey"

Lord Huron "The Night We Met"

The Score "Legend"

Jon Pardi,"Dirt On My Boots"

Blue Foundation "Eyes On Fire"

Spiderbait "Black Betty"

Dorothy "Wicked Ones"

Rednex "Cotton Eyed Joe"

William Clark Green "She Likes the Beatles"

ABOUT THE AUTHOR

E. J. is a wife and mother, a foster parent, a reformed corporate lackey with a degree in something unhelpful, and is a twenty-year veteran of the horse training industry. Currently, she works part time trying to teach adults and children how to not damage themselves on horseback. In her spare time - when she's not ignoring laundry, bathing one of the multiple dogs and/or children, or acting as an unpaid chauffeur - she gives in to her persistent craving to tell a story she hopes you can lose yourself in.

Connect with EJ:
website: ejnickson.com
instagram: @author_ej_nickson
twitter: @EJNickson1
facebook: EJNicksonWritesSometimes

Itching to spend more time at Crooked Brook Ranch? Visit www.ejnickson.com to sign up for EJ's newsletter and she'll send you the secret password to access the *Tour Crooked Brook Ranch* link.

www.BOROUGHSPUBLISHINGGROUP.com

If you enjoyed this book, please write a review. Our authors appreciate the feedback, and it helps future readers find books they love. We welcome your comments and invite you to send them to info@boroughspublishinggroup.com. Follow us on Facebook, Twitter and Instagram, and be sure to sign up for our newsletter for surprises and new releases from your favorite authors.

Are you an aspiring writer? Check out www.boroughspublishinggroup.com/submit and see if we can help you make your dreams come true.

www.ingramcontent.com/pod-product-compliance
Lightning Source LLC
Chambersburg PA
CBHW072222170626
46813CB00003B/1057